THE CADIEUX MURDERS

THE CADIEUX MURDERS

A Historic Homes Mystery

R.J. KORETO

First published by Level Best Books 2024

Copyright © 2024 by R.J. Koreto

All rights reserved. No part of this publication may be reproduced, stored or transmitted in any form or by any means, electronic, mechanical, photocopying, recording, scanning, or otherwise without written permission from the publisher. It is illegal to copy this book, post it to a website, or distribute it by any other means without permission.

This novel is entirely a work of fiction. The names, characters and incidents portrayed in it are the work of the author's imagination. Any resemblance to actual persons, living or dead, events or localities is entirely coincidental.

R.J. Koreto asserts the moral right to be identified as the author of this work.

Author Photo Credit: Dutch Doscher

First edition

ISBN: 978-1-68512-768-8

Cover art by Level Best Designs

This book was professionally typeset on Reedsy.
Find out more at reedsy.com

To Wren Fontaine's godmother, Cynthia Zigmund

Chapter One

Wren stood on the shore and stared, trying to sort out her feelings about the ineffable house in front of her. She was only vaguely aware that while she looked at the house, her companion looked at her.

"So, Ms. Architect—what say you?" Bronwyn finally asked. Wren saw her wry smile. She knew she'd have to answer, and Bronwyn would expect it to be clever.

"Architecture should speak of its time and place, but yearn for timelessness," Wren said.

"Is that an original observation?" asked Bronwyn.

Wren laughed. "You flatter me. It's the great modernist architect Frank Gehry. This house is very much of its time and place. Look at the white stucco walls, the glass and steel, the absolute cleanliness of lines. The geometric arrangement of the layers is mathematically perfect."

"Why do I sense a 'but' coming?" asked the woman, arching an eyebrow.

Wren knew there could be no softening the message. "I don't find it welcoming. There is something very self-aware about modernist homes. A look-at-me arrogance about them, as if they are doing you a favor of letting you inside." She paused, wondering if she had gone too far. "But maybe I'm being unfair. I haven't been inside it yet. And there's no doubt that it's stunning." She looked at Bronwyn, waiting for her reaction.

"Are you saying I may have made a mistake buying it?" asked Bronwyn. Wren heard the teasing in her voice.

"No. Nobody ever made a mistake buying a house that spoke to them." *Yes, even if they spent thirty million dollars for it.* "If you are honest with yourself about what you want, you will be happy here. And if you are honest with me, I guarantee I can give you what you want with the renovation."

"Fair enough," said Bronwyn. "Was that Frank Gehry again?"

"No, that was entirely me."

"Ah. But as Gehry said, it should yearn for timeliness. Has this succeeded in that?"

"We'll need to give it another century."

Bronwyn nodded. "Maybe it's because I'm a writer. I become obsessed in making sure my books, the plots and subplots, are exciting. This house looks exciting. I was happy in my nice, simple co-op, and then my financial advisor told me I could do better. Much better. I fell in love with this right away. The more I walked through it, the more I liked it, the idea that I will be able to stay in it a long time, and keep finding something new about it."

"Then you absolutely did the right thing. Indeed, that is the very purpose of a house like this," said Wren. She mulled over her next statement. "When I was a girl, however, I wanted to live in a Victorian manor house, with a great hall with a huge hearth and handmade wooden furniture. I'd wear long dresses and be attended to by maids in starched uniforms." *Did I just sound silly?*

"That's very romantic," said Bronwyn, and Wren wondered if that was a criticism, a put-down for a flighty young girl. "But then again, I feel romantic about this, about men in classic tuxedos and women in Chanel dresses, with cigarettes and dry martinis and Dave Brubeck playing in the background. I guess we're both *emotional* that way, so despite our differences about favorite eras, I'm thinking hiring you is going to turn out to be a good decision as well."

Wren felt relief wash over her. She felt confident building houses but closing a deal—that involved people. She still didn't trust her abilities when people were involved. Of course, there was still one more feature of the house they needed to discuss: The "tragedy." That's how the papers had described it.

But Wren wasn't going to bring it up first.

CHAPTER ONE

Bronwyn hugged her leather jacket. "It's a great view, but it's getting cold. Let's go inside."

Yes. Wren always looked over the outside first, but she was especially excited about seeing the interior. Until Bronwyn had bought it a few weeks ago, no one had been inside the house since the 1950s, except for the caretaker staff.

The house overwhelmed Wren despite herself. Oh yes, she thought, Marius Cadieux knew it would. He would be so amused. So very proud. No—*smug*. Even if it wasn't to her taste, there was no denying what Cadieux had achieved here: the soaring ceiling, the clever use of windows filling the house with light even on a dreary day, the unexpected curves and angles, the steel staircase, which also served as a sculpture. Wren just stared. There really was nothing to compare it to—a Cadieux house was always unique. She could see him standing over her, "Very nice, isn't it, little one? And, of course, your client is overwhelmed by it, as she should be."

"I'm glad I bought a house that even knocks the socks off another architect," said Bronwyn, grinning.

"It certainly does," said Wren. "I've seen pictures, but they're not the same as really being inside it." Wren took in Bronwyn, with her attractive, angular face and the matching pixie haircut. Did the author indeed have a modernist personality, a match for this home, a connection with Cadieux? Indeed, did Bronwyn know how perfect she looked in her new house?

Wren walked among the rooms, taking note of the artful ways Cadieux had divided the house—very few true walls and doors, just a series of levels and passages, rectangular pillars clad in stone. Cadieux loved granite and marble, quartzite and sandstone, and merged them with oak and walnut, teak and lyptus. Wren saw Bronwyn marveling over it, even though she had already visited her new home several times. That was the thing about a Cadieux home that Bronwyn had already realized: You could live there forty years and marvel over it every day for the rest of your life.

"I'd like to see upstairs." Wren smiled. "But as you no doubt noticed, 'upstairs' is relative in a Cadieux house, with its intersecting layers. It just flows. That was a hallmark of Cadieux, but none I've seen are quite as…"

She let her voice trail off.

"You can't find the word?" said Bronwyn.

"You're the writer—can you? Architectural journalists struggled to describe him. But here we go…'intriguing.' No other Cadieux house is as *intriguing* as this one. It may take me a while to figure it out."

"You mean, how it's put together?" asked Bronwyn.

"Oh no. That's easy. I meant, what is its personality? Marius Cadieux stamped a *personality* on this house. It has a reason, and I will find out what that is. For now, we look at it: See the extraordinary flow of the house, the ways the rooms are separate and yet merge into each other, the way the light plays along the floors and walls. The materials blend into each other, and Cadieux is taught in every architecture school—as if you could teach this."

"It sounds like you studied him," said Bronwyn. "It sounds like you knew him. Did you?" She fixed her eyes on Wren, who gave that question some thought.

She didn't want to go there, not yet.

"He died before I even started studying architecture," said Wren, not quite answering her. "Still, he lived a long life, past his nintieth birthday, and was active until the end. He designed this house in his early forties. He was already well-known, but this elevated him to the top ranks." They walked along the hallway into a broad suite, cantilevered from the main structure, with floor-to-ceiling windows granting a two-hundred-and-seventy-degree view of the grounds.

"This is the master suite," said Bronwyn.

Yes, everyone knew that. In the wake of the death, this room got more photos in the press than any other. Wren was aware Bronwyn was eyeing her. But for now, she'd stick with the architecture.

"It's signature Cadieux," said Wren. "Overwhelming, isn't it? He always was extravagant. Beyond that. He was *indulgent*." She glanced at Bronwyn and wondered again about what she had been saying. She had to remind herself that she was not a professor lecturing a class but an architect closing a deal with a client. And despite her mixed feelings about the house, she still wanted to work on it. If for no other reason than to amuse Cadieux's ghost.

CHAPTER ONE

"Extravagant?" asked Bronwyn, looking amused. "I toured the Biltmore Estate. It has over two hundred rooms. I'd say that was extravagant. Or are we just talking about taste?"

Wren knew that question was coming. She smiled back. "The Biltmore house was built in service to an ideal, a desire to impress, to overwhelm, to rule. That isn't the case here. It's still extravagant in its own way but designed for a different message. I have not found the ideal Cadieux was serving here. Though I do have a sense of *what* he wanted to achieve. I'm lost on the *why,* but I expect I'll figure it out as I work on it." Bronwyn raised an eyebrow. "For now, I will say there is a refreshing *openness* about this house. I know Dennis and Rebecca Blaine, the first owners, were celebrated for their parties. So, I'll amend my original statement. Even if I don't find this a welcoming house, I find it a hospitable one."

Bronwyn laughed. "I like you, Wren! I like the way you look at my house."

"Thank you," said Wren, who felt a little warm inside, but didn't know what else to say. "Hospitable." That wasn't always high on her list for homes, not for the teenager whose goal in life was to live in Manderley—by herself. But now she was living in an apartment with Hadley. The girl who had desired a mansion to herself had grown into a woman happy to share a bed. *It has made me a better person. And perhaps a better architect as well.*

"Anyway," continued Wren, "with older homes, there's often major structural work that needs to be done, everything from water damage to rotting beams to ancient electrical systems. But I'm guessing that the house is in good shape, although I'll need to take a closer look. It's less than eighty years old and was well-built. Not all houses at that time were, but Cadieux would've insisted on it. We can upgrade plumbing, electrical, and heating systems. And I imagine you'd like a central air conditioning system. Even by the beach, summers can get hot."

"Oh yes, I'd like that. You can do that even in a place like this without changing its design?"

"Absolutely. What else would you like to do?"

"Well, you talked about how open the place is. I had the same thought, but I wonder if some of it is too open? Like, this bedroom—it isn't entirely private, is it?" Bronwyn seemed hesitant now, as if she were afraid of sounding like a Philistine.

"I agree. You're not the first person to say that about a Cadieux. Even in his lifetime, some thought his approach was a little too much. I've been in a number of his other homes, and this one is more open than most." *Did the house deserve some blame for the death? That was a very deep rabbit hole...*

"Off the cuff," continued Wren, "I'd say we can add some pocket doors—they're unobtrusive, and we can design them to match the walls, so they'll reflect the tone of the house. That is, they won't spoil the overall appeal." Just as well that Cadieux wasn't around to argue the point.

"That's good to know. It sounds like you have this well in hand. Now, when we last spoke, I mentioned something about a new structure, a 'she-shed,' as I think I put it. My lawyer assured me that was legal from both a zoning and landmark position."

Wren had been thinking of that. A bestselling author, who was single and childless and had just purchased a ten thousand-square-foot house, was not looking for a place simply to do yoga in private.

"A she-shed is simple," said Wren. "I'm guessing you want more of a little guest cottage?"

Bronwyn shook her head. "Forget the 'guest' part. It's for me—just me. I like to socialize. I plan to have guests at the main house. But I need a place to write in private. A place with a lock on the door and no room for anyone but me, perhaps for days."

Wren felt an instant kinship with Bronwyn. "I understand that very well. I also love private places where I can work. In my office, I put my phone on mute, close the door, and just work. You want what is formally called an 'accessory dwelling unit'—an A.D.U., and more casually a 'tiny home.' It will have heating, electricity, and plumbing, but be just one bedroom."

"Not even one bedroom," said Bronwyn. "I want it to be impossible to put someone up."

Wren nodded. "All right. I'm seeing a single room with a desk on wheels that can be rolled away and a custom-designed Murphy bed. A kitchenette off to one side with a small counter. Bathroom with toilet and stall shower.

CHAPTER ONE

We have several choices for location, with a view."

Bronwyn smiled. "Exactly. I know you will oversee the renovation of the house. Can you recommend someone to design the tiny house, another member of your firm, perhaps?"

Wren felt her heart pounding. She had been thinking of this ever since her first talk with Bronwyn, and now she forced a casualness to her tone. "I was planning to do it myself." Bronwyn looked surprised—but not upset.

"Oh! I thought you only did renovation projects, not new ones."

"This tiny house will need to be in the same style as the main house. It will have to complement it. I plan on knowing Cadieux House intimately in the coming days, better than anyone, and I am best positioned to create the proper tiny house." *And I knew Cadieux. I can honestly say that.*

"That is, to be the same as Cadieux House."

"No, not the same," said Wren. "*Complementary*. A tiny house is not just a big house on a smaller scale. It needs to have its own consistent design that merges with the main house without merely echoing it."

She watched Bronwyn think that over. What if she said, "Never mind, then. I'll find someone just to copy it."?

But no. She just smiled. "I thought only writers cared about the right words. But it seems architects do, too. I look forward to planning it with you, Wren—the renovation of Cadieux House and my 'she shed.' Very nice." Bronwyn gazed over the lawn that led to the rocky beach. Wren now felt a sort of prickling inside at the thought of designing the tiny house. What would Monsieur Cadieux have said? Would he throw a fit that someone dared imitate him, tamper with the perfection he had created? His tantrums were the stuff of legend, but she liked to think that after a moment, he'd laugh and kiss her on both cheeks.

He did like her, after all.

Then Bronwyn quickly changed tack. "Of course, I suppose at some point we have to talk about the *tragedy*, as they call it. It was only mentioned in passing—someone was killed here? It made me think of Norman Mailer, who almost killed one of his wives. It was something like that?"

She looked at Wren with a raised eyebrow. Wren was surprised. She would've thought anyone, especially a novelist, would've looked that up. Still, it had happened long before Bronwyn had been born, and all the principals were no doubt dead by now. Who knew or even cared about the Blaines anymore?

Or maybe Bronwyn did really know but was testing her to see if she was well-versed in the home, maybe even knew something as an architect she could share. Could she smoothly fence with Bronwyn? No, that was out of her element. All she could do was answer her.

"The Blaines were wealthy and well-connected socialites with a very old New York pedigree. One night, with a party in full swing, Dennis Blaine was killed," said Wren.

"Angry wife? Something like that?" asked Bronwyn.

"I'm afraid it was blander than that. Although the newspapers had a field day with it, the police arrested one of the hired waiters, who had been dismissed. He had a criminal past, had done time in prison, and it was seen as a burglary gone wrong, or perhaps just revenge. He denied it."

"You know a lot of this then?" asked Bronwyn. She looked closely at Wren.

"The Palace of Holyrood House in Edinburgh is the British monarch's official residence in Scotland. In 1566, jealous courtiers murdered David Rizzio, private secretary of Mary, Queen of Scots. You can see the exact place where it happened. It's important to know the past of a house."

Bronwyn looked a little stunned, which pleased Wren.

"It would've been fascinating if there had been a trial, if Rebecca and Dennis's relationship and their friendships in their inner circle all came out. Indeed, Marius Cadieux himself was there that night at the party. He was a frequent guest at the house he had designed. Would he have been called as a witness? But the suspected waiter died in a prison fight before the trial even started. And that was the end of it. There didn't seem to be any other motives. No one seemed to have a reason to kill Dennis. There was talk of infidelities on his part and Rebecca's. People wondered about her and Cadieux."

"There is always talk about the beautiful people—the beau monde, the jet set, whatever we've called them over the years. Nothing changes," said

CHAPTER ONE

Bronwyn, with a smile. She should know—that's what her books were all about.

"I'm sure. Anyway, they recovered the handgun, but there were no prints. The case was closed. There were murmurs—it was too neat to have a criminal servant who conveniently died himself. These were powerful and wealthy people, and there was talk of a cover up."

"You've researched this carefully indeed," said Bronwyn. *So—it was a test. All right then. She was good at tests.* "This was about more than simple history, though. I mean, Cadieux House isn't as famous as Holyrood House."

"I need to know the home's personality. Yes, houses have personalities. The people who live in a house affect it. And the house affects the people in return. The parties. The famous people who lived here. And finally, the death." Some clients found Wren's philosophy confusing, or even silly, but not Bronwyn.

"Where did it happen?"

"The room we're in right now."

Wren watched Bronwyn force herself not to look down.

"What do you believe? Do you believe that waiter killed Dennis? Or was it someone else?"

Wren smiled and shrugged. "I'm an architect, not a detective. Someone else might've. Rebecca could've killed her husband, I suppose, but she'd need a reason. There didn't seem to be one."

Bronwyn seemed surprised at what Wren knew, which pleased Wren despite herself. The famous author was cool and sharp and self-possessed… but she had gotten to her. Wren wondered if Bronwyn would challenge her on that, ask how Wren could possibly know. But no. At least not today.

"So what's the next step?" Bronwyn asked.

"We talk in more detail, and I look this over with my contractor, Bobby Fiore. We draw up plans, provide an estimate. That's just for the main house. I'll get started designing the tiny house and work with the local authorities on getting the necessary permissions. Just one more thing—you know, of course, that this has landmark status. There's little we can do to the exterior, although the interior changes you want should be okay. But Cadieux hasn't been gone all that long, compared with the 19th-century architects who designed the homes I usually work on. I just mention it because he had a lot of disciples. Actually, more like acolytes, as they pretty much worshiped him. They became prominent architects in their own right, and even though we have legal authority on our side, they may scream if we so much as change a lightbulb."

Bronwyn nodded. "I can see that. The price I'll pay for living inside a modern masterpiece."

"The most fanatical of them works right in New York, in fact. He'll have something to say."

"Oh, but I'm hiring the distinguished Wren Fontaine—everyone says you're the best," said Bronwyn with a dramatic wave of her arm. "Surely you can stop by his office and soothe him—architect to architect—before he shows up here with a picket sign?"

"I'll give it a try—I know him pretty well, you see. He's my father."

* * *

Now that Wren had moved out of the family home and into an apartment with Hadley, she and her father had gotten into the habit of weekly lunches that were half business and half personal. This week's restaurant was Italian, and Wren ordered the Osso Buco alla Milanese.

"That's a new one for you," said her father.

"Living with Hadley has made me more adventurous about food."

"Another reason to like her," said Ezra.

"Another?" asked Wren.

"I have observed that she has made you a happier person."

"On behalf of Hadley, thank you. We will have you to dinner again soon." She paused and eyed him carefully. "You aren't lonely by yourself?"

"I have friends over from time to time," he said and gave her a wry smile. "Some of them are female—"

"I don't need to know about that," Wren said, more sharply than she intended.

CHAPTER ONE

"It's nice to know I can still embarrass you. But onto business—how did the Long Island trip go? I assume some 1920s Jazz Age mansion? For houses close to the shore, you'll have to watch out for salt damage."

"Not exactly," said Wren. "Something a little more modern—1950s."

"Really? Doesn't seem old enough to require your particular expertise."

"It's a rather special house, requiring someone who really knows what they're doing. It's not just adding heated floors in the bathroom and a new range in the kitchen."

"What makes it so special?"

"A special design." She paused and looked at him closely as he brought his wine glass to his lips. "A special architect."

He stopped.

"Wren." The heavy finality on her name—the mark of a serious conversion since she was six. "You aren't about to tell me you're going to update the Cadieux House." It wasn't a question.

"The Blaine family has finally sold it," said Wren. "It's been uninhabited since before you were born. The new owner wants to bring it back. I can do it for them."

"What exactly do you plan to do? More than heated floors and a new range?" His eyes drilled into her.

"You never saw the inside of Cadieux House. I have. It's open—very open, even for Cadieux. We were talking about some sliding doors."

"And you, Miss Fontaine, are up to the task of improving on *Marius Cadieux?*"

Wren sometimes missed tones—but not from her father. She knew that in one form or another, that question was coming, and she had already planned on how she'd have to answer.

"Look at it this way, Mr. Fontaine. Even if we assume that Cadieux is perfect—and I know there's no 'if' about it for you—the client is still going to want changes. If we don't take the job, someone else will, and it won't be as good."

Ezra drank some wine. "Your confidence does you credit. I don't like this, but I do accept it. We'll work on the bid together and I will want to tour the house as soon as possible. You no doubt did your homework—it was designed for the Blaines. They were friends of Cadieux's, powerful and influential people. Rebecca Blaine, in particular, was quite a piece of work, I heard. They met Cadieux in France in the 1930s. He was young but already being talked about. And she already had something of a reputation, bright and beautiful, making friends and winning admirers everywhere she went, always with something witty on her lips, it was said. There was talk about him and Rebecca."

"Really? Is this a monument to his love? His Taj Mahal?"

Ezra laughed. "It seems my daughter has a romantic streak! Anyway, Cadieux was handsome and charming, and there had always been talk about him, too, so it was probably inevitable the two of them were matched in the minds of gossip columnists. He never stayed with any woman very long. Still, he remained close with her for the rest of his life, although it was clear there was no romance, at least not anymore. He mentioned her in passing from time to time, but never discussed his feelings for her or their history. That was something he was silent about. She died in 1985, I think. I remember because he bowed out of an important panel discussion to attend her funeral. Marius looked forward, not backward, in his work and his life, so that was very uncharacteristic of him."

Her father didn't seem to understand the details of their relationship, and he knew people, knew Cadieux well. What chance did she have of uncovering it?

"Who's the client, by the way?" asked Ezra.

"The novelist Bronwyn Merrick. I'll have to get a signed copy of her latest for Ada." Their housekeeper adored her books.

"Really? Judging from the book covers, I'd thought she'd buy an English castle. De gustibus non est disputandum—no accounting for taste. If she bought a Cadieux, my estimation of her goes up."

"There's more," said Wren. "She also wants a freestanding accessory dwelling unit—a tiny house where she can write in private."

He nodded. "Sensible for a writer, even though the house is large. Do you feel up to designing it yourself?"

CHAPTER ONE

Wren felt almost giddy that her father assumed she would do it—that she *could* do it.

"Yes. Something to complement the main house."

"'Complement.' I like that word. You didn't say 'copy.'"

"If I copied a Cadieux all I'd get is, at best, a second-rate Cadieux. The ADU is going to…*partner* with Cadieux House. Different, but matching its tone."

"And that tone is…?"

"I'm still working on it. I know people are not my strong suit, but I do know that Rebecca Blaine was a strong personality and so was Cadieux, of course. That house was a match of their personalities. I think the ADU can be a match as well."

"Between Marius Cadieux…and you?" Ezra seemed amused.

"I feel confident," she said, daring her father to disagree.

"You'll have to be, adding on to a Cadieux. He'd have a fit if he thought someone was adding even a birdfeeder without consulting him."

"Maybe he threw tantrums in your presence, but not in mine." She grinned, in both amusement and relief. "If you recall, he rather liked me."

Her father was going to say something…but then stopped and chuckled. "You know…you're right. This is going to sound silly—"

"You've never said anything silly in your life," said Wren.

"I'm about to give you a compliment, so don't interrupt. I was going to say that even though Marius Cadieux mentored a score of world-renowned architects, I believe that if he had to choose someone for this job, he'd choose you. He liked you, as I remember."

They ate in silence for a couple of minutes while Wren thought that over, until her father said, "When you've recovered, I'm interested in any preliminary thoughts on the ADU."

* * *

"Leftovers from a job, I'm afraid," said Hadley. She had bags looped over her shoulders.

"What do you mean, 'I'm afraid?'" asked Wren. "When do you have to apologize for your leftovers?"

"Thank you, Little Bird." She gave Wren a kiss. "I just like making something special for us."

"It's that word, 'leftover.' We need something better. When you think about it, I work on leftover homes. Let's call your leftovers 'classic.'"

"Oooh. Clever girl. Anyway, another music client tonight. We created the whole album release program. It's Southern Rock. I hadn't even known that was still a thing, but if it works for them…anyway, fried chicken—which I actually like better cold—potato salad, and coleslaw."

Wren's dream furniture had always been late Victorian, but for a one-bedroom apartment, it wouldn't have worked. So she had suggested an industrial style, an old-fashioned factory look, retro enough to be charming and practical for a small living space. Wren set the trestle table as Hadley unpacked the food.

"What a wonderful partnership we have," said Hadley. "I cook great food and you've set a great stage to serve it on." She poured them glasses of Fiji water and they clinked glasses. "So you told your father about the Cadieux House? Did he take it well?"

"Better than expected. I think he'll be breathing down my neck for this one. Any house designed by Cadieux is not just a home; it's a church where his followers can worship him. He wants to see it as soon as possible. I bet he's jealous I saw the inside before he did."

"Well, you're the renovation boss. It only makes sense. And now, from the sublime to the ridiculous. Any insights into the Blaine murder? There are still murmurs there was some kind of cover up."

Wren laughed. "I have a feeling that now that the Cadieux House has been purchased, and by someone famous, the Blaine case will be back upfront. I saw a piece that said Dennis was shot at very close range. How and why could that happen? That he was that close. And there was a tragic aspect about it—Dennis and Rebecca lived a storybook life, and he was so handsome, even in his middle years. That somehow, the gods struck him down before he could get old and ugly. 'Live fast, die young, leave a beautiful corpse.'"

CHAPTER ONE

"Wow, Little Bird, quoting James Dean."

"It's older than that," said Wren, laughing. "But all this is beyond me."

"It's about the house, for you," said Hadley. "If you understand the people, you can understand the house. But it's really about understanding the house so you can understand the people."

"Fair enough," said Wren.

"You're too hard on yourself. I think you know people better than you think. Anyway, were Rebecca and Cadieux hot and heavy?"

"Could be. Rebecca and Cadieux had been close. He was a notorious womanizer, and she was still very attractive at fifty. But police could find no evidence that they had ever slipped off to some hotel. Even afterwards, there was no sign of an affair."

"Okay. But about the Blaines. Great, great wealth. Did Rebecca want control of her husband's money? I've never met any of them, but back in the day, they moved in the same circles as my family."

"Of course," said Wren. "Two houses, both alike in dignity. But Rebecca was wealthy in her own right. So neither Rebecca nor Dennis had a financial reason to want the other dead. There was talk they had an agreement they could both have affairs as long as they were discreet—they were very sophisticated. Again, according to the accounts at the time, there were flirtations—but then, again, talk like that always happens around the beautiful people, going back to the Renaissance."

They cleaned up, and then Wren sat in a corner of their leather couch. Hadley kicked off her shoes and lay down, with her feet on the wooden couch railing and her head in Wren's lap.

"So you have a mystery," she said. "A mystery about the house."

"Every great house has a mystery. Just think of the mysteries in some European castles that were already old when Columbus sailed. This one is more modern, but still, it was over sixty years ago. Pretty much everyone who was there that night is probably dead."

"You'll figure it out." She looked up at Wren, who idly flicked a strand of blond hair off her girlfriend's forehead. You will insist on understanding this house and since modernist is a little off the beaten path for you, you'll look at all connections. You always say it comes down to the house, right, and you need to figure out Marius Cadieux." She giggled. "I know my Little Bird."

Yes, she did.

Wren was thinking of an answer when her phone rang.

"Wren? It's Bronwyn. I hate bothering people in the evening, but I wondered if you had a moment. Something came up…I got a call earlier from a Woody Blaine. He doesn't seem happy…that is, he has some questions about the house and its, ah, future. He wants to meet…with his lawyer. I was hoping you could come?" It was a half-question.

Thoughts ran through Wren's head. She wasn't good at tone, but there was something off about the straightforward Bronwyn. Nevertheless, she was waiting for an answer.

"Bronwyn…I'm not a lawyer. And we're still in the proposal phase. You haven't actually hired me—"

"Oh hell, you know I'm going to hire you. Who else could do this? And it's not really a legal thing. Believe me, I had lawyers make one hundred and ten percent sure we had clear title. No. It's just that—well, one of the Blaines, not the Blaine I bought it from, has a problem, and I'd like to resolve it quietly. I'm something of a public figure, and I don't want this blown out of proportion. It doesn't…anyway, I thought if you could just explain a few things…" Her voice trailed off.

"Explain what?" asked Wren. "At this stage, I only have the most general ideas for what I'll be doing with the house or the ADU. Of course, the exterior is covered by landmark regulations, if they want to know about that."

"Actually, it's not that…" said Bronwyn. Wren let her hang. People would speak when they were ready. "It's about the history…it's about the tragedy, what we talked about, the unsolved murder. They have certain concerns and want to make sure we're all on board. I know they don't have a legal leg to stand on, but I don't need a fight right now, at the start of your work on the house. They want to talk and hear your insights."

Insights on what? Is there a message behind her words that I'm just failing to grasp?

CHAPTER ONE

"Anyway, do you have about an hour tomorrow?"

Wren looked down at Hadley, who saw her concern and blew her a kiss. Wren winked at her and then thought of her father. He wouldn't stand for this kind of nonsense.

"I want to help. But I need to be prepared. I need to know what they will want from me."

"I know it sounds silly after all these years…but there are concerns about the tragedy—and all that. I know your firm has worked with so many prominent people, you'd of course be sensitive. But they're concerned."

It was true that rich people could be odd, but these weren't even the owners. Her father would want her to stand up for herself, but also to oblige a client.

"Yes. I can certainly give you an hour tomorrow."

"Oh, thank you so much. We tentatively agreed on ten—if that works for you. It'll be at an office in Midtown. I'll text you the address."

Wren clicked off.

"What was that all about?"

"I'm not really sure. But I spoke too soon. It suddenly seems that I may have to deal with the Blaine tragedy after all."

Chapter Two

Wren knew the address right away: 230 Park Avenue, the Helmsley Building, a century-old jewel that straddled Park Avenue, just uptown of Grand Central station. She had never been inside one of its offices, so getting to visit was a plus.

She wore one of her good pants suits—standard for office meetings—and slung her large leather bag over her shoulder. Wren faced her usual internal battle between her own obsession with punctuality and her father's advice to make people wait for her. She was a little annoyed at the secrecy of this odd summons, so why not be a few minutes late? She arrived a few minutes early but spent the time savoring the splendidly ornate lobby before getting on the elevator five minutes late.

The law firm of Archer, Voight, and Cleveland was, as Wren expected, replete with Victorian-style furniture. Who had decided that that should be the default for law offices? She'd love to do an office in High Renaissance.

"I'm Wren Fontaine, here to see Mr. Archer," she told the receptionist. A moment later, an executive assistant came and ushered her into a conference room—more Victorian wood.

"Wren Fontaine," announced the secretary. "May I get you some coffee?"

"No, thank you," said Wren.

Bronwyn, another woman, and two men sat at the conference table, and the men stood up. One was in his mid-fifties, a little portly, and the other was taller, and spare, and probably around seventy.

The older one spoke first. "Ms. Fontaine—I'm Tristan Archer. I am the attorney for the Blaine Trust," he smiled his welcome. "This is Woodrow

CHAPTER TWO

Blaine," who shook her hand, and nodded, but didn't smile. "He is both a beneficiary of the trust and its financial manager. You know your client, of course, Bronwyn Merrick." She smiled at Wren. "And this..." a brief hesitation "...is Rebecca and Dennis's daughter, Shoshana Blaine."

Now—*she* grabbed Wren's attention. The face was very old, but not the eyes, which hit Wren like a pair of searchlights, and she sat straight in her chair. She wore a robe-like dress, vaguely Asian, and her wintry white hair fell across her breast in a long braid, over a beaded African-looking necklace.

"Ms. Fontaine," she said. Her voice didn't waver, a clipped upper-class city accent. "I understand your father was a follower of Marius Cadieux. I'm sure he'd be pleased that the work on his house was being handled by the Fontaines." She smiled slyly—and launched into French. *"My mother spoke fluent French, as do I. She could speak with Cadieux in his native language as he designed this house. She felt French was important to fully understand the house. Do you know any French?"*

Wren took a seat—and switched to French herself: *"A little, even if I don't get to practice it very often. And I flatter myself, Madame Blaine, that Monsieur Cadieux would fully understand my Parisian accent. I heard he could be quite critical. I hope he didn't make fun of your French...Marseillaise, I think, from the south? Oh, and call me Wren."*

Shoshana just stared at her for a few moments, and Wren looked right back, hoping the old woman couldn't see how fast her heart was beating. Then Shoshana slammed her hand on the table and burst out laughing.

"Oh, I deserved that, Wren! That was terrific. Yes, my mother had a perfect Parisian accent, and I did not. I'm glad to see you're just as sharp-tongued as Marius was. Let's see if you're as talented."

Archer cleared his throat and shuffled some papers, rather nervously. Well, if Shoshana was an example of the family, a lifetime of serving them would make anyone nervous.

Wren glanced around. Woodrow looked just plain annoyed at the exchange. In an expensive and traditional blue suit that did its best to masquerade his plump physique, he didn't resemble his cousin Shoshana. However, the expression was the same. *These are people who are used to being in charge, and*

Woodrow was not happy with the interruption.

Meanwhile, Wren didn't know if Bronwyn knew French, but she could tell at least that the old lady had been put in her place and was amused.

"Okay then," said Archer, clearing his throat. "I think we'll start with a little background, especially for Wren, for whom a lot of this will be new. Now, after Dennis Blaine…died, his widow, Rebecca Blaine, and their only child, Shoshana Blaine, inherited some funds outright, and Rebecca had considerable family funds of her own. This was back in the day when my father, Percival Archer, represented the trust." Establishing the long history of the Archers, Wren realized. "Also, substantial sums had been set aside in a trust for any future grandchildren. The house itself was part of that trust, although the house was part of Shoshana's legacy. The family chose to commit to upkeep, rather than living there themselves."

"It's a *Cadieux*," said Wren. "No one wanted to live there? You couldn't sell it or rent it?"

"The death and resulting publicity didn't exactly make it a hot property," said Shoshana. "My mother wanted to get away from it all. We moved to California and led a quieter life. We had plenty of money even with it sitting there. We left everything there. We just…didn't care anymore. Now, maybe I'll die tomorrow, or maybe I'll make it to one hundred, but it seemed ridiculous to have this spectacular house unoccupied. I don't want to live way out here, however. Perhaps once…but I'm too well-ensconced in Manhattan, where I've lived for the past quarter-century." Did Wren hear some regret there? "Anyway, it's time to let go. With the trustees' permission, we should sell it. I'll have some funds to distribute to various philanthropies I support. I'm going to be moving on soon, in a final sense, so let's wrap this up."

She looked around, daring anyone to disagree with her.

Woodrow spoke first. "My father—Dennis's nephew, and your first cousin—was a trustee, before his retirement. Now I am, too. As you know, I never thought much of this house. I thought it was a waste of money—"

"Do *shut up*," said Shoshana. "No one cares about your opinion of the house—"

CHAPTER TWO

"It's a ludicrous house, and we were damn lucky Cadieux's dubious fame allowed the family to recoup the costs. I just wish that going forward, the money from the sale would be kept in the family trust," Woodrow snapped back.

"The idea of the trust was to prevent reckless spending of any proceeds. It's now decades later, and it's well past time to distribute. Whom are we protecting anymore? You got your share anyway. The whole idea of a trust was to protect me and any descendants, and that is no longer an issue. I don't even see why we're having this meeting."

"Ahh...although I wouldn't have put it that way," said Archer, "Ms. Blaine is technically right. As I explained a year ago, and several times since, there were no legal grounds for preventing Shoshana from selling the house and distributing the proceeds."

"It's not that, as I've explained myself," said Woodrow. He leaned forward on the table. "My concern isn't financial—"

"Ha!" said Shoshana. "I've known you since the day you were born and never knew you to make a decision that *wasn't* financial. You are your father."

Woodrow pulled back. "Do not mention my father. I mean it." Shoshana just rolled her eyes. "Dear Auntie, you were very lucky to be able to live a life without ever worrying about money. But every now and then, someone in this family has to do the boring work of seeing to the various family businesses. I have a very advantageous, and very sensitive, deal in the works with a French consortium, and I don't need the publicity that the sale of this house is continuing to generate. That's bad enough, but ongoing attention could make my position even worse."

"That was nearly seventy years ago," said Shoshana. "Who the hell even cares anymore?"

"That's my point exactly," said Woodrow. "People will rake it up all over again. There are still plenty of Blaines around. You are still around. You were even there then, and we never did find a way to keep your mouth shut."

Wren shrank at that, and it wasn't even aimed at her. Shoshana smiled without humor.

"What I would like," he continued, "is for the parties here to understand that the house is not just a house. It is part of the family history, a well-known and influential family." He turned to Wren and Bronwyn. "Ms. Merrick, I have no right to ask about what you will do with your property. But I know you are an author. I know in your literary endeavors you often fictionalize real-life events for your books." Bronwyn raised an eyebrow. "And I don't criticize that," he quickly added. "And I know that I have no right to question your work. But this is a family that is still very much present. It is my family. You will hurt people, especially as some of your readers may not understand the various…subtleties and think of your book as an authorized family history. Please consider my—our—situation. In return, I have some family papers relating to the unfortunate death of Dennis Blaine that may be of use to you. My father was very close to Dennis, and I can be of help to you." He turned to Wren. *What is he going to ask of me?*

"Ms. Fontaine, again, I have no right to control your work as an architect. But I know your firm has dealt with some very distinguished families that have no doubt appreciated your tact and discretion. I hope you will exercise that here. You may come across certain aspects of the family that are not technically part of your work. In any case, I hope I can count on your discretion. And of course…" he smiled at her. "…because of my family connections, I am in an excellent position to recommend your firm widely."

The Fontaines don't need your help, she wanted to say, but she realized that was needlessly antagonizing. She thought for a moment, organizing her words, while Woodrow looked back and forth between her and Bronwyn.

"Some of my clients want a lot of publicity up front, and I make myself available for interviews. Others want complete silence about the project. I always follow my client's wishes. For anything related to the house, I will defer to Bronwyn Merrick."

Bronwyn looked at Wren and nodded, then turned back to Woodrow. "I understand your concern," she said. "I am careful. I do want you to know I've never been sued for libel. Not successfully, anyway. I suppose Mr. Archer's presence here is to imply that I can be sued for libel?"

But Tristan waved that away. "I am legal advisor to the family. I am not a litigator. I just facilitated this to do what I can to protect the reputation

CHAPTER TWO

of the family. This is a special case—a house so intimately connected to the family, even if it is no longer owned by them."

Wren watched Bronwyn. *She's like me, really. I work with houses. She works with people. She's studying them.* Bronwyn looked at Shoshana, who gave her a wintry smile. Woodrow just looked stiff. Tristan—did he look a little tired? Again, managing this family must be exhausting.

"I just bought a house," said Bronwyn. "This has nothing to do with my writing. Nevertheless, I like keeping everyone's goodwill, and I'll say now you won't have to worry about me, even if Wren finds something in the course of her work." She looked at Wren, who nodded in agreement.

"Well, I think we all have what we want," said Archer. "Ms. Merrick, Ms. Fontaine, thank you for your time and for being so understanding."

Wren thought that was it but hadn't counted on the family. She had unfortunately found herself in the middle of family arguments before, as descendants found themselves in bitter arguments over tiny details. She had thought it ludicrous that such minor issues could lead to so much rage. Her father had explained: "Wren. Arguments like that have nothing to do with where you put the kitchen counter and everything to do with childhood wounds and decades-old resentment on how you were raised. It's a home, Wren, for better or worse. How much of our home is connected with memories of your mother?"

It could be a suburban split level or a mansion, it ended up the same, and Cadieux House was going to be no different.

Woodrow turned to Shoshana. "Dear cousin, there's a good chance the recent home sale will revive interest in the family history. I can count on you to behave?"

She just stared at Woodrow for a few moments.

"I dislike you. And I disliked your father before you."

"I told you not to mention my father. You are your mother's daughter, Shoshana, a true Rodriguez, and had little use for your father, Dennis. But I am a Blaine, and my side was close to Dennis."

"I'm astonished that after all these years, you remain appallingly unaware of our family's history. I admit I can't tell if it's just unimaginable stupidity or self-delusion that borders on psychopathy, but I do promise whatever I do, I'll stick with the truth." Woodrow just pursed his lips and stared. "Perfect," continued Shoshana. "I see even the thought of the truth scares you. That says everything, doesn't it?"

Woodrow sighed dramatically. "Fine." He turned to Archer.

"And I can assume your professional ethics will allow you to remain silent on this?" he asked.

"As you know, I represent the trust and a variety of other Blaine interests. As my father did before me. I will always do what is best for the family."

Woodrow frowned. "Before I die, I want to hear a lawyer give me a straight answer to a question. I guess I'll be satisfied with that." He looked around the room and then stood. "Thank you all for coming and for your cooperation. I believe we are done here." He shook Archer's hand, nodded at everyone else, and left quickly, as if he was afraid someone would change their mind.

Archer raised an eyebrow. "Ms. Fontaine, Ms. Merrick, once again, I appreciate your cooperation. It was above and beyond."

"I'm glad we could resolve it so easily," said Bronwyn. Wren didn't know what to say. Wealthy people could be strange, but this level of weirdness, gathering people at a lawyer's office to prevent knowledge of a scandal that happened decades ago, was beyond explanation.

Archer cleared his throat. "And, ah, Shoshana. On behalf of the family, thank you." She rolled her eyes. "He's a jackass. And his father was a jackass before him. Anyway, I'd love to have a meeting with these two ladies. I'm sure you have things to do, and if they have a few minutes, I'd like to talk with them, so some good can come out of this meeting."

"Oh…yes, of course. Take all the time you want. Let me know if you have any questions." He left quickly, closing the door behind him, no doubt pleased to get away from the family for a while.

"Bronwyn, so glad to see you again," Shoshana said. "We met at the closing but didn't really have time to talk. I'm not sentimental about homes, but you seem to have a sense of the importance of Cadieux House, and that pleases me." She turned to Wren. "I know this largely because Bronwyn chose you. I looked you up. You're making a name for yourself. Your father was a student of Cadieux's and is said to be almost as talented. And almost as arrogant."

Wren smiled back at her. "You're right on both counts."

Shoshana laughed. "Bronwyn, you've chosen well. Now, since I have you both here, I have some curiosity about the old place. I suppose I could've arranged for a visit before it was sold, but I never wanted to. And now I'm not sure I can visit, not after all this time. There are memories. I was there the night my father was killed. I was only twenty. I didn't see anything—a few of the young set had gone for a walk on the beach. But still, I was there. I saw them carry his body away."

Bronwyn glanced at Wren and then said, "I understand. But If you change your mind, and if it's okay with Wren while she's working, you can stop by."

"That's not a problem. It will be some time before we start actual work anyway," said Wren. She looked into the surprisingly clear eyes of this old woman. "Also, I'd like to know more about the house and its history. And as I promised your cousin, I will be very discreet."

"Of course, of course. Don't worry about my idiot cousin. But I would've thought you'd just be interested in the structure, materials, and wiring, not our gruesome family history."

"As I explained to Bronwyn, houses have personalities," said Wren. "They stamp them on the families who live in them, and the homes themselves absorb the personalities of the people who reside there. When I renovate a house, I need to know as much as possible about those relationships to connect with the soul of the house. It is important for any house, but especially for a Marius Cadieux house. Every house he designed was a gift of his brilliance to an individual. For this house, that person was your mother, Rebecca Blaine, so the more I know, the better the renovation will be."

Wren stopped and looked at her audience, suddenly afraid she hadn't read the room. Her father could. Her father knew how to speak to everyone. Bronwyn's eyes were practically popping out of her head. Shoshana just stared, and Wren wondered if she had just given the old lady a stroke.

"That was...something," said Shoshana. "I thought that you were handing me a line to find out about our scandalous past, but you look so damn serious.

I don't think you have the talent to deliver something like that unless you were actually sincere. That's a frightening prospect in itself. You know, I've met a lot of crazy creatives in my life…but wow. All right then." She turned to Bronwyn. "Did you know about this?"

"A little," said Bronwyn, "but people have said I'm a crazy creative too. So we should get along."

"Well, I'm here," said Shoshana. "What do you want to know?"

Wren took a deep breath. "I am not asking about the death or who was responsible. I want to know about your parents' relationship with Marius Cadieux—especially your mother. I believe she was the main point of contact for the design. I want to know the extent of their friendship. I know he was a frequent guest here, and that tells me they were more than architect and client. That is unusual. I guess you could say this house was a child of that relationship. If you had a sense of that friendship, it would help me understand this house better."

Shoshana nodded. Wren caught Bronwyn's eye—*she's as curious as I am.*

"You're right about my mother. My father had vague ideas about a showplace, but that's as far as his imagination ran. It was my mother who worked closely with him. You know, they had known each other for many years, even before my parents married. It was rumored…" She smiled slyly and cast a glance at Bronwyn. "You know what I'm going to say, don't you? A writer like you probably knows everything about us."

"Not really," said Bronwyn. "Wren here seems to be the family expert." A quick smile and a sidelong glance at her architect. *Okay, I'm on stage now.* "I don't gossip myself. But I can tell you, and I'm sure you know too, that there has always been talk that Cadieux was your father."

Shoshana laughed. "Of course, of course. I hate to disappoint everyone, but that's not true. You could look at where everyone was when I was born, but even so, Marius was only about twenty years older than I was and seven years younger than my mother. Although she did meet him when he was young—my parents visited France in the thirties and Cadieux was already a firebrand. Some big names in architecture had taken him under their wings, and, as my parents knew everyone, they met. I think they found him

CHAPTER TWO

amusing. He was always an entertaining and charming man and incredibly handsome." She focused on the past for a moment, then recalled herself. "Anyway, even then, Marius Cadieux was very sophisticated. He had caught the eye of every woman he met, and my mother was older than him. He didn't actively pursue her. She was older and married. But I think she caught his attention. And, of course, she loved him, but she was also sophisticated. She wasn't going to make a fool of herself chasing after a younger man while she was married. But I can tell you—there was love there."

"Like…siblings?" asked Wren.

Shoshana looked at her coolly. "Is it necessary to classify it? They loved each other, and that was enough—make of that what you will. There was a lot of love there at the time, and not everyone knew what was happening. My mother was fifty, still very handsome, of course, not too old for…feelings. I was twenty and had many admirers." She gave them a secretive smile. "There is more to the story, and maybe someday I'll share it with you." She glanced at Bronwyn briefly and looked smug. "Anyway, I'd have thought that you, with a long-term girlfriend, would understand the silliness—the futility—of classifying love." Wren felt the heat rising to her face. "Young women still blush!" said Shoshana. "I thought blushing went out sometime during the Eisenhower administration."

"Thank you for your frankness," said Wren, trying to move the conversation along. "That will be something I will definitely keep in mind for both the renovation and Bronwyn's 'she shed.'" She felt proud of herself for daring to ask, despite the embarrassment.

They all stood. Bronwyn said she had a car waiting for her downstairs and would be happy to give both of them a ride home. Shoshana said she had her own car waiting, but Wren accepted.

Shoshana's car was an older but well-kept black Cadillac. The chauffeur wore a traditional outfit and helped his employer into the back seat.

Bronwyn owned a massive Mercedes SUV, in a dark green.

"I know—it looks like it belongs on the veldt. This city girl didn't learn to drive until she was thirty, and I went over the top for my suburban move."

Her driver wore a sports coat, unbuttoned. Wren was surprised at what she saw but decided not to comment. He opened the door but didn't help anyone in, barely glanced at them. Rather, he looked around the crowded street, shut the doors, and drove off quickly. Bronwyn gave him Wren's address.

"Will do," he said.

"Rather odd," said Bronwyn. "I mean that little meeting. You work with old homes. Is that par for the course?"

Wren smiled. "It's like what F. Scott Fitzgerald said, 'The rich are different from you and me.'"

"Ah, but I'm rich. That's what my accountant says, anyway. And I don't understand it."

"Yes. But this is different." Wren organized her thoughts. Her father handled talks like this smoothly. With panache. Could she? "My clients are wealthy. You have to be wealthy to buy a historic home. But I'm concerned with the old money that built the homes I work on." Bronwyn seemed interested. Wren took the next step. "There is a phrase—'the kind of people who buy their silver.'"

Bronwyn laughed. "Oh, what a nice way of saying nouveau riche. I love it. So you're saying that it's old money that can be a bit odd. The Blaines go back, I know."

"Yes, that's it exactly," said Wren, pleased that Bronwyn seemed to get it and wasn't offended. "I'm an architect, not a psychologist, but I feel I build a connection to the old families through their homes."

"You wish you were back there, don't you?" asked Bronwyn. Wren felt a sudden jolt. But, of course, she was dealing with a best-selling author who knew a thing or two about motivations.

"I'm afraid so," said Wren.

"Don't say 'afraid so.' I've written enough historical fiction and often would like to be in another time myself. Anyway, I liked what you said inside about Rebecca being the point person on the house. Now, she was only a Blaine by marriage. Is she from money, too?"

"Actually, yes. Different from the Blaines, but far more interesting. She was a Rodriguez."

CHAPTER TWO

"Spanish?"

"Sephardic Jews—Iberian ancestry. Moses Montefiore, as in Montefiore Medical Center, was a financier and philanthropist of Sephardic ancestry, and so was actor Jerry Orbach. I'm not an expert, but they have different traditions, different outlooks, from the East European and Russian Jews who came here later. The Sephardim were in the U.S. much earlier. "

"I…that's fascinating. Maybe that explains Shoshana's attitude about all of this. Anyway, I see you're not just an architect. You're a historian."

"Not really," said Wren, and then heard her father's voice telling her not to be self-effacing. "But I do research houses. Every house exists in its own particular time, and you can't understand it unless you are intimate with that time."

Wren felt warm under Bronwyn's gaze. "Wow. An architect AND a historian AND a philosopher."

"Fontaine Partners only bills for the architecture," said Wren. "The history and philosophy are free."

Bronwyn laughed, and Wren felt relief, as they pulled up to her apartment.

"We'll talk soon," said Bronwyn. "I'm very excited about working with you and taking the next steps."

The driver let Wren out, and she noticed again he didn't look at her, but around the street. He didn't talk to her at all. Walking into the lobby, Wren mulled over the oddities of the Blaine family, the singular Shoshana, and Bronwyn's curiosity about the family.

And why Bronwyn felt she needed an armed chauffeur.

Chapter Three

"We are missing so much by not keeping ourselves buried in social media twenty-four/seven," said Hadley with a grin. "Fortunately, as we provide social media help to our clients along with catering and event planning, we employ a social media consultant from time to time. She's rather odd, as she spends the better part of her life scrolling through Facebook, Instagram, Pinterest, Twitter, and so on, but she knows her stuff. And your Bronwyn has been front and center lately. It's not altogether good."

Hadley placed her laptop on the table and served the potstickers. She admired how deftly Wren handled the chopsticks. Wren's father had said that if you didn't have the dexterity to manage chopsticks, you weren't qualified to be an architect.

"It seems Bronwyn wrote a book last year about a young Englishwoman, Eliza Charteris, from a good family who comes to New York in the Victorian era and becomes a leader in New York society. Lots of romance, some R-rated sex, a duel or two, and plenty of dinner parties. Business as usual in one of her books, I understand."

"Not my cup of lapsang souchong," said Wren. "But okay. Don't tell me Bronwyn killed her off, and now everyone is upset? That was the plot of the Stephen King novel *Misery*, right?"

"Exactly. Apparently, fans take books and movies very seriously, and thanks to social media, they can find each other and organize. In the book, our Eliza was being courted by a 'bad boy.' Lots of 'bad boys' in Bronwyn's books. Tall, dark, and handsome—the whole nine yards. The fans were

CHAPTER THREE

waiting for Eliza to capture and tame this man and lead him down the aisle. But that's not what happened. Eliza found out he betrayed her, so she killed him and went off, presumably to have more adventures as a proud single woman—Christ, Wren, don't tell me you're upset too?"

Wren paused. She put down a prawn and drank tea.

"Not about my client's murderous protagonist. Not directly. But that's the tragedy in the Cadieux House. Rebecca Blaine was one of the suspects in the death of her husband, Dennis, although she was never charged. She lived the rest of her life as a proud, single woman. What is coincidence, and what is planned?"

"Ohh...wow. I hadn't even put that together. It's so much more exciting to think that this was more than a coincidence."

"When was this published?" asked Wren. Hadley clicked to Amazon. "All right. So I'm thinking that it took some months between writing this and having it published, and I know when she bought the house...so it certainly adds up. She could well have found the house, learned about the history, and then put that incident in her novel. I—" She stopped.

"What were you going to say?" asked Hadley.

"I think she lied to me. I'm not good at being able to tell..." She gave a self-deprecating laugh, and Hadley gave her shoulder a squeeze "...but you know that. I'm thinking now she knows more about the house than she let on and more about the Blaine and Rodriguez families. She pretended she knew very little and I found myself wondering if she was testing me. Maybe she was curious, or even worried, about what I knew. I wonder if this connects with that odd meeting, worrying about the secrets."

Hadley giggled. "We know something for sure. Someone besides Wren Fontaine was affected by a house."

Wren smiled. "I think you're right. I can see Bronwyn in that house she just bought, wondering about the people, about the death, and deciding to end her book that way. Even if it did upset her readers. So much so that she goes around with an armed bodyguard."

"It might explain that meeting," said Hadley, who continued to click away. "That Woodrow Blaine had a sense that this would make headlines again, although frankly, I can't see a murder that old getting everyone worked up. I mean, Shoshana Blaine is probably the last one left who knows about it first-hand. Now, here's something interesting…according to this old account, the Rodriguez family was represented by Archer, Voight, and Cleveland—we knew that. But there were various branches of the Blaine family represented by Calvin, Cromwell."

"Why is that name familiar?"

"That's where my brother works. He just made partner. Of course, not in an exciting area like criminal law. He plans estates and does trusts."

"Well, I like Trey a lot. And I love his wife."

"We all like Trey and Marcia, and after all," Hadley dramatically put the back of her hand against her forehead and struck a histrionic pose, "only one Vanderwerf at a time can be interesting, and I'm afraid the burden for this generation is mine."

"Fair enough," said Wren, laughing. "But I'm wondering if Trey can give us some background. If there's a Blaine connection there, it may spill over to Rebecca and Dennis. Does client confidentiality last over sixty years? I'd like to avoid any further surprises, and Trey might have some insights."

"All this happened before our parents were born, Little Bird, but that's the funny thing about people like us—the Old Money set. We're clannish and have long memories. It's our strength *and* our weakness. From what Trey, and my father, have said over the years, all the lawyers at that level know each other. Everything is connected. Now I've burned a lot of bridges, but Trey has been a good boy, and the Calvin, Cromwell name can open a lot of doors. I'll give him a call and put him to work."

Wren nodded. "Good. There are other doors, too. As I explained to Bronwyn, Rebecca Blaine was born a Rodriguez—Sephardic Jews with a long history in this country and plenty of money of their own. You know…" She looked at her girlfriend. "The day after tomorrow, Bronwyn and I are planning to meet at Cadieux House for a more detailed look. Can you come?"

"Oh! Yes. I have an evening event, but if it's in the morning, sure. How will you explain my presence? Your cultural consultant?"

"You're an event planner. You are advising me on the use of space. And it

CHAPTER THREE

just so happens you're my girlfriend. I'd like you to meet Bronwyn. I'd be interested in your reaction to her."

"I'd love to see the house, I admit." She fixed her eyes on Wren. "Has your father seen it yet? You told me he was almost obsessed with it, with Marius Cadieux."

"He's tied up with some clients of his for the next few days, but as soon as he gets a moment free, he'll be joining me. Just as well, I'd like to know a bit more about it before he shows up. For now, you and I will drive with Bronwyn in the morning—her and her chauffeur/bodyguard, and then she'll take us back to the city."

"Do I detect a note of anxiety?" asked Hadley.

"Never mind school. I really learned to be an architect from my father. There's a special place in his heart for Marius Cadieux, and I wonder how he'll cope with his daughter working on his house."

Hadley knew her Wren.

"Little Bird, you're wondering how *you* will cope. I've watched you. You just know how homes are put together. And if I can see that, surely your father does as well."

Wren squeezed her hand. "Thank you. I'd feel better if it were a 19th-century house, like what I'm used to. There is something I don't understand about the house." Then she laughed. "Actually, I think that's why he's so eager. He's only seen the plans for the house, and I imagine there's something he saw there that he didn't understand, before I was even born." She winked at Hadley. "Who knows? Maybe I'll uncover it first."

Chapter Four

They went through the usual routine, with the driver looking up and down the block as he let Wren and Hadley into the car. His jacket was open—Wren presumed to make it easy to reach his gun. Wren introduced Hadley and Bronwyn.

"So glad you could come," said Bronwyn. "I'm still getting used to the place myself. Wren says you're the space expert, event and party planning."

"That's what I do. Wren asked me for some advice on the flow of the house."

"I want to make sure that any changes we make work for your purposes—any entertaining," said Wren. She looked closely at Bronwyn. Getting clients to be open and honest about what they wanted to do with a house could be a puzzle. It wasn't that they lied to her. They lied to themselves about grandiose plans they wouldn't have the time, energy, or interest to do. Hadn't her father installed twenty thousand dollar ranges in houses for homeowners who ate out every night?

"I'm a bit of a loner," said Bronwyn with a smile. "Actually, that's not fair. I have friends, but I don't throw many parties or have large events. I don't have much of a family, either. I'll be rattling around here."

Fair enough, thought Wren. But if the house would be empty, why should she need a special tiny house? There was still a lie there.

"Still, I suppose I'll have a housewarming," said Bronwyn. "You can do that?"

Hadley quickly produced a card. "I take care of everything. I'm the chef. We don't just bring in frozen foods."

CHAPTER FOUR

Bronwyn looked at Wren. "Living with a chef? That's very nice. I'm thinking you two are lucky."

"We are," said Wren softly.

"Glad to have both of you here. I'm still understanding this place. And your father is coming too. Has he gotten over the fact that I'm daring to change a Cadieux?"

Wren smiled. "Right now, he's just so excited about seeing the house. He's always wanted to, but it's been closed up. Cadieux had a cadre of followers, but they were children, or not even born when this house was closed up. My father will be the first to see this, which thrills him."

Wren tossed off some ideas she had and was pleased to see Bronwyn listening carefully. Hadley contributed some entertaining ideas.

In less than an hour, they arrived. The driver quickly got out, looked around, and then motioned for the passengers to leave.

Am I crazy or is he paranoid, wondered Wren. He produced a key and motioned them inside.

"Ms. Fontaine?" he asked as she went through the door. She looked up at him—he had seemed imposing, but his smile softened him, and now looked almost shy. "I was wondering if I could impose on your time to discuss locks?"

"Oh, I'm terrible!" said Bronwyn. "I never introduced you. Darren doesn't like being disturbed while working, but that doesn't excuse my bad manners. Ladies, this is Darren Cavetti, hired to make sure my crazed fans don't attack me. Darren, architect Wren Fontaine, and her girlfriend, Hadley Vanderwerf, event planner and spacing consultant."

"A pleasure," said Wren.

"My apologies for the drama," he said. "It goes with the job. But if you have a moment, can I ask you about the locks here?"

"Of course! This is a mortice lock embedded in the door. Very secure and hard to pick. The mechanism was standard, but Marius Cadieux would've designed the hardware himself. That was very typical of him."

"What about installing electronic security?"

"This is something Fontaine Partners is used to. We work with wealthy people in the public eye, or who have expensive artworks. My contractor, Bobby Fiore, and I can go over the options with you. We have contacts among the top security companies."

"Good," he said. He brushed a finger along the mortice and caught Wren looking at him.

"It's perfection," she said, "and that's why you couldn't resist touching it. Everything Marius Cadieux created was perfection. If he's watching us, he would laugh, watching you appreciate his work." She hadn't her father's gift for casual conversations with clients and was aware of how serious she sounded. Darren seemed surprised, even confused, but he then slowly smiled.

"Can I see the master bedroom? I want to check it out."

"You two go upstairs," said Bronwyn, "while Hadley and I look over the living room."

Darren let Wren lead the way up the winding staircase, and she watched his reflection in the windows, looking over the house. She didn't think he was looking at it from the point of view of a security expert. She had seen enough people look at magnificent houses to know he was appreciating it as a piece of artwork.

"The glass isn't bulletproof," said Wren.

"Excuse me?" said Darren.

"I assumed that's what you were considering. Whether the glass was bulletproof. Glass can never be bulletproof. There are heavily resistant materials, polycarbonates, that can offer a lot of protection, but nothing is one hundred percent, , and anyway, I'm not going to subject Cadieux House to that."

She couldn't read Darren's expression. She thought it was surprise and then amusement.

"Are you a typical architect, Ms. Fontaine?"

"No," she said.

Now, he laughed. "Okay then. Anyway, that's not what I'm worried about. I'm concerned with crazed fans, not assassins."

Wren showed him into the bedroom. The curved walls and windows made

CHAPTER FOUR

her almost dizzy. Was that what Cadieux intended? What had he told her, all those years ago?

She watched Darren watch the room, take in the unusual shape.

"Is this the original furniture?" he asked.

"Yes. The homes I work on rarely have more than a few pieces of original furniture, but this has all of it. They just closed up in 1955 and left. Cadieux chose the items when he built the house, even designed many of them himself."

"Really?" he said, then turned to take in all three hundred and sixty degrees. Cadieux would've been so pleased. "It's a big bedroom." Wren smiled to herself. She had wondered what was going on here, but she knew now. It was funny how people took houses for granted and so gave themselves away there.

"That's unusual. Frank Lloyd Wright believed bedrooms were just places for sleeping. Cadieux mostly followed that. But not here. He was generous with this bedroom—lavish."

"Why?" asked Darren.

"That's the big question, isn't it?" said Wren with a smile. "Figuring out why Marius Cadieux did what he did, and how he made Rebecca's dream come true."

She saw he was about to ask something about that...but then cocked his head and took off at a run. Wren wanted to run after him but heard her father saying architects didn't run—it wasn't dignified, so she followed at a fast walk. She heard shouts, Darren's deep voice and quite a sight waited for her in the foyer. Bronwyn was shrinking against the wall. Hadley was running in with her phone in her hand.

And Darren was holding a woman face down on the floor. She was wailing, and Darren was grabbing her arms and cuffing her with an efficiency that, despite the fracas, she had to admire.

"Shut up," he said with a quiet firmness. "Struggling makes it worse. I am calling the police now."

He pulled out his phone—he had someone on speed dial. He hung up and looked around.

"What the hell happened? How did she get in? I locked the door."

"It was my fault," said Bronwyn, with a hint of a whimper. "We were looking over the space. Hadley had to take a call, and I wanted to see the outside again, and she was waiting there. I should've waited for you. I'm sorry."

Wren looked down at the woman, who was beginning to calm down. She looked middle-aged and was neatly dressed.

"She killed him," said the woman. "It didn't have to happen. Not here, not here....I just wanted to talk to you…Ms. Merrick. You know where you are. It doesn't have to be like this. Just because of what happened here, it doesn't have to be…"

So it was about Bronwyn's recent novel, with her heroine killing her faithless lover instead of settling down with him. Shooting him, like Rebecca supposedly did to Dennis.

Wren looked out the window and saw a strange car there. Had the woman been stalking Bronwyn? The purchase of the house had probably become public knowledge by now. Had this woman driven by regularly and finally caught Bronwyn there? Dear God…

The woman's speech became muttering, and then they heard the police sirens and two Nassau County police cars pulled into the driveway. Four officers got out of the cars and entered the house. They had a brief talk with Darren, changed his cuffs for theirs, and led the woman away, her head down and apparently still talking to herself. The cars drove away.

"All right, no one was hurt," said Darren, forcing a smile. "Everything is fine. She was more frightening than dangerous." He turned to Bronwyn, still shaking in the corner. "You're all right?"

Bronwyn nodded, took a step toward Darren, then stopped. She was seemingly lost for a moment, but then Hadley put an arm over her shoulder. Bronwyn took a deep breath.

"Thank you," she said. "I should've been more careful. I never thought…but thank you."

"Come into the kitchen. Have something to drink and some light food," said Hadley.

CHAPTER FOUR

"I don't think we have anything," said Bronwyn.

"I'm a caterer. I always have something with me," said Hadley. She led Bronwyn away, then looked over her shoulder and gave Wren a wink. *It'll be okay, Little Bird.*

"Christ," said Darren, still staring after them. "Anyway, I hope they work out something with her so Bronwyn doesn't have to be questioned."

"It's the house," said Wren. "It inspires passion, for good or evil." Darren raised an eyebrow.

"I think this was about Bronwyn's book, not the house," he said.

"I know. But that woman saw the house—and she entered and confronted Bronwyn. There was already a passionate death here. Cadieux always inspired passion."

Wren was quietly amused by Darren's reaction. He looked confused, started to speak several times, and stopped.

Bronwyn and Hadley came back, and the author was munching away, carrying a plate of the special canapes Hadley so excelled at, and had brought with her.

"My God," Bronwyn said. "You are definitely doing my next book launch and the housewarming here."

"And my secret recipe lemonade," said Hadley, handing Bronwyn a plastic flute. She seemed restored now. Hadley's food had a way of doing that.

"I'm sorry, folks," said Bronwyn. "And sorry for you, Darren. I'll be a good girl going forward."

A "good girl," thought Wren. *Interesting language. It seems I was right.*

They heard another car in the driveway. Darren raised a hand for everyone to stay where they were as they looked out the window. *Surely not another crazed fan?*

But it didn't look like a fan: A thirty-something man in a jacket and tie got out of his car but didn't enter the house right away. He shoved his hands in his pockets and looked at the house. Wren could see the wonder in his face as he tried to take it in. He smiled, shook his head, and walked to the door. He reached into his jacket pocket and pulled out a badge as he rang the bell.

"Adam Fitzgerald, New York State Police," he called out.

Darren opened the door. "You're a little late," he said. "The county boys already took her away. I assume that's why you're here."

"Oh, I'll get to speak with her later," said Fitzgerald, with a vague wave of his hand. He continued to look around the house. "I'm really interested in this place. Always wanted to see it, but it's been closed for years."

Darren looked a little stunned. "I'm sorry. I thought you were here about that woman who attacked Bronwyn…Ms. Merrick."

"That's what brought me here. There's a…I guess you'd say, a *tab* on this place if anything happens, the state police get alerted. There was an incident here once many years ago, I'm sure you know. What you may not know is that it was never officially closed. And now, as soon as the house is occupied again, something happens." He smiled wryly. "It's become trite, but police really don't like coincidences."

"I understand," said Darren. He stuck out his hand. "I don't think we've been introduced. Darren Cavetti. I provide security for Ms. Merrick. I was an NYPD detective, first grade."

"A pleasure," said Fitzgerald. "If you don't mind, you look very young to have retired from such a distinguished position."

"Personal reasons," said Darren.

"Of course."

"I'm being rude," said Bronwyn, jumping in. She put down her plate and drink, and Hadley handed her a paper napkin. "I'm Bronwyn Merrick. I just bought the place. Welcome to Cadieux House." She extended a hand. "This is my architect, Wren Fontaine, and Hadley Vanderwerf, an associate of Wren's who's advising us on space usage."

Fitzgerald gave Hadley a speculative look. "Vanderwerf? One of the New York Vanderwerfs?"

"Sadly, yes," said Hadley, laughing.

"I bet some of your family visited this house in its heyday."

"I have no doubt," said Hadley. "Again, sadly, I now work for a living. Are you a historian of the New York social scene?" she asked.

"Something like that," said Fitzgerald. "I'm glad to meet all of you, but I am so sorry about your invasion earlier. My mother and sister are big fans of yours, Ms. Merrick, and I know they'd be very upset to hear you were attacked. I'll be questioning the suspect myself later."

"Thank you," said Bronwyn. "But tell me, is there something special about this house that gets state police attention?"

"The 1955 death wasn't wrapped up as cleanly as we'd have liked. You may have heard the suspect himself died before he could be brought to trial. Then this very valuable house stood empty for so long…" He shrugged. "Something we keep coming back to."

"You should've been here earlier," said Darren. "Wren gave us a history of this place. It seems the brilliant Marius Cadieux, who designed this place, did it as a gift for Rebecca Blaine, who presided over events here. I was just asking Wren how she could be so sure about that." He looked at Wren. She glanced at the wondering eyes and steeled herself.

"Yes. This house was specifically designed with Rebecca in mind. That doesn't mean she created it—it's all Cadieux. But he understood her. That's the way he worked. Cadieux *read* her. He knew what Rebecca wanted—something I doubt she even knew herself. I didn't know her, of course. But I expect I will start to see her through his eyes as I work on it. The pleasure of working on this house will be the solving of that mystery." She smiled. "I know all this, you see, because although Marius Cadieux was my father's mentor, he was my friend."

Chapter Five

The little girl, dressed in green corduroy pants and a white button-up shirt, sat on the floor amidst neat piles of Lego blocks and looked at her plans. From the living room, sounds of laughter, chatter, and clinks of ice cubes floated in, but they didn't register. The only sounds for the girl were the muted clicks of the plastic pieces snapping together.

A bathroom door closed down the hall, and a few moments later, she heard a cough. She looked up: an old man was watching her from her doorway. His face was lined and his hair a shimmering white. Like her father, he was wearing a tuxedo.

"You are Mademoiselle Fontaine?" he asked.

"Yes. Wren Fontaine."

"My name is Marius Cadieux."

"I know. My father says you're the best architect in the world."

He laughed, but the girl didn't laugh with him. Her face was serious—no, more than that. Solemn.

"Your father is right. Are you making a house for your dolls?"

That same unnerving stare. "Dolls don't need a house. And I don't have any dolls anyway. This is a *model* of the house I will build for myself when I'm older."

Cadieux looked around. The room was almost bare except for the model; it had likely been a maid's room once, now repurposed as this little girl's workspace. He sat on the only chair, no doubt an orphan from some long-ago kitchen set. He picked up one of the Lego boxes.

"You're not building what's on the cover," he said.

CHAPTER FIVE

"No. I made my own plans." She showed him the pages. "The master bedroom is going to be on the first floor, because I want to be able to leave easily. The main salon will be on the second floor. It'll still be High Victorian but with my arrangement."

"All right. The other bedrooms…"

"Over here…"

They went over the plans for a few minutes. Cadieux wanted to know about every room, built or planned. The little girl had a reason for each decision and seemed happy to explain them. No—happy was too strong a word. She was content. After the explanations were done, Wren went back to building. Cadieux just watched her for a while.

"Can I give you some advice, mademoiselle? Not about your plans. They are yours, and I will not criticize. About what you need to know, *in general*, for building homes. After all…" he smiled, "…I am the greatest architect in the world."

"Thank you," she said, but again, without a smile.

"Then listen to me, mademoiselle. Listen closely." He sounded strict now, like her father when he was giving her a lesson, so she stopped working and looked at him. "I am going to tell you some things that maybe only ten people in the world understand. I think you might be one of them. You are building a home that is for *you*, right? It is the home *you* want."

"Yes. It's the home I am going to live in."

"Every home I built was a gift for someone. But it had to be exactly right. I had to understand the people very well, so the house matched them. My talent was my gift to the owner of the house. I had to figure out the owners and give them the homes I knew they wanted, even if they didn't know themselves. Because I was smarter than all of them. And watching you, I think you will be smarter too than your clients. You will see what they want, what they need, just as now, you know what you want for yourself. Do you understand, mademoiselle?"

Those wide, serious eyes just stared at him.

"Yes, Monsieur Cadieux."

"A long time ago, I built a house for a friend, someone I knew very well."

"Like a birthday present?" asked Wren.

"Yes, exactly like a birthday present. I wanted her to like the house a lot. So just like you put the rooms where you'd like them, I put the rooms where I thought she'd like them."

"Did she?"

"Very much. I made her a house she liked very much, and she liked living there. But I did something else. I wanted it to be such a beautiful house that she would think about me every time she looked at it. That was very hard, but I did it. I guess you make birthday cards for your mother and father, and they keep them. They think about you when they look at those cards, right?" The girl nodded. "Think of how hard it would be to build a whole house where someone thinks of you. Could you do that? Give a house to your friend, so they would think of you every time they looked at their house?"

"I can make special houses," said the girl.

"I think you can. Again, I am telling you this because, looking at what you're building here, you may understand this. You are thinking seriously about houses, and that is a good thing. If you don't understand it today, then you will someday and, if the fates decree it, I will live long enough to discuss it with you again when you are older. But enough philosophy for now." He waved his hand to sweep away the previous talk. "I have given you plenty to think about. I have some more interest in your house. Let's talk about arches. Tell me why you added them like that on the first floor…"

Eventually, Wren's father found his way to them.

"Marius, is everything all right—oh!" He watched his mentor gaze at his daughter and her house. Wren looked up to see her father's surprised expression, and then he smiled at her. They watched Wren work in silence, but soon, others made their way down the hall, and then she saw half a dozen adults had crowded into her room, including her mother. She always felt a pang of pride looking at her mother, so beautiful, tonight in a long black dress that set off her honey-blond hair so well. Her mother raised an eyebrow at the scene.

"I stopped to watch your daughter work, Ezra," said Cadieux. "You promised to show me something new in architecture if I came back to

CHAPTER FIVE

New York, but I didn't realize it would be in your own house. Not *you*, however, but your daughter."

Everyone laughed.

"As long as it stays in the family," said her father. More laughter, but not from Cadieux, who stood.

"I wish you success, Mademoiselle Fontaine. I enjoyed meeting with you, and I am confident about your future success." Everyone headed back to the living room except her parents.

"You impressed Monsieur Cadieux," said her father. "You should be proud of yourself."

Wren didn't know what to say to that. She just thought for a while and then said, "He was nice."

Her father smiled, and her mother laughed. "That's probably the first time someone called him 'nice,'" she said. From the doorway, she blew Wren a kiss. "I'll be in later to tuck you in," she said. They went back to the party.

Wren wasn't sure what had happened or why people laughed. It wasn't worth thinking about, though, although what Monsieur Cadieux said about presents was interesting. She looked at her plans and resumed building.

Chapter Six

Wren showed up the next day on her own. She hadn't been able to put her father off any longer—he was coming that afternoon. But meanwhile, she could spend the morning alone, "communing" with the house. Her father would laugh at that word, but he'd do it too, even if he didn't use that term.

Marius Cadieux. Her mind kept going back to him, trying to remember every word he said to her when she was ten. Rebecca Blaine was his client—she and Cadieux were old friends. Also, it was widely accepted that while Dennis was a lively host and witty conversationalist, Rebecca was the creative half of the couple. This house was Cadieux's gift to Rebecca. What had he told Wren all those years ago? That he knew what clients wanted better than they did themselves.

Wren laughed. Her father believed that about himself as well. What architect didn't? She sat on a Knoll chair—she knew the design well: It was featured in the Cooper-Hewitt museum. The chair enveloped her, and she closed her eyes, thinking of the little girl with her Legos. Yes, she remembered the old man's face. Was it just idle bragging? She was no better at judging people then than she was now, she reflected. But Marius Cadieux, of all architects, really did know best—she had to admit that.

She opened her eyes and looked around the room. It was definitely a Cadieux, but something more…a gift. Endless space—what did that say? Was that what Rebecca wanted? Space to move, to go in any direction? Space from her husband? It was always assumed that the marriage was a happy one. Cadieux, of course, was an infamous womanizer…was he having an affair

CHAPTER SIX

with Rebecca? Did this house say love? She smiled. She never could figure out people, but she knew houses, and this house did not speak to her that way. Perhaps the bedroom said something different. She walked up the stairs, which seemed to float above the room. Did the stairs say anything? Wren took in the light along the hallway, leading her to the bedroom designed for Rebecca. Specifically for Rebecca. *Intimately* for Rebecca.

She stepped into the bedroom…and stopped. She stopped, and she stared. Later, she would realize with dark humor that she was an architect down to her very soul, because the first thing that registered with her was that so much blood would never completely come out of the carpet.

* * *

"I'm really okay," Wren said. Why shouldn't she be? She was sitting on a living room couch that Cadieux had designed for that house. You couldn't find it anywhere else, and Wren couldn't believe how comfortable it was. "But I'd appreciate some water."

"Of course," said the young cop, who didn't look old enough to shave. He came back a few moments later with a tumbler of water.

"It's Baccarat," said Wren. "That's a three hundred dollar glass you're holding."

He didn't say anything. He probably thought she was in shock, but mercifully, left her alone. She remembered her father was coming and didn't want him frightened seeing the police cars out front, so she texted, "I'm fine, but police at house." He responded, "Okay. There soon."

She lay back and closed her eyes, until she sensed someone standing in front of her. Adam Fitzgerald, the state police detective.

"Are you up to speaking?" he asked.

"Yes. A little shaken, but all right. I told everything to one of the Nassau officers."

"Yes, I'm sure. But could you repeat it?" He pulled up a Cadieux chair.

"Not much to say. I came here to review the house. I entered the bedroom and saw the man lying there. After a moment of shock, I checked for a pulse—nothing, of course." Fitzgerald raised an eyebrow.

"You have medical training, Ms. Fontaine?" She couldn't be sure, but she thought she detected a slightly patronizing tone.

"As a matter of fact, I do," she said. "Every job site must have someone trained in first aid, and my father insisted I get the proper certification. I worked for a contractor one summer when I was in college."

"Ah. That explains it. You were right, he's been dead a while. Did you recognize him?"

"His name is Tristan Archer. He's the lawyer for the Blaine family, which owned this house until Bronwyn Merrick bought it. Bronwyn Merrick and I met him in his office—his client, Woodrow Blaine, wanted reassurance about the house."

"Reassurance about what?"

"He was concerned about adverse publicity for this house. I told him I would follow my client's lead. Architects do have a code of client confidentiality."

"So this wasn't about your client, Bronwyn Merrick. It was about Woodrow Blaine. Do you have a contract, any kind of business relationship, with him?"

"No. Nothing, with the Blaines. Bronwyn is my sole client for this. She has clear title."

"Ah, you check these things?" He smiled at her. She smiled back. "I'm guessing it was rather odd for a third party to request privacy like this and that it was about the 1955 Dennis Blaine death."

"You're right on both. It's unheard of for a third party to go as far as to ask the architect to get involved in something like this."

"And something as old as the Dennis Blaine case. This is…interesting." He frowned and looked thoughtful. Wren didn't meet many people who just stopped to consider something. She rather liked meeting a fellow thinker. "Thank you," he said. "We'll probably talk more later." He left.

Wren looked around. There was quite a crowd, police and crime scene staff. She was trying to figure out the next step when a uniformed officer joined her. "Excuse me. We can't let anyone in right now, but your father is

CHAPTER SIX

outside." Did she sense a bit of a smirk—my God, the cop was thinking that as a grown woman, she still needed Daddy to help her when she was upset.

"He's my business partner…he's here on business," she said, but the cop didn't care.

Wren sighed and stepped outside. Her father was standing on the front lawn, hands shoved in his pockets, looking appreciatively at the house.

"Wren. You're okay?"

"Yes. Just a bit of a shock. I found the body of the Blaine family lawyer in the master bedroom, apparently shot." He nodded.

"The carpet was wool?" That was so like her father, looking at it from an architect's viewpoint.

"Do you think Cadieux would've had anything else?"

"Of course. I was a fool to ask. It's a pity, though. Did the police favor you with their thoughts?"

"No. But I told you about the meeting. They asked a lot about that."

"I'm sure. Wren. I am not happy about your working here if there are such…deadly passions surrounding this house." He looked away from her. Her father was smooth, but statements of paternal love didn't come easily to him. Wren actually found that rather endearing.

"They weren't after me. And anyway, once we get started, I'll be with Bobbie and his crew. And besides—" she gave him a wry look "—I know you're hoping that working on this house and building the ADU will convert me to the Church of Cadieux. You know, father, it just might work."

Her father raised an eyebrow. "I suppose. But don't visit this alone again. Do you think this has anything to do with our client and the stalker who was found here?"

"I think…" said Wren. "I think it goes back to Cadieux." She was aware of her father staring at her, felt the color crawl up her neck.

"What makes you think that?"

"Don't laugh. But it's the house. This is absolutely…Cadieux. Whatever happened with the Blaines, Cadieux was there. And that house says something to me, about him and about the Blaines."

She glanced up at her father. He looked amused. "That didn't take long, did it? Letting Marius Cadieux get under your skin. Now, I'm not a detective, but you have an attack and then a murder, just days apart. Do you think that apparently deranged woman stalking Bronwyn Merrick knew Cadieux? Was she seduced by the house, too?"

"Come now, father. Everything is connected. Cadieux taught you that."

"Quoting my mentor back to me?"

"You're just jealous because even though I was just a child the one time we met, he liked me more than he liked you."

Ezra laughed. "You know what, Wren? You might just be right."

"And you did show me that article once, saying he preferred having women as clients. He said women had a more intuitive understanding of his work. Very sexist, but…" She let the sentence drop as she studied her father.

"Again, Wren, sexist or not, you and Marius may both be right. But come—they seem to be wrapping up. Maybe they'll let us back inside."

The police were leaving, and Adam Fitzgerald stepped just outside the door, looking expectantly at Wren.

"Detective Fitzgerald—this is my father and business partner, Ezra Fontaine. Father, this is Adam Fitzgerald of the state police, who has a particular interest in this house—and the people who once lived here."

"A pleasure to meet you, Mr. Fontaine." He looked up at the house. "I've done some research. Marius Cadieux designed this house, and you were his greatest student."

Ezra smiled. "Greatest? Some might dispute that."

"But not you," said Fitzgerald, and Ezra laughed. "Someday, at a better time, it would be a pleasure to take a tour of this house with you."

"By the time the renovation work is done, I am sure my partner will know more about it than I do," said Ezra.

Wren fought not to blush at her father's vote of confidence.

"Of course," said Fitzgerald.

"Can you tell me," said Wren, wanting to change the subject, "what your interest is? Is it about the attack on Ms. Merrick? This new murder? Or the original 1955 death?"

"My interest is in the house. I think we have that much in common," said

CHAPTER SIX

Fitzgerald. "I am sure you can enter the house, although the bedroom may be off-limits for a little while more. A pleasure meeting you, Mr. Fontaine, and good seeing you again, Ms. Fontaine." He waved to the officer at the front door and then walked toward his car.

Ezra raised an eyebrow and turned to his daughter. "He's right. Our interest is in the house."

The police were apparently still in the bedroom, and so they had most of the house to themselves.

Ezra just stood in the doorway and looked—and looked. Wren had never seen him like this, so captivated by the house, even though they had together been in some of the greatest buildings in the world. She didn't interrupt his thoughts.

"As I said, Wren, by the time you are done with this, you will know more about it than I do. But that's not true today. I am going to give you an architect's tour of what might well be the finest home in North America."

Oh yes. I will learn about the house...and because of that, I will learn about Marius Cadieux...and, because of that, about Rebecca Blaine.

Chapter Seven

"They're having an affair," said Wren. "Rather trite—famous woman falling for her hunky bodyguard, but considering the books she writes, a trite romance is no more than we can expect."

They sat on a couch in their living room, drinking Hadley's special recipe Arnold Palmers. Hadley was lying with her head on Wren's lap. She looked up at her girlfriend for a moment—and then laughed. "Oh, good one, Little Bird! I love it when you tap into your nasty streak. And pat yourself on the back. You figured out a personal relationship, and you say you're bad with people."

"You figured it out, too, didn't you?" asked Wren.

"Oh, God, yes. I hope they don't think they're fooling anyone. I watched the way they looked at each other. You saw that as well?"

Wren shook her head. They had just finished a restaurant lunch with Bronwyn and Darren. It was billed as a "social" meeting, so she had told Wren to bring Hadley.

But maybe, as Wren had finally realized, Bronwyn thought at some level, if she was bringing a "significant other," Wren could as well. Either way, she had made it clear she wanted Wren to continue—as long as Wren was comfortable.

"No need to worry," Wren had said. "Once we start, we'll have a crew there all the time, and our contractor, Bobby Fiore, has known me since I was a little girl. He's very protective of me." Bronwyn seemed reassured, and they parted, optimistic for the future of the house.

"All right then," continued Hadley. "I don't know about that lawyer—that's

CHAPTER SEVEN

clearly a Blaine issue, and I'm sure the police will figure that out soon. As for the fan, I imagine this bit of nuttiness will pass."

Darren put a reassuring hand on her. "And I've already looked into security issues—motion detectors and cameras. I'll go over the details later with Wren." He looked at her. *We'll take care of Bronwyn.*

Hadley continued to reflect back. "People who are involved always give it away. If you know how to look, you can tell. It's a look, the way they stand. You are vulnerable when you're with someone. Now, it's one thing when you're a writer, but for a tough guy like Darren—I could see. It wasn't that he was just nice to her. He let her be nice to him. She gave him a bread roll he particularly liked, and he took it. Even with little gestures like that, food is love. Take it from a chef—a chef in love."

Wren laughed and thought about that now, focusing on what Hadley said. It made sense. She never saw things like that herself in human interaction. "Okay, I see what you're saying. But for me, it was the house. People look at houses differently based on what they need to see. If Darren had been interested only in security, he would've looked at windows and doors. I work with rich people, and they or their people will look at it that way. But not Darren. He looked at it like a man who planned to live there. In that house. In that room."

Wren knew someone else might've laughed at that, or at least looked at her oddly, but Hadley just sat up, gave her a hug, and said nothing for a while.

"At least, that's one mystery solved," Hadley eventually said. "But we're still dealing with a crazed fan and a dead lawyer. Not just a dead lawyer—but a dead lawyer in that house. A house that should've been empty."

"It's all connected," said Wren. "I told my father that. The house, the intruder, and especially that murdered lawyer."

"All right, sweetie, we all know you're the 'house whisperer.' But how could you know that?"

"It's a Cadieux," said Wren. "These people all are connected somehow with that house. Nothing happened by accident in one of his houses. Everything is planned. That was his genius. I bet we find that Bronwyn and Darren came together at that house, possibly because of it. That intruder—I think

53

she was ultimately inspired by the move."

"Okay, Little Bird. At least I'll give you the lawyer. How did he get in there? Why? He's a city-based lawyer. What got him here? And how?"

"That's a very good question. Think about that place. Whenever I work on a house where no one has lived for a while, it's empty. But Cadieux House looks like Rebecca Blaine just walked out one day with nothing but her clothes. The artwork is still on the walls—there's a Picasso hanging there. A Matisse. The dishes and glassware alone are collectibles and worth a fortune. God knows what the insurance company is charging. I know the house managers—they wouldn't be just keeping the keys on a hook in their office."

"But as the family lawyer, Archer may very well have had a copy," jumped in Hadley. "His law firm is one of the old city firms, probably representing the Blaines even before that house was built. I bet there have been keys collecting dust in a drawer there."

Hadley glanced at Wren—she recognized that look. Wren had fallen deep into herself, and she was back at Cadieux House, assembling pieces in her mind.

"I'm sorry, I'm being silly," said Wren, finally coming back.

"Wren, being silly? Perish the thought. But you have something, don't you?"

"It's what I don't have. A reason for that house. I look at grand mansions, and I see the power of the families that built them. But this Cadieux—there's something else there. Something I can't understand yet. And I need to before I do any work on it, and especially before I plan Bronwyn's tiny house."

"Oh, well, I have some news that may help. Trey texted me—he thinks he has some information he can share with us."

"Great! Maybe there's a break there. Let's have Trey and Marcia over. We haven't seen them in a while anyway, and we'll question your brother over a nice dinner. Also, there was something interesting about that woman who attacked Bronwyn. She said, 'Not here' and made other references to Cadieux House. Now, Bronwyn's purchase was not widely publicized. She told me she didn't put it in her newsletter or website, so I find it odd that her crazed fan managed to make that connection. I know I always go back to the house…but I wonder…" Hadley let her think. "You know, if this woman, Karen, had heard about the purchase in some way, she could've found pictures online. Even the photographs show a stunning house that could've turned her head—they are…bewitching."

"And what does that tell you?" asked Hadley, looking amused.

Wren laughed. "It tells me that despite my doubts, my father may have been right all along about the power of a Cadieux House."

* * *

"How are my ladies!" said Marcia. She was tall, with a brisk pace, and bore down on Wren and Hadley to give them hugs. Wren had thought the hug was a first-time meeting event, but Marcia was a dedicated hugger, and Wren accepted that after realizing that Marcia was *genuine*. Wren long had trouble realizing who was genuine in her life. She now knew that Marcia truly loved her husband's sister and was delighted to extend that love to the sister's partner.

"Look—" Marcia had said at their first meeting. "I grew up with two brothers. I now have a husband and two sons. I'm thrilled to be able to welcome ladies into my family life."

Trey followed her into the apartment at a more sedate pace, wearing a wry look that made it clear he was Hadley's brother, despite so many other differences.

"Dear sister, dear Wren," he said, giving each of them a kiss on their cheeks. "You both look well. I assume you can offer me a glass of whatever carrot juice concoction you have going?"

"A guava juice concoction, as you say, that is out of this world," said Hadley. Marcia gave a thumbs up, but Trey only raised an eyebrow. When they moved in together, Hadley had told Wren that she didn't mind if Wren wanted to keep alcohol in the house—she was far along enough in her recovery to handle that.

"I drink very little myself," Wren had said. "And that tends to be at dinners with clients. So we'll make this a teetotaler household and eventually develop a reputation in the building as those strange Baptist spinsters."

Trey loosened his tie and took off his jacket. He took a sip of the guava cocktail and pronounced it "surprisingly good."

"And healthier than a martini," added Marcia. Hadley also provided artfully cut vegetables and her own hummus.

They caught up on family, especially their two boys, at Chadwick Prep, which had educated generations of Vanderwerf men: blazers with crests on the pocket and a school song in Latin.

"Wren—you went to Denis-Loft in Brooklyn, didn't you?" asked Marcia. She pronounced it correctly, of course: Denee-Loft.

"For my sins," said Wren. "It's Chadwick's semi-official sister school, I know. Plaid skirts with matching floppy bowties and well-tailored jackets."

"Did you fit in?" asked Marcia.

"Not entirely, but to be fair, I don't know anywhere I might've fit in better. I kept to myself, and for those years, that worked." She shrugged. "At least I didn't have to worry about dressing to look cool."

"Looking cool—ha! You didn't realize it at the time, but you were way too cool for Denis-Loft and our funny little world," said Marcia.

Wren smiled. "At least I liked the neo-gothic architecture."

Dinner was soon ready, and Hadley had outdone herself with her own take on Indian cuisine. Wren was especially aware of the scent, which drifted through the apartment. It's what a home smells like, she thought.

"Okay," said Trey as he took a last forkful of rice. "I'm a lawyer, and I know it's a tit-for-tat world. You expect me to sing for my supper. And you're trying to figure out what happened at Cadieux House."

"We have something in common, Trey," said Wren with a wry smile. "We work in heavily regulated professions. I know what's in your firm's files has to remain secret."

"True," said Trey. "Still, there's a lot that's public knowledge, and it would take you weeks to pull it all together. But because they were a longtime firm client, I know. So, if you don't mind me mansplaining it to you—"

Marcia patted his arm, "Your feminist credentials have been confirmed."

CHAPTER SEVEN

"Glad to hear it," he said with a laugh. "Because this is not going to be an entirely pleasant story."

Chapter Eight

Trey took a sip of Hadley's special brew coffee ("made especially for me by my personal coffee sommelier"), sighed in contentment, and steepled his fingers. Wren smiled to herself—it's what her father often did. Hadley had said it was a "straight white man thing."

"This wasn't just a marriage. It was a union. The Blaines were old WASP money." He glanced at his sister. "I'm sure if we went back far enough, we'll find the Blaine and Vanderwerf family trees crossed at one point. The Rodriguezes, on the other hand—I bet you know, Wren."

"Just a bit," said Wren. "They were Sephardic Jews, been here for ages."

"You're right. Now, how about this—do you know what the Buttonwood Agreement was?"

"Wren is not a schoolgirl here to answer your test questions," said Marcia. Wren laughed.

"It's okay. My father is the same way. Anyway, I do! It's the agreement made by a handful of stockbrokers in the late 18th century establishing what would become the New York Stock Exchange."

"Ha! I meet hardly anyone outside of Wall Street who knows that. Yes, twenty-four merchants met to organize the growing stock trading business. Five of them were Jews, who all belonged to the oldest Jewish congregation in the United States—Congregation Shearith Israel. The Rodriguezes belonged, too. Helped to found it, in fact. I believe they were even related to one of the signers. They were merchants with extensive international connections that only grew over time."

"What were they *like?*" asked Wren.

CHAPTER EIGHT

"I'm sorry..." said Trey.

"Dear," said Marcia, "She's politely saying that she doesn't want a financial history of New York but would like some insights into the woman who owned that splendid house."

"Fair enough," said Trey, with a laugh. "But I just wanted to give some background. Wren gets to give background when she describes her homes. I get to give background on money." He winked at Wren. "Even if money is boring. But where was I? The Rodriguezes and the Blaines. Our firm was on the Blaine side of things, but when families, especially wealthy and prominent families, intermarry, their affairs tend to blend. And these families were indeed wealthy and prominent, both of them with deep roots in this country's social and business life. After you called me, I talked to a few people who knew them, or at least about them."

Of course, Wren realized. Trey would move freely through the old-line clubs, mingling with the men who had ruled the city since it was New Amsterdam. They all know each other, Wren was well aware. Their parents knew each other, and so did their grandparents. They were even mostly related to each other.

"So, a word here and there. Certain...gentlemen quietly told me that this was a lopsided affair. It was said that Dennis fell head over heels for her. Everyone fell in love with Rebecca Rodriguez, according to the lore of the day. There are enough old men in the clubs who remember her—she had a reputation for being...exciting. Charming, bright, shrewd—and stunningly beautiful. For her part, she seems to have liked Dennis well enough. For her, the marriage may have been less of a love match than a partnership."

"*Just* a partnership?" asked Wren.

"There was no *just*," said Trey. "Not with people like that. You've worked with old homes and old families; hell, you've paired up with a *Vanderwerf*"—Hadley laughed—"so you should know."

Wren nodded. "I don't know people very well. But, I suppose they don't change much. Of course, she was Jewish, and he was Episcopal. But that didn't seem to matter to the signers of the Buttonwood Agreement." She smiled wryly. "I suppose money and power covers all that up."

"Oh yes," said Trey. "I'm guessing Rebecca walked a fine line. She never forgot who she was because she knew no one else would. So we have a very unusual home for a very unusual woman. And here we are, trying to figure out the home and the woman. Look, Wren, as you've often said, you view people through the lens of their homes. So think of Cadieux House as less of a residence and more of a…*temple*." He seemed very proud of his metaphor. Hadley rolled her eyes at her brother, but Wren looked serious.

"That is very telling," she said. Trey took a mock bow. "This was a Cadieux house, so I can actually see that happening."

"Why do they call it 'The Cadieux House,' anyway?" asked Marcia. "Aren't grand houses usually named after their owners? Or location? This was named after the architect."

"That's a good question," said Wren. "It was the house that cemented his growing reputation. But not just for his architectural skills. It was *how* he built it, merging his ideas with the…psychology, the *personality*, of the people who hired him with the houses he built for them. No one had done it like that before—or since."

Hadley giggled. "'Or since.' I think your father would disagree."

Wren laughed, too. "You may be right. But at least he'd give his mentor precedence."

"There may be more to that," continued Trey. "It seems that Marius Cadieux made himself very much a part of the house. He was very tight with Rebecca. Very." He leaned back, looking pleased with himself. "They were having an affair, it seems."

Wren leaned back and idly ran a finger along her chin. Then she smiled.

"I was a quiet girl with big ears. Over the years, I heard enough gossip from my parents to understand Cadieux was a lifelong philanderer. He never married, but was linked to many women over the years, all the beautiful people. The *beau monde*, as my mother would say with a smile."

"A bit of a scandal," said Trey. "The Blaines were quite the couple, and eyebrows were raised because she was fifty—"

"And naturally, women are no longer attractive to men at that advanced age," said Hadley. "How heteronormative of you."

CHAPTER EIGHT

"I was about to say," Trey continued, sounding a little nettled, "that she was fifty and Cadieux was six or seven years younger. I'm not saying that was wrong, but it was unusual. And I know enough about Cadieux to know that most of his...girlfriends were noticeably younger than he was. Rebecca was an outlier."

"I barely understand same-sex relationships," said Wren, smiling and reaching for Hadley's hand. "And I certainly can't speak to straight ones. You're right—Cadieux generally did favor younger women. But Rebecca was in a class by herself; she had no trouble turning heads at fifty. And the word most often used with her was 'sparkling.'"

Trey threw his hands up in mock surrender. "Okay then. I'll stick to the legal details and let you figure out the romance. You've probably looked through all the old accounts online: A waiter who had had some sort of argument—stealing the silver, or something like that—had been arrested for killing Dennis Blaine. It was convenient, and it made a lot of sense, but it was thin. The lawyers were...nervous. There was no proof, that waiter stole anything there, although he did have a record, it seems. However, it was all circumstantial. A Bar Association insider told me that prosecutors were nervous about the case. They were keeping an open mind about other suspects. They were thinking about Cadieux, possibly in connection with the widow Rebecca."

"But quietly," said Wren. "No one was going to make charges against people like that unless they were one hundred percent sure."

"Oh, absolutely. Anyway, whatever was going on, Cadieux gave Rebecca an alibi—he was with her when Dennis died. No one else could be sure—that is—and this is lawyer gossip: no one could refute Cadieux and say Rebecca definitely was away from the crowd when Dennis was shot. Everyone had been drinking—this was the 1950s, after all."

"But if Cadieux was known to be Rebecca's lover, wouldn't that have made him worthless as an alibi?" asked Wren.

"Bingo!" said Trey. "And that's the problem. They both denied they were having an affair. It was just something everyone *knew*. But when push came to shove, the police couldn't find anyone who had actually heard either of them discuss it. Or find anyone who saw them in a compromising position, or seen them at a hotel, or found an incriminating note. They must've been very cautious, because the police couldn't prove anything. Indeed, everyone said Cadieux had been a good friend of Dennis's. He didn't seem to have a reason to lie to protect Rebecca. There was no motive for her to kill her husband. No financial reason. No evidence of an affair on either side. So it was unhappily closed after the death of the only solid suspect."

"They just let it rest after that?" asked Wren.

Trey shrugged. "Dennis and Rebecca's daughter Shoshana apparently told police that she was close to her father and couldn't offer any reason— no secret that may have indicated why he was killed. She was questioned privately about infidelities and said her parents seemed happy together. I can tell you that Shoshana had a reputation back then for being 'difficult,' and there was a sense she knew more than she was saying."

"Being rich and beautiful and twenty will do that to you," said Hadley. "Believe me, I know."

"Oh yeah," said Trey. "Let's not even go there. Anyway, that's the bare bones. The county D.A. looked at Rebecca and Cadieux and were bracing themselves. But the problem with that was that there was no motive. Was there an affair? Not a problem. This was 1955, not 1855—she could've walked away. She had the Rodriguez fortune; she didn't need Blaine money. There was no motive. Let's just say it became very convenient when a lowlife loser working as a waiter picked a fight with a fellow inmate who had a homemade knife."

"It's called a 'shiv,'" said Hadley.

"I bow to your superior knowledge," said Trey, and they shared a sibling laugh.

"I keep thinking about their group—the Sephardic Jews," said Wren. "So connected, at least in this case, with the old money New York world, and yet always separate. There is something there, I think. Maybe I'm fantasizing, but maybe that's her secret, her unwillingness to give herself completely to anyone, at least outside her faith."

"I couldn't say," said Trey. "I can tell you she never tried to deny her

CHAPTER EIGHT

heritage. She gave generously to charities—there was a paper trail—both Jewish and secular. Toward the end of her life, she gave a lot to the newly established Statue of Liberty-Ellis Island Foundation."

"That makes sense," said Wren. "The poem on the statue, 'The New Colossus,'—the one that starts 'Give me your tired, your poor'—was written by Emma Lazarus. Like Rebecca, she came from a wealthy Sephardic family. The Sephardim could be pretty worldly, open to those outside their community. And they could be sharp and tough. British statesman Benjamin Disraeli was of Sephardic background and was once the subject of an antisemitic insult in Parliament. According to one account, he responded, 'My ancestors were building the Temple of Solomon while yours were still living in caves and painting themselves blue.'"

Everyone chuckled at that.

"Perhaps there's something about her background in the house," said Wren. "I don't mean literally, but maybe Cadieux sensed that, a sense of otherness."

"I'm just a lawyer digging up facts," said Trey. "The house is your bailiwick. What any of what we found has to do with the house today, or the current murder or your client's stalker, is beyond me. I hoped I could help. Cheers." He raised his coffee.

"You've been very helpful—thank you," said Wren. "Maybe we have to turn to the next generation. I met Shoshana. She's a piece of work. Of course, she must've only been in her early twenties when her father was killed, but she wouldn't have gone to pieces. I see it was already noted she was difficult. Maybe I'm not good with people, but when we met, she was clearly very self-possessed. I imagine she was, even then. If she knew something and wanted it kept secret, she'd have kept it secret."

"And fortunately, you are also the 'house whisperer,'" said Hadley. "You always know what's going on by looking at the house. What does that house tell you about the family?"

Wren gave a wry smile. "Sorry to let you down, but I'm still figuring out that place. How Cadieux would laugh at me mulling over it. But that's the funny thing, really. He did tell me what the house was all about when I was ten years old. If I can piece it all together."

63

"Oooh…that's a fascinating possibility," said Marcia. "But you said that it was a secret about the *house*, not his love life. I don't think even Marius Cadieux was crazy enough to confide an illicit romance to a child. But about a house…dear Wren, you're always telling people that they need to listen to what the house tells them. So never mind the Blaines for now; what does Cadieux House tell *you*?"

"Fair enough," said Wren, smiling. She became aware that everyone was looking at her closely. *What can I say? They're expecting something profound.* "I have been in a lot of Cadieux's homes. My father saw to that. There is always a sense of airiness in them, and yet, you feel protected. 'To be in a Cadieux House was like having a lover,' one critic once said, and considering Cadieux's reputation as a…libertine—" *Did anyone even use that word anymore?* "—that's not surprising, I suppose. But in none of those homes did I ever see that same sense as strongly manifested as in Cadieux House. The question, I suppose, is why? I just don't know…at least, not yet."

"I bet Shoshana does," said Hadley. "Fathers and daughters, right, Trey?"

"Ha! You always read Dad better than I did. Now, what about you, Wren? Can you read your father?"

"Just on houses," said Wren. "Otherwise, he's a mystery to me. But to be fair, I'm probably a mystery to him too."

Talk turned to various Vanderwerf cousins, and Marcia sidled up to Wren to get some furniture ideas for a planned living room redecoration. Eventually, Trey looked at his watch and said they should be heading home.

They got their jackets, then at the door, Trey suddenly put his hands on Wren's shoulders. "I don't think we've ever really said it, but speaking for the family—" he glanced at Marcia, who gave him a "don't be pompous" look "—we are so grateful Hadley found you."

"Not as grateful as I am for finding her," said Wren quietly. Trey laughed and kissed Wren on her cheek, then Marcia did as well, and they were gone.

"They like you," said Hadley.

"I know. I just wish your brother didn't treat you like that—that somehow, you didn't deserve to be happy because of your difficult teen years."

"Big brother's prerogative, and let's face it, I was hardly hanging around

CHAPTER EIGHT

with the best people for years, most of them with police records. You're so…normal." She laughed. "I don't mean that as an insult."

Wren laughed, too. "No insult taken! I suppose it's some sort of progress that even a lesbian connection is considered normal today."

"Oh, Little Bird, that's hardly new. I look back on the family, and I think of a so-called 'maiden aunt' who lived with a 'good friend' for companionship. A 'confirmed bachelor' cousin who vacationed with other men to save money by claiming the double-occupancy discount, even though he was a very successful attorney. Deep down, the family knew. All we've done is talk about it. You've said that architectural styles change radically, but what we want from a house—the peace, comfort and security—doesn't. It's the same about people." She flashed a cheeky smile. "Even in the dim dark past of the 1950s."

"I suppose you're right. But as interesting as all this is, I'm just going to focus on the renovation and the ADU. I'm going to assume the unfortunate late Tristan Archer had another client who wanted to kill him, and the house became a convenient place to do it."

"Perhaps. But the Blaine death, the Archer murder, the attack on Bronwyn—all centered on Cadieux House. I thought that when everything connects to a house, you have to look at the house." Then Hadley giggled. "At least, that's what a wise woman said to me."

Chapter Nine

Four months later

"This," said Bobby, "is going to be fun." Wren's contractor looked over the interior of Cadieux House. His look was no less professional than Wren's, but she could see it was different. She focused on what the space made her feel, but Bobby considered how it was put together.

Wren put on a fake pout. "I'm hurt. I thought you liked living in the 19th century like me. And here you are, falling for a post-war house. I thought we were friends."

And Bobby laughed. "Be fair, boss. I've been working with your father since you were a little girl. Some of this modernist jazz had to rub off on me."

Wren laughed in return. "All right—I'll accept that. And I admit there is something about this place...I just don't know what."

"Well, let's ask the chief."

Ezra had wandered ahead of them, hands thrust into his pockets, taking in every angle, every curve. Wren knew she wasn't good at reading people, but she knew her father, could see the numbers running through his mind, considering the ratios that defined the space, the mental pathways his mentor had traveled to create it.

"You're right," said Wren. "Father, you've been back several times with me to see this. I'm still trying to figure out what this place was about. No one knew Cadieux better than you. What was he saying here?"

CHAPTER NINE

Ezra turned and smiled wryly at his daughter and his contractor.

"You're a partner in this firm, Miss Fontaine. If Monsieur Cadieux made a connection with the Blaines, that's for you to figure out. I expect you to figure it out and explain to our client why it is the way it is. I told you this wasn't going to be easy."

"All right," said Wren. "But if Bronwyn Merrick wants something different, can I change a Cadieux?"

"No. And again, I'm counting on you to change Miss Merrick if necessary. Not to change the house to suit her. There is a price to pay for the privilege of living in a Cadieux, and you must explain that to her as you proceed."

It might have been amusing coming from someone else, but her father was dead serious.

"She'll be here soon. I'll make it clear to her. I'm going to unveil some initial thoughts for the ADU today."

"Of course," said her father, but vaguely, as he was contemplating—again—the loop of the staircase.

"You didn't say anything about it," said Wren.

"Renee, no doubt, sent it back to you with my signature."

"Without comment," said Wren, hedging on whether or not that was a question.

"Dear daughter, if you have any questions or need advice, you know I'm always available to you."

Wren glanced at Bobby, but he was deeply involved in reviewing the state of the floor, making it clear he wasn't going to involve himself in a discussion between two firm partners. Between father and daughter.

"I don't need any advice or questions answered," said Wren, hearing herself sound more nettled than she meant. "I want to know what you think about the ADU—Bronwyn's tiny house. It's just a preliminary, of course. I want to discuss it with Bronwyn before going further with it."

Ezra laughed. "What I *think*? Twenty years ago, Marius Cadieux told my little girl how impressed he was with the house she was building. You didn't need my opinion then. I don't think you need it now. But if you do want advice, watch out for salt damage. Even Marius Cadieux was no proof against the elements. I'm going to look again at the bedrooms." He started walking upstairs.

"Was I just complimented?" asked Wren.

"Hmm?" said Bobby.

"Don't pretend you weren't listening."

"Oh, all right. I'm thinking that maybe your father has finally decided he's almost as good as Cadieux. And he's a tough man but a fair one, so at the same time, he might be thinking you're almost as good as he is."

Wren started to contemplate that, but then the door opened, and Bronwyn and Darren entered. Darren was looking around, but Bronwyn made a beeline for Wren.

"So you have the plans?" she said.

"Yes, I have some drawings and want to show them to you here while you're looking at the spot we'll be building it on. But first, let me introduce you to the man who will be building it, Bobby Fiore. We do nothing important without him."

Bobby shook hands and told them he was looking forward to the job.

"Those are your people out there?" asked Darren.

"Yes. All of them good. And I know you're worried about crazy fans, but this house is going to be surrounded by my crew, and I know them well. No one is going to get near this place."

"Good," said Darren. "I know that we, that Bronwyn, will want to visit over time as you proceed." He briefly bowed to Wren. "Of course, we don't wish to interrupt your work."

It would. Wren worked best uninterrupted, but her father had frequently reminded her that a certain flexibility was necessary. As the Spanish said, "With the rich and mighty, always a little patience."

"Not at all. I look forward to keeping you apprised."

"Excellent," said Bronwyn. "Now for my tiny house—I'm so excited." Wren wondered if her father would come down to watch the presentation, silently praying he wouldn't. It was hard enough to reveal her first house, but to have her father watching and silently judging...

She heard his footsteps on the stairs. He saw the arrival of the clients and

CHAPTER NINE

put on his patented, welcoming smile.

"Bronwyn Merrick? I'm Ezra Fontaine, senior partner of Fontaine Partners."

"Oh! A pleasure. And this is my...driver/bodyguard, Darren Cavetti. Your daughter—or I should say, partner—was just about to reveal her plans for my tiny house."

"I'd love to stay and watch, but I was just doing a quick review today on my way to a meeting in the Hamptons." He gave his daughter a brief smile. "Anyway, this is Wren's show, and she doesn't need me looking over her shoulder. I know you'll be as delighted as I was with her revelation, and I have no doubt you'll be completely happy with the renovation and the new house."

Wren wondered if she'd ever reach a time when her father didn't surprise her. She watched him leave, then shook herself out of her funk.

"Come," she said. "I want to show it to you. We'll lay it out on the table in the main living room. You'll see the plans in the same sunlight that will brighten your tiny home. Of course, this is just preliminary, but I want to make sure I'm on the right track with what you want."

It was funny, thought Wren. Bronwyn had just bought one of the finest modernist homes on the East Coast but seemed more excited about this "cottage." Darren didn't seem nearly as worked up. Well, Wren didn't want even Hadley around when she was working on a house. Maybe Bronwyn didn't want Darren around when she was writing a novel.

Wren felt her heart pounding. She had worked on new houses before, but always in conjunction with her father. And this was a major client. She spread the papers on the table.

"Oh!" said Bronwyn. "Oh!" A small smile and her fingers traced the paper as if she could touch the house.

"As we discussed, it's just one room, with a small balcony where you can drink a morning coffee or a late-night brandy, as the weather allows. Plenty of light, but blackout curtains to make it completely dark. Murphy bed or fold-out couch, if you prefer. The couch gives you another place to sit, but a Murphy bed is more comfortable for sleeping. It depends on how often you plan to sleep there." *Was Darren wondering the same thing?*

"Yes, I see," said Bronwyn, but vaguely. She was still looking at the picture. Imagining herself there? "It echoes the house," she finally said.

"Yes. 'Echo' is the word. It is not a repeat. The clean lines of the house, but not the…" Wren struggled for the word, then stopped. She had already decided not to apologize—her father would've hated that. *Well, Marius Cadieux designed the main house, but for this, you're stuck with me.* "Let me just say that Cadieux was lavish, and I am not."

Wren wondered if that would confuse Bronwyn. Make her laugh? But she just nodded and then looked around the room. "Yes, Wren. That's the word: *lavish*. Not fussy, but indulgent." She smiled. "I'm no architect, but I know something about settings and the words to describe them. And we are talking about words, aren't we?"

Wren nodded.

"Anyway, it's just what I need," said Bronwyn.

"Thank you. I'm glad you like it," said Wren. She smiled. "But I'm thinking of words. You said it's what you *need*, not what you *want*. Is there a difference?"

Bronwyn raised an eyebrow, and Wren suddenly feared she had gone a bridge too far. She had watched her father so many times, envying his ability to work so smoothly with his clients. Had she said too much? She watched Bronwyn cast her eyes around that perfectly proportioned room, that perfectly proportioned house.

"You tell me that Marius Cadieux built this for Rebecca Blaine? Did he give her what she wanted? Or what she needed?"

Wren gave that a moment's thought. "I expect that as I proceed with your main house, I'll find out."

Bronwyn laughed, and Wren felt relieved that she had handled that correctly. "Yes, Wren, I expect you will."

Wren glanced at Darren, standing a few steps back. He seemed pleased that Bronwyn was happy.

"Again, these are just preliminary. It is not perfect. When I understand the main house perfectly, I will be able to finalize the tiny house. At that point,

CHAPTER NINE

the tiny house will be perfect." She looked closely at Bronwyn, hoping she had made that clear. Bronwyn nodded.

"I understand what you are saying. That's how I approach my books. I have an imperfect draft and then a final one. My editor and agent tell me if I'm at least on the right track. And you are on the right track with this."

"I'm glad you think so." Relief rushed through her.

"But I am curious—what do you need to know about the house to know whether my little studio is perfect?"

"I need to get into the head of Marius Cadieux. There is something about this place—houses can show freedom as well as protection. This shows both at the same time. I am trying to figure out how he did it." Wren's father had to remind her on multiple occasions that she had a tendency to over-explain. But she glanced at Bronwyn, who seemed interested, so she continued. "It's not just looking and making a note of the measurements and materials. It's how he put everything together, the proportions and materials. There is a sense of indulgence here, as you noted. Is it about Rebecca? Who inspired it? I don't know. It's certainly something special. I will figure it out."

"I am sure you will," said Bronwyn.

The doorbell rang, and Darren motioned for them to stay put. "I'll get it," he said. Even with Bobby and his crew, he wasn't going to take any chances. Was it going to be like this throughout the job, Wren wondered.

For now, though, it was okay. Darren came back with Detective Fitzgerald, who didn't look happy.

"I'm afraid I have some bad news," he said, looking back and forth between Darren and Bronwyn.

"Don't tell me that stalker is after me again?" asked Bronwyn.

"Oh no, that won't happen," said Fitzgerald. "She received a suspended sentence after showing she was under the care of a psychiatrist and being medicated. But that's moot now, because she's dead. Karen Weston was murdered."

"When and how?" asked Darren, the ex-cop.

"She was shot last night. She had a condo right here on the island, not far from you at all. There's a little park across from her building, and she was found there. Neat and quick. Now, here's the interesting thing. She was killed with the same gun as Tristan Archer."

"Do you mean the same kind of gun?" asked Darren.

"No, I don't," said Fitzgerald. "I literally mean the exact same gun. The ballistics are clear. It would seem the same person who killed Mr. Archer killed the stalker Weston." He looked at Bronwyn. "The only thing they had in common was you, Ms. Merrick."

And the house, thought Wren.

Chapter Ten

"I hope you're not suggesting that Bronwyn—that Ms. Merrick—had anything to do with the death of that stalker," said Darren.

"Of course not," said Fitzgerald, with a thin smile. "I don't think that someone who writes about death in books is necessarily a killer. But you, Mr. Cavetti, you are well-versed in firearms."

"I was detective first-grade with a spotless record," said Darren. Even Wren could hear the danger in his low tone. "Are you accusing me of murder?"

"Of course not. I'm simply looking at all the connections. You should know that, especially as a detective first-grade. Now you know I have to ask this—but where were both of you last night?"

"I was alone in my apartment," said Darren. Fitzgerald looked at Bronwyn.

"Same here," said Bronwyn, looking a little flustered. "That is, alone in my apartment. Darren saw me home, and that was it. I was writing all evening."

"Did either of you have any contact with Ms. Weston since her arrest? Phone, in-person, email, social media?"

"Believe me, you would've heard," said Darren.

"All right then. This is enough for now, but there will be follow-up. Are you here for the rest of the day?"

"No, we were just here so Wren could discuss some of the ongoing work. We were heading back to the city," said Bronwyn.

"All right then," said Fitzgerald. "I'll be in touch. Thank you." Darren gave a final look at Fitzgerald as he and Bronwyn turned to leave, but then she stopped for a moment.

"Thank you again, Wren. It's really lovely. I'm so sorry for…" She waved her hand vaguely and then left with Darren.

"Well, well," said Fitzgerald, more to himself, then seemed to remember Wren was still there.

"What was she thanking you for?" he asked.

"It'll be part of the public record soon anyway. I'll be building a special 'tiny house' for her. On this property."

"Really? A house of this size, and she wants more?"

"Creative people," said Wren with a smile. "They often like a place apart to work."

"Ah. Personal issues. You must know something about Bronwyn Merrick's life."

"I do. It's very important when designing or renovating a home to know about the client's life and how they're going to use the house."

"And I suppose Marius Cadieux had to know something about the Blaines to design this. I wonder what it was?" They stood in silence while Wren watched Fitzgerald scan the house. "That wasn't a rhetorical question, Ms. Fontaine."

"You overestimate my knowledge. Even my father wasn't born when Dennis Blaine was killed here."

Fitzgerald shrugged. "Maybe our jobs are similar in that we work with patterns. I think of the Blaines and that death and now two deaths linked today, both apparently centered on Bronwyn Merrick. So I'd like to know certain things about her that you may know from working with her."

"There are client confidentiality issues regarding my work," said Wren. Fitzgerald laughed, and Wren suddenly felt embarrassed.

"I'm sorry. That wasn't nice of me. But everyone thinks their work has a special confidentiality clause. A baker once tried to refuse me a look at an inscribed birthday cake, because frosting was covered by the First Amendment. But very few professions really have that ability."

Wren wondered how to respond to that. Perhaps interpreting her thought as doubt, he tried smiling again and said, "I won't reveal to anyone that you were the source of the information. And look, we're all on the same side here. You want to keep this house—this worksite—safe, as well as keep your

CHAPTER TEN

client in good health, and so do I."

"All right then, detective. Come with me."

"Something to show me?"

"Sort of," said Wren, and enjoyed the bewildered look on Fitzgerald's face. He followed her up the stairs to the master bedroom.

"What do you look at here?" Wren asked.

"Are you asking me as a detective?" he asked.

"That you ask that question tells me a lot. I don't know if you live in a house or an apartment, but when you moved in, you probably looked at it with an eye to how comfortable you would be there."

"I guess so. And I suppose this is leading somewhere?" asked Fitzgerald.

"I'm sorry—of course." *When it's a social situation, I never think of what to say, but when it's work-related, I can't shut up.* "I notice how people look at houses. That tells me what they hope to get out of it. I saw Bronwyn look at it as a place where she could settle. And I expected Darren, given his profession, looked at it as a place he would need to guard. But I could see what he looked at and how. He saw it as a place he was going to live. That is, with Bronwyn."

"That's...interesting. But is that all you have? You didn't catch them giving each other a—I don't know—special look? A quick kiss?"

"No. I...don't read people very well. But with houses, with people and houses, it all makes sense." Wren suddenly wished she didn't say anything, realizing how silly she must sound. But she was relieved that he didn't seem too upset after all. He nodded.

"All right then. You're the expert, and I respect experts. Tristan Archer, the murdered lawyer, and Karen Weston, the murdered stalker, I don't suppose you have any insights into their views of the house?"

"I'm afraid not. I would have needed to see them in the house—and there's no guarantee. I mean, I'm not a mind reader."

Fitzgerald chuckled. "Of course not. Anyway, thank you. How about the Blaines, especially Rebecca, who worked closely with Cadieux?"

"Is that a change of subject? I thought we were talking about the stalker and lawyer—which, as you say, seem to be connected?"

"I think it's all connected, going back to Dennis and Rebecca Blaine," said Fitzgerald. "Could you figure out Rebecca's connection to this house? I mean, eventually."

Wren wanted to hedge. But she heard her father's voice in her head. This wasn't a profession for modesty.

"Yes, I will," she said. "Eventually."

* * *

"It was my understanding that homes had to be a lot older to rack up so many deaths," said Hadley, standing over the sizzling shrimps in their apartment kitchen. "Never mind Bronwyn, you need a bodyguard, Little Bird."

Wren set the table. "I don't think it's me they're after. It seems to have something to do with Bronwyn. As for the house, killing Tristan Archer accomplished nothing. He was set to let it go forward, and nothing has changed. And that was Bronwyn's stalker, not mine."

"But what about the death of Dennis Blaine?" asked Hadley. "As you said, Detective Fitzgerald sees it as all related—now, zucchini on the side with my patented New Potatoes a la Hadley. I may need to work on that name." She served the plates.

"It doesn't matter," said Wren. "It's extraordinary, whatever you call it. You continue to spoil me." She reached over the table and gave Hadley's hand a squeeze, then laughed. "Do you think Rebecca cooked for Dennis like this?"

"From what I've heard about Rebecca, she doesn't sound like someone who spent a lot of time in the kitchen."

"If there is a house connection," said Wren, "we need to speak to someone who has a connection to the house then and now. Shoshana Blaine. She was in her early twenties then, so she may have known what was going on."

"Would she talk about her family, though? You met her—what was she like?"

"A studied eccentricity that only wealthy, privileged people can afford, along with a no-doubt inherited arrogance. I may be deluding myself, but I think she liked me. We should arrange a meeting—she'll know more about

CHAPTER TEN

the house, and I'd appreciate your take on her."

"Sounds like fun—and are we moving along on the extrovert scale?"

"I don't know if I can say I'm actually looking forward to a social meeting—I haven't gotten that far—but I am curious to know more about the house, especially as the Dennis Blaine death seems to be connecting to the present."

"All right. I'll cook for her, if you want, but if she's as grand as you say, she might prefer a high-end restaurant."

"No. I think she'll invite us to her house. She'll want to discuss something like this on her home territory where she feels comfortable. Where she feels powerful. She gave me her card—a remnant of another time when even people who didn't work had cards. She has a westside townhouse, and judging by how she decorated herself, I imagine it'll be something."

"All right then. But first, some pineapple—they're great this time of year."

It was indeed. Then Wren sighed and picked up her phone and Shoshana's card, and called her.

"Ms. Blaine's residence." Of course, she wouldn't answer her own phone.

"This is Wren Fontaine. I am the architect renovating Ms. Blaine's old house on Long Island and was hoping to speak with her."

"One moment, please." I wasn't immediately dismissed, thought Wren, so that was something. About a minute later, Shoshana got on the line.

"Wren! So pleased to hear from you. But not surprised. I imagined you would want to know more about Cadieux House, so you'd call. I have some knowledge I can share with you. Would you like to come to my home? I think as an architect you might find it interesting."

"Oh yes—thank you," said Wren, mentally giving herself a pat on the back. "If it is all right, my girlfriend, Hadley Vanderwerf, is an event planner and chef and advises me on space usage, especially regarding kitchens."

"Ha! I heard the concern in your voice that I'll be upset about your being a lesbian. I've seen a lot of changes in my long life, what was acceptable and what wasn't. Or more to the point, what was discussed in public and what wasn't." There was a pause, then she spoke more quietly, quickly. "We change and adapt or try to. We even acknowledge mistakes when necessary. Not everyone can see the full picture, though. You know, every generation thinks they invented sex." She then resumed her former tone. "Saturday at one? I prefer lunch meetings at my age. See you then."

Wren clicked off. "It's going to be some afternoon," she said.

Chapter Eleven

When they moved in together, Hadley had taken charge of Wren's wardrobe, and after some discussion, Wren had given in.

"You know so much about 'dressing' a house? And for your Edwardian cosplay club you do yourself so nicely. But for each day—you don't care."

"You're right. I don't care. I'm interested in clothes as a subject, but ultimately I just don't care."

"You care when a beautiful house has the wrong curtains. And you're beautiful. What's the difference?"

"I'm not beautiful," Wren had said quietly, as if afraid to vocalize it.

"I'm forbidding you to say that ever again," said Hadley in a rare moment of anger. But she couldn't keep it up long, the scowl quickly turning into a smile. "I do love you, you know."

"And I love you. I love the way you take care of me. But I don't know why you love me."

"Jesus, Little Bird. For a smart girl…you know, you tell me that you see the extraordinary beauty even in a house that is falling apart, and just like that, you were the first one to see the beauty inside this ex-drug addict. I don't mean my pretty face—'cause let's face it, I'm a doll—" and Wren had laughed despite herself. "But you saw all the way into me. Okay? Have we settled that now? Because we've gotten off topic, which is all about improving your wardrobe."

And so Wren had gained fashionable clothes. For the summer, she slipped into her deep green linen pants suit ("It suits your coloring," Hadley had said), and Hadley put on a dress with red and yellow flowers, and it was off to Shoshana Blaine's.

Their hostess lived in an Upper West Side brownstone shaded by old trees.

"A big house for one lady," said Hadley, then laughed. "Of course, in my family's ridiculous history, that would've been fine."

"But today—you're right. I wonder who will answer the door. Do you think she still keeps a butler?"

But no, it wasn't a butler, or even some ancient family retainer, but a brisk woman of about thirty, dressed in khaki pants and a Ralph Lauren Polo shirt. She seemed to read Wren's mind.

"I know—expecting a man in a frock coat who'd take your calling cards on a silver tray." She held out her hand. "Millie Blandings. I'm Shoshana's assistant—or factotum. She likes that word. You must be Wren Fontaine and Hadley Vanderwerf. Come on in."

Wren wondered if the house's décor and upkeep were going to reflect the casual—if cheerful—welcome. She had seen many old homes whose owners had given up, rooms left to fall apart as they retreated into a little apartment. But not here. Wren saw everything was well-repaired and cleaned. And updated: No Gilded Age portraits of women with tiaras or men in muttonchops. It was all modern art.

"That's a Kandinsky," said Wren, stopping by one picture. "Oh! And that's Paul Klee."

"Nothing gets by Wren," said Hadley proudly.

Millie laughed. "Well done," she said. "Shoshana likes it when people notice the art she's collected. Of course, not many people visit anymore. Most of the people she knew are dead. Anyway, she has a sort of receiving room upstairs where you'll eat. There's a cook-housekeeper who lives in, and I show up on an as-needed basis."

"Are you joining us today?" asked Hadley.

"I'm not paid enough for that," said Millie as they headed up the stairs, and that ended the conversation.

At the end of the hall, Millie opened the door and led the women in.

"Wren Fontaine and Hadley Vanderwerf," she announced.

CHAPTER ELEVEN

Wren's eyes scanned the room. A little different here—the walls were covered with photographs, mostly black and white. The furniture was... *jarring*, she concluded. All mid-century modern, as if it had been taken right out of Cadieux House. Perfect in that house, but somewhat at odds with what Wren expected in a brownstone.

And Shoshana herself, sitting on a chair, wearing a beautifully embroidered jacket with an East Asian look, loose white hair over her shoulders, and half leaning on a silver-topped cane that Wren suspected was more for show than use.

"Welcome," she said with a smile. "Thank you, Millie. You can finish that next chapter, and I'll review it after lunch."

"Sure thing, Shoshana," said Millie. She turned, rolled her eyes at Wren and Hadley, and left, closing the door behind her.

"I'm working on my memoirs. Millie is invaluable. Less than half my age but understands my sensibilities."

The *bohemian* sensibilities, realized Wren, who noticed Millie called her employer by her first name. Shoshana, she remembered, had come of age at an interesting time, as the great families were adapting to the post-war years and adjusting to a less formal world. They would naturally make poverty-chic their own.

"Come, ladies, have a seat."

A lavish spread covered the glass and chrome table, like a delicatessen had exploded. Exotic breads, caviar, half a dozen cheeses, egg salad, tuna salad, white fish salad, smoked salmon and fruits, all artfully arranged. On the side stood a pitcher of orange juice and a bottle of white wine.

"Wren, good to see you again, in a social situation."

"Me too," said Wren. "Thank you for seeing us. This is my girlfriend, Hadley Vanderwerf. She's a chef and event planner."

"A pleasure," said Shoshana. "But I thought 'boyfriend' and 'girlfriend' were out. Don't young people say 'partner' now?"

"A linguistic problem," said Wren. "I'm in business with my father, so I refer to him as my partner, in a legal sense. Working on a better term is one of my priorities."

Shoshana laughed. "I like that. Anyway, this is how I eat nowadays. I browse. I enjoy it. Please sit and help yourself. The lox is very good."

"Better than lox," said Hadley, peering at it. "This is nova."

"I never did understand the difference," said Shoshana.

"Nova salmon is smoked. Lox, true belly lox, is not smoked, but cured in salt."

"You girls today are so literal. Wren—you are less interested in the food than in my home? Fair enough. You're an architect. I know this furniture isn't of this time. I bought it because it was comfortable."

"Surely more than just comfort," said Wren. "The chair you're sitting in was designed by Mies van der Rohe. The one in the corner by Eero Saarinen. Two of the 20th century's greatest architects, who were also furniture designers."

Shoshana leaned back in her chair and smiled broadly. "Oh, you ladies are very sharp. You see what is."

Wren helped herself to some caviar. "Thank you. I like the pictures on your wall. By that window—that's you with Jack Kerouac, the great Beat writer, isn't it?"

"Very good," said Shoshana, like a teacher praising a pupil. "I wasn't sure anyone remembered him anymore, just vague references to 'On the Road.' I met him once or twice." She waved away the subjects. "But you wanted to talk to me about Cadieux House, about my parents and Marius Cadieux. Have some wine and ask away."

Hadley glanced at Wren, who gathered her well-rehearsed thoughts. *You have this, Little Bird.*

"Marius Cadieux was known for his ability to channel his clients' thoughts and desires, even when only vaguely expressed, into architectural brilliance. It is always assumed that your mother, Rebecca, was the primary contact with Cadieux over the house. That is, it was her vision. Is that true?"

Shoshana laughed. "Oh, absolutely. Not all rumors are true, but that one is. My father didn't care much as long as there was a generous bar. The Blaines were never very imaginative people. My mother was a Rodriguez, as I'm sure you know. Cadieux House was absolutely a *Rodriguez* residence. My mother was proud of her Sephardic ancestry."

CHAPTER ELEVEN

"Yes," said Wren. "I read about her."

"I knew you would've researched it. My mother was not religious, but in many ways, she was a very traditional woman. Home and hearth and family were important to her, even in an ultra-modern home like that. But we were also an imaginative family. That house was an extraordinary achievement for Marius, but it was a Rodriguez vision. My mother's personality."

"And what was that?" asked Wren. She tried to sound calm. Shoshana raised an eyebrow.

"Really? I asked about you, Wren. I heard you could read people from their houses. But not my mother. Interesting."

"Perhaps this is a special case," said Wren. "You said at the law office that your mother and Marius Cadieux loved each other. Maybe that allowed him to put more of her into the house than I can understand. Or maybe I'm too close to it—as I said, my father was one of Cadieux's disciples, and Cadieux remains an important influence on his work. At any rate, I can't figure it out."

Wren felt her face get warm, as Shoshana studied her.

"What about me and this house? Read this house, Wren. Read me." Wren gave a quick glance to Hadley, who gave her a wink in return.

"Very well," said Wren. She took a breath. "This house is in…misalignment. I know this because I grew up in a brownstone in Brooklyn."

"A *misalignment?*" She clearly didn't expect that word.

"Do you know what a brownstone really is? It's a kind of sandstone. It was widely available not far from New York and easy to work with, making it a good substitute for the more expensive limestone or marble. You could get the elaborate façades the 19th-century homeowners desired at an affordable price. These houses are worth a fortune today, but when they were built, they were for respectable middle-class people." She paused, and her eyes swept over the room. "With respectable middle-class furniture."

Wren hoped that last remark would take the edge off her brief lecture, which sounded heavy even to her, and inspire Shoshana to laugh.

But it didn't.

"You don't like my furniture?" she asked, daring Wren to confirm.

"I love your furniture. But—" and she knew she better finish quickly, or she'd lose courage—"but that's really immaterial. You asked me to read you. *You* are misaligned, Shoshana. You and this house are not right for each other. And what's more, I think you know that."

She gave a quick glance at Hadley, hoping Shoshana—clearly upset—wouldn't notice, and her girlfriend winked at her. *You have this, Little Bird, and you don't need me to tell you that.*

"You…you don't know me at all. You have no idea about my life…" The amused fencing was gone. Shoshana was genuinely angry.

"You are right, I don't," said Wren, forcing her voice to remain steady. "I don't know people well at all. But I know houses very well. I know *homes*. And I know enough about you to see you don't fit here. You fit in Cadieux House, but not here. So it makes me wonder."

Shoshana sat up straight. The studied languid look was gone. Wren knew she had gone too far. She never did judge it right. At least this wasn't a client or prospect—she wouldn't have to explain this to her father.

"How dare—"

"Oh, come on, Shoshana," said Hadley. "You asked Wren to read you, and she got it right. You wouldn't be so angry if she hadn't. But what the hell—the Vanderwerfs never liked hearing inconvenient truths, and I suppose the Blaines are no different."

Shoshana turned a skeptical eye on Hadley as she clicked a ringed finger on the side table and then turned back to Wren.

"You did get one thing wrong, though. It's not about the Blaines. They were really not anyone, just a bunch of Episcopalians who got lucky in business. I take more after my mother, a Rodriguez, as I said. Cadieux House was a Rodriguez vision, as I made clear. I bet you know what I'm talking about, Wren, or are there limits to even your knowledge?"

"I know one of your ancestors belonged to Shearith Israel, the first Jewish congregation in North America."

"Exactly. Again, I'm not a religious woman, but that congregation is still around, and I belong. The Rodríguezes were important people in this city. My mother was important. My mother—" Then she seemed embarrassed.

CHAPTER ELEVEN

"But never mind, that's a conversation for another day. I haven't forgotten you insulted me and my house."

"I didn't," said Wren, forcing herself to remain patient. "I said you were misaligned. You liked Cadieux House. You and your mother could've stayed there. You never sold it or even rented it, so it wasn't financial. You are matched with that house. I see your personality there, not here. Why did you leave?"

"I didn't want to be in a place where my father was killed. Nor did we want strangers there. Surely, Miss 'expert at houses,' you can understand that."

"Let me tell you what I do understand. I believe that Marius Cadieux built that house for your mother, that she was the inspiration for it. That is how he worked. I can look at that house and see that they loved each other. That's what Cadieux House says to me."

Wren feared another outburst, but all Shoshana gave her was the nastiest smile she had ever seen, smug and almost vicious.

"Look, both of you, at that picture on the bookshelf." She pointed to a silver-framed black-and-white photo. "That was me. I was gorgeous. I was stunning. You don't seem to understand anything, but I got news for you, ladies. I am now ready to give you the real story. He and my mother were thick as thieves, as the gossips said. My mother may have helped Marius *plan* the house, but it was me who *inspired* it. It was *me* Marius loved. It was *me* he took to bed the day we moved in." She paused. "It was *me* he gave a child to."

Wren may have had trouble reading faces, but there was no missing Shoshana's look—not love or wistfulness—just pure triumph. Without even meaning to, Wren had pushed her over the edge. She had been dying to brag to someone. *How old could Shoshana have been back then? Probably just old enough, but that's not where to go right now...*

"I am happy for you," said Wren. It was a strange thing to say, she knew, but what else to say to an elderly woman bragging about a sixty-year-old sexual conquest? "But again, we've gotten off topic. You and your mother left that house. You went to California, and you eventually set up residence here, trying to recreate Cadieux House in a brownstone. I want to know why you didn't go back. Until recently, everyone—rich or poor—died at home. The houses I worked on probably have seen scores of deaths. You and your mother left your dream home after one death—a tragic one, I know. But in my experience, people take comfort in their homes." Wren felt almost dizzy. "My mother died in the home she and my father built together. He didn't leave it. He never will. She is a part of it. And I know Cadieux House is part of your life, because if it weren't, you wouldn't have tried to recreate it here. I wanted to know the true story of Cadieux House so I could properly work on its renovation and build a complementary tiny house for my client. But I see I will not learn it from this house. Or from you."

Whether it was a one-room shack or a Gilded-Age mansion, Wren had always felt comfortable in homes, but suddenly she felt the brownstone's walls closing in on her. She stood and hoped she wouldn't faint.

"I won't take any more of your time. Thank you for your hospitality." She glanced at Hadley, saw a mix of pride and sympathy, and knew she would make it out.

Shoshana gave away nothing, at least not to Wren, who turned and headed for the stairs. She heard Hadley behind her.

"Yes, thank you very much. Wren and I really appreciate your time and assistance. And by the way, the nova salmon was super."

Chapter Twelve

Back in their apartment, Hadley made Wren strong tea with honey and didn't say anything, which made Wren marvel yet again at how well Hadley knew her. They sat in silence until Wren was halfway through it.

"Wow," Hadley finally said. "I mean, just wow. Every now and then, you still surprise me, Little Bird."

"You didn't think I had it in me?"

"Oh no, I knew you had it in you. I wanted to see you let it out. You really are your father's daughter."

"No. He would've been more diplomatic."

"That'll come with time. But you were as brilliant as he was, sticking to your artistic vision, your wisdom in houses. I promise you, you gave Shoshana something to think about. You forced her to think about herself, and that's no small thing."

"Thank you. I'd like to think so. I feel so drained. The whole point was to find out what Cadieux House was really about, and I'm seeing now that question is a lot deeper than I realized. That death was about something very deep." Wren suddenly laughed. "I became an architect so I could deal just with buildings and not people. I know, that was very naïve of me. But here I am, seeing that the profession may have been a big bait-and-switch."

Hadley laughed, too.

"Anyway, even if I can't read people, I can hear words. Shoshana referred to her father's death but didn't discuss how he ended. Does she believe there was a cover up? Was she part of it?"

"Oooh...maybe she killed her father?" said Hadley. "Her father didn't like the idea of his architect screwing his barely legal daughter."

"That's a chilling thought. You wouldn't want to live in a house where you committed a murder, would you?" She shook her head. "You know, Cadieux and Rebecca were each other's alibis. But from what I understand about Cadieux, he never loved any woman enough to kill for her or cover it up. And there would've been talk if he continued to socialize with either Rebecca or Shoshana. Indeed, just a year later, he made the gossip pages when he was found in a villa in La Croix-Valmer, in the south of France, with the estranged wife of a Belgian duke."

"Busy boy," said Hadley.

"I know, right? Still, there is something there...that quartet, Dennis and Rebecca and Marius and Shoshana. Anyway, was she just posing? Or do you think she was really having an affair with Cadieux?"

"Oh...unless she's really psychotic, I think she was together with Cadieux. I don't think anyone is that good a liar," said Hadley.

"Well, she was beautiful, and Cadieux was quite the lady's man, as my father would delicately put it. And given his...predilections, it makes sense he left a child or two along the way. But I wonder—we haven't heard of that child. Are they still in touch?"

"Another player," said Hadley. "Do they get a piece of the pie?"

"Exactly. Also, Shoshana got something wrong, although I doubt if she realized it. She said her mother planned the house but that she herself inspired it. That isn't true for a house, especially for an architect like Cadieux. The whole point of a Cadieux house is that there is no line separating inspiration from planning. He would plan a house based on his inspiration. Now, whether it was the mother or daughter who inspired him, I couldn't say."

"So Shoshana lied to us?" asked Hadley.

Wren thought that one over. "You know, I don't understand that house yet. And I don't think that Shoshana understands it either. But there is something about her mother there, about Rebecca, as if she were in competition with her. Or maybe I'm not thinking about it correctly. I just can't imagine.

CHAPTER TWELVE

Anyway, even if we assume Shoshana is not lying to us, she may be lying to herself. That happens enough when people are asking for a house."

"Very wise, Little Bird. But where do we go next?"

"You know, I really don't care about Shoshana's love life or why someone may have hated Dennis Blaine. But Marius Cadieux did something with this house. I want to make sure any changes I make are aligned with what Cadieux intended. And I may have to dig a little deeper for that." She looked at Hadley. "Am I foolish?"

"Do you know how many horrific neighborhoods I've wandered into looking for a unique dish whose rumors had reached me in Manhattan?" She struck a histrionic pose. "We are those who are willing to suffer for our art." And they both giggled.

"Okay then," said Wren. "We will see what we can do to get inside Marius Cadieux's mind. I think we got as far as we can with Shoshana. I'm not going another round with her. But there are other ways to take a look back—Lavinia would love this. I'll give her a call and see what she can turn up." Lavinia Suisse, professor of history at Columbia, is a leading authority on the history of New York. She was Wren's former professor—and now, Wren was proud to say, her friend.

"Oh yes. If the Rodriguezes are as great as Shoshana and my brother says they are, she'll know plenty."

"Yes. But we can't forget the present either," said Wren. "The stalker and the family lawyer, killed with the same gun. We wonder about Shoshana's connection, but what about my client's? Bronwyn may have stalkers, but maybe there's another connection to Cadieux House. It's funny, her wanting it so badly. Was she going to reveal something about this place? And that bodyguard of hers…what else is she hiding? It's an awfully big house for one woman or even one couple, and she wants a tiny house too."

"Maybe she loves it just like you. You once told me that the Palace of Holyrood House in Scotland had over two hundred and fifty rooms, and yet you wanted to live in it by yourself."

"I admit it!" said Wren, laughing. "Okay then. She loves this house. But how does she love it? For its architectural perfection? I'm not sure. Maybe because she has a connection to the people. She never said she was writing about the Blaines, but it would be just the kind of thing she'd do, based on her past books. She did admit to slipping in a reference to them, but I bet she's going further…you know, I'm going to have to talk to her again."

"You don't sound thrilled with that prospect," said Hadley.

"I know. I keep having to deal with people. It would be easy to leave this whole thing alone, but then I wouldn't really understand the house. And I couldn't bear that."

"Because you'd disappoint your father?" teased Hadley.

"Because I'd disappoint Marius Cadieux. He knew I could figure it out. He knew when I was ten. Now, I'm seeing maybe I don't have to talk to Shoshana again—I can talk to Bronwyn. She comes regularly to have a look, and I'm thinking she knows more than she's saying. I think we can strike a deal. It can't be as bad as Shoshana."

"That's the spirit! You'll sweat it out of her?"

"No. I'll listen to her. I think she likes to talk. I had a volleyball coach who told us God gave us two ears and two eyes but only one mouth, as a sign we're supposed to listen and watch twice as much as we talk."

"Pretty deep," said Hadley, then giggled. "I wish I had seen you play volleyball."

* * *

Bronwyn certainly likes the house. Wren could see that. But even people who liked homes could like them for different reasons. If Wren liked it for its extraordinary design, why shouldn't a writer like it for its story? Indeed, Marius Cadieux might have been amused at that, his house merging with a story it inspired.

Or did the house inspire the story?

"You've done me a favor," said Bronwyn. "Not only do I like seeing this house, but you've given me an excuse to not write today, and any novelist will tell you that's most welcome."

"Oh, but will your fans blame me if your next novel is late to the

CHAPTER TWELVE

bookstores?"

"Could be. As you've seen, fans can be very unforgiving." So that still rankled.

"I think they're calming down," said Darren. "No more incidents recently, and we're hardly getting any more angry emails and texts." Ah, but you're still guarding her!

"I'd like to show you first what's happening with kitchens and bathrooms. Back then, no one took those rooms very seriously, not even Cadieux. They were utilitarian. As I told you, we'll be updating them to reflect the overall theme of the house with glass, wood, and stone. There's plumbing work we need to do, but meanwhile, I can show you some of the fixtures."

They walked upstairs to the master bathroom, still with its original green tiles, but Bobby had already unpacked the beautiful new sink, and Wren watched Bronwyn's eyes get big. But not Darren's. To him, an appliance was just an appliance. Fair enough.

"That's something," said Bronwyn. "I know I saw it online, but to see it like this—it's almost a shame to wash your hands in it. I don't know what my mother would make of it."

"That's the thing about houses. Some elements age faster than others. You know, I used to feel my father standing over my shoulder, reviewing my work. I got over that, but now, with this house, I feel Marius Cadieux here. He has a sarcastic smile as he questions every move I make, in that perfect Parisian accent of his."

She saw Bronwyn and Darren were looking at her a little oddly, a typical sign she had spoken too long, on a peculiar tangent.

"Come with me. I want to show you what we're doing in the master bedroom." She turned to walk down the hall, assuming they were following her. At least it was about the house, so she was comfortable. Inside the room, she turned. "We're installing a curved sliding door to separate the bedroom from this—dressing room, I think we'll call it. God knows what Cadieux called it. Probably only he and Rebecca knew what it was. There was a strong sense of honesty between them—this house would not have been possible without it. And that's why Marius is leaning over my shoulder.

He wants me to demand the same honesty from you."

Okay—Darren wasn't the one with the imagination, but he knew before Bronwyn did what was happening. He smiled.

"All right, we're busted. We have more than a professional relationship. We're two single adults, so I don't see why we're going through this."

"I think I know," said Bronwyn. "From one artist to another, okay? You can't do a proper job on this house without knowing about who is living there and how, right? So yes, I hired Darren, and then we fell in love, but we didn't want a huge press thing all over it, especially with the messy stalking issue."

"I am a widower with two children," said Darren. "I left the police when my wife died. This job offers more flexibility. I am curious about how you knew?"

"The house. You looked at this house as someone planning to live here."

Darren nodded, and Bronwyn laughed. "I like that. I like that a lot. A connection with this house. You're the 'house whisperer,' Wren. Again, I see how smart I was to hire you."

Wren gave a little bow to cover up her blush.

"If I may," said Wren, deciding to take advantage of the current goodwill. "I have a sense of what Bronwyn sees in this house and wants from it. But you are different, Darren. What do you think? What do you want?"

"You mean, as a detective?" He smiled. Wren did not smile back.

"No. That is immaterial to me as an architect. I mean as a person. Being a detective is part of who you are, of course, like being a writer is part of who Bronwyn is. But I work on homes for people. As a person, what do you think of Cadieux House?"

"That is…rather heavy, Wren," said Darren, and she once again thought of how much more smoothly her father might've handled this.

"Yes, it is," she said. "And I can tell you that for all his good cheer, Marius Cadieux was rather heavy. Anyway, I'm curious."

"I am going to get used to it," he said after a few moments of thought. "My children are adaptable, and I think they'll see this as a sort of playground. I'm more of a traditionalist. But oddly, I feel safe here. And that's something

CHAPTER TWELVE

for a person who is, in fact, a detective. I don't know why—it's a very open structure. But that leads me to believe I can get used to it, even love it."

The couple exchanged fond looks.

"Cadieux would be pleased with what you said," said Wren. "Anyway, I assure you, I won't share anything you tell me. But this is just the beginning of the story. There's more. I'm thinking back to the late Tristan Archer and that odd meeting we had in his office about privacy, where we all promised not to discuss the home's history. It seemed strange, because none of this material is private. Anyone could've dug this up, but Woody Blaine is especially worried about it now."

She looked back and forth between Bronwyn and Darren. Could she tell what they were thinking? Darren was unreadable, especially to her, but Wren figured he'd probably be unreadable to everyone. A detective must be trained to do that. And Bronwyn? Perhaps a half smile. After all, weren't they both artists?

"To me, he seemed overly anxious," said Wren. "After all, this was well over sixty years ago. Who would care, or even remember those people anymore? But then I visited Shoshana Blaine. Do you know she has done her best to recreate this house in her brownstone? It's ridiculous. She has a connection there. I can tell about people and houses. She had years to discuss this however and yet, nothing. But now she grudgingly promises to give Woody a year, just a year, of privacy. I'm wondering why, after decades of silence, she's difficult, about a year. After years of owning this empty house, she cooperates in its sale. It all came together to me."

There was no missing it now, that wry smile on Bronwyn's face.

"All right," said Bronwyn. "I should've known that this would come out. I didn't expect it from you, however. But it makes sense, your connection to the house. I flatter myself, but I think you and I have the same connection."

"Uhh…do you think you should reveal this?" asked Darren.

"Why the heck not? We haven't done anything illegal. And I think we can trust Wren to be discreet. So yeah, it was a nice coincidence. I read some old article about the Dennis Blaine death. I slipped in a reference, but as I kept digging, it looked like something fun to write about in a big way. I approached Shoshana. I feared she would throw me out of her house, but she seemed excited I'd tell the story and would give me some inside info as long as I made her look good."

I'll bet, thought Wren. Imagine having someone as popular as Bronwyn Merrick writing your story, your passionate love affair with Marius Cadieux. Probably even lead to a TV movie.

"When I was visiting Shoshana, she said she had a secretary working with her on her memoires."

"Oh, yes. Gathering the info. You know, she may be old, but she still has her wits about her. She knew it was going to be hard to get attention for such an old…scandal. Is anything even scandalous anymore? But there we were, talking about the house, and the next thing you knew, we were visiting it. What do you know—I fell in love with it." She gave Wren a cool look. "But you'd know all about that, wouldn't you?"

"Of course. I'm afraid though, I've been very inconstant regarding my love affair with houses. I've fallen in love with so many."

"Interesting—polyamorous with houses, but I imagine very steady with Hadley. I watched you two. You'll grow old together, I'm sure…oh, I'm truly sorry I embarrassed you. Being too observant is an occupational hazard with writers. But it's true, and I'm happy for you."

"Thank you," said Wren, painfully aware of how vulnerable she was about her private life while realizing how silly it was, feeling like a teenager whose crush was just made public during homeroom. "I hope the same for both of you, but not being a writer, I am not able to predict the future as confidently as you can."

Even Darren relaxed enough to laugh along with Bronwyn at that, and Wren felt better.

"So you're working with Shoshana," said Wren. "That explains why both of you were okay with the one-year limit. I imagine it'll take at least that long to write and publish that book and thus allow Woody Blaine to complete whatever deal before it all comes out."

"Exactly. But there's something else. As you're the architect, and I'm your client, I do have to tell you there is something special here. Something about

CHAPTER TWELVE

this house and the story, about the way they lived—and the way they left so quickly."

Wren looked around the room and imagined Marius Cadieux standing next to her, crossing his arms over his chest and looking at her with his superior smile.

"I asked you two about what this house said to you. But the real question is what they said to Rebecca. Yes, I think the house was really designed for her, but what did Cadieux see in her? If these walls could talk..." said Wren. "That phrase goes back at least to the mid-nineteenth century. I suppose that's why I like old houses."

Chapter Thirteen

"You fall into the most unusual things, Miss Fontaine," said Lavinia. "A great compliment indeed," said Wren. "I know you have a high bar for 'unusual.'"

"Yes, rummaging through the city's history has left me a little jaded," said Lavinia. Wren imagined her old professor had been jaded and sarcastic even when she had been in kindergarten. "Anyway, more for my book." Lavinia Suisse, professor of history at Columbia University, continued to work on what would be her magnum opus, a history of the great families of New York.

Although Lavinia had an office at the university, she preferred working at the nearby apartment she shared with her wife, Angela. Her home office was lined with books, and every spare surface boasted a pile of manuscripts. But Lavinia made room on her desk for her wedding photo. It was the only time Wren had ever seen either woman looking self-conscious. And Wren herself, a proud and nervous twenty year old standing in front of them as their bridesmaid. *Look at me now,* thought Wren.

"The Blaines are somewhat dull," pronounced Lavinia, bringing Wren back to the present. She clicked on the keyboard to bring up notes, documents, and genealogical tables onto her screen. "Despite being an old New York family, they never did anything very interesting. Ran a variety of tedious family businesses. The men were good at tennis. The women set a good table. They tended to marry well and went to St. Thomas on Sundays. Dennis, I think, may have been a little sharper than the average Blaine. Took the family money and invested it in a variety of European ventures—especially

CHAPTER THIRTEEN

in France. Apparently, he spoke good French and did very well for himself."

"Oh!" said Wren. "That connects at my end. I was sworn to secrecy, but I guess I can tell you. Woodrow Blaine, who seems to run the family investments, has a big deal happening in France and doesn't want the family scandal to interfere. And then there's Marius Cadieux, who designed the house—another connection to France. More than coincidence?"

"Yes, Marius Cadieux." Lavinia leaned back and smiled. "I ran into your father the other day." Ezra was adjunct faculty at Columbia's architecture school. "He mentioned your work on a Cadieux House. I gathered he's rather proud of you."

"Not...anxious?"

"Your father has never been anxious in his life. You know that."

"I mean, concerned about me working on the house of the great Marius Cadieux."

"You are obviously comfortable working on the 'house of the great Marius Cadieux.' And yet you are concerned that your father is not on board. Interesting." Wren flushed. "I'm sorry. I didn't mean to embarrass you—that wasn't nice of me." She touched Wren's hand. "It's the way families work, most of them. Probably all of them. I have families on my mind right now. The Rodriguezes, mother and daughter, are quite a pair. The whole family is interesting. Not your strong suit, I know, but I do have some interesting insights."

"Hadley's brother Trey told me something about the family, about the Rodriguezes and the Blaines. People thought Rebecca killed Dennis, but they couldn't find a reason, and..." She looked away.

"And what, Wren?"

"And there would have to be a reason. There would have to be a very big reason."

"And what do you consider a good reason, Wren?"

"I didn't say a good reason. I said a big one. There is no such thing as a good reason."

Lavinia just stared at her, and Wren knew she had gone too far with one of Columbia's most distinguished professors. But then Lavinia just burst out laughing.

"Touche, my dear! I had that coming. I taught you well, and it's coming back to haunt me. But I agree."

"Thank you," said a relieved Wren.

"Okay, then. If we want to think there was a big reason, what do you think it could've been?"

"That's a little hard for me," said Wren. "I'm not…I suppose betrayal. That sounds very biblical, I know: thirty pieces of silver and a kiss. If Dennis was having an affair. But actually, she may have been. With Marius Cadieux. At least that's what I thought. But now her daughter Shoshana tells me that she was the one having an affair with Cadieux. If she can even be believed."

"That is interesting, Wren. Do you think she's lying to you?"

"I think she may be lying to herself."

"Ooh. And you say you're not good with people."

"I'm not. It was the house. Actually, two houses. There is something…off about the way Shoshana lives, and maybe this sounds like an overstatement, but there's something dishonest about the way she is living."

Lavinia shook her head. "That may not be an overstatement at all. In fact, it is rather shrewd. But we're getting a little ahead of ourselves. The Rodriguezes have a fascinating background. Shake that family tree and out fall some very successful entrepreneurs and financiers. Trey probably told you an ancestor signed the Buttonwood Agreement."

"A big deal in that set."

"Oh yes. But there's more to them than that…including yet another French connection." Wren watched Lavinia slip into her lecturer mode. "They're an interesting group, the Sephardim. They've kept a separate identity while mixing with a larger society and have been doing that in the New World for more than three hundred years. The Rodriguez clan consisted of some canny risk-takers. They may have been here since this was New Amsterdam, but the Rodriguezes didn't forget their European roots. Rebecca's paternal grandfather put together some rather nice import/export deals. His son—Rebecca's father—expanded the business. He was the one who started working with the Blaines. They also had been in the United

CHAPTER THIRTEEN

States since forever, and despite their American bona fides had maintained good connections among the English monied class and aristocracy."

"Not always the same thing, is it?" said Wren.

"Good girl. Exactly. A rising commercial class and the old land-based aristocracy—which was becoming less relevant year after year. But don't count them out. They're a clannish group with a lot of influence, even today. But the Rodriguezes made room for everyone. That's the way they worked. Business documents are often public, if you know where to look. And I do. Our Rebecca graduated from Bryn Mawr in 1927. Then her name started appearing in corporate documents."

Wren laughed. "I don't know what her father thought of a woman in the family business, but from what I heard, Rebecca wouldn't be content just leading her synagogue's sisterhood committees."

"Oh no. She was in the thick of it." Lavinia's fingers danced across the keyboard, calling up scanned copies of business documents from the 1920s and 30s. "Here is her name again and again."

"So she joined right before the Depression," said Wren.

"Yes," said Lavinia. "And that's when things get interesting. The Rodriguezes remained sharp. Who knows? Maybe generations of having to watch out as minorities had made them cautious. Rebecca's father pulled back just in time. The Blaines did okay—they had a lot of land, and that's always worth something. But their world was disappearing, the old connections falling apart. As wealthy as the Rodriguez family was, they could see the advantages of partnering with one of the old WASP families. And then we had a merger, of sorts."

"A family marriage."

"You saw it coming. They were married in 1930. But you seem unhappy with that."

"I am," said Wren. "Not entirely surprised. Trey—Hadley's brother—already told us about the importance of the two families. But do you think Rebecca felt something for him? I guess I saw her as rather heroic—she inspired Cadieux, so she must've been something. I wouldn't have thought that she'd just get married for a family alliance. You make it sound like an arranged marriage. The Blaine name and connections and Rodriguez cleverness. I was hoping you'd find she was more progressive than that. I heard Dennis fell hard for her—she was stunningly beautiful and charming—but what did she feel for him?"

"Oh, Wren," said Lavinia, shaking her head. "I'm making some allowances because, to put it nicely, you're not a people-person, but try to add a little imagination to this. It's 1930. Angela and I were born more than half a century after Rebecca, and yet we were both lesbians before you could go public with it."

"You're not saying Rebecca and Dennis were—"

"Again, use your imagination, Wren. Straight women have problems, too." Lavinia smiled. "Or so I've been told."

"Okay, then," said Wren, slowly. "So it's 1930. We have a single woman…" The room was silent for a few moments. Then she smiled. "She's a single woman. I don't suppose it was very easy being a single woman back then."

"It never was," said Lavinia dryly. "Let's think about Rebecca, not just a woman, but a woman from a small religious and cultural minority, especially as the Eastern Jews, the Ashkenazi, started outnumbering the more established, worldlier Sephardim. I'm a historian, not a psychologist, and I never knew Rebecca. But I can get a sense of how she might have navigated the communities she sailed through, open, but keeping her own counsel and not forgetting where she came from."

"And people expected certain behaviors from a single woman, no matter what background she came from," said Wren. "A married woman, with a flexible husband, actually had more freedoms. He apparently adored her, so no one would question her behavior, technically under husband's authority. It was a Brownstone marriage."

Lavinia raised an eyebrow. "Explain."

"I've been thinking about Brownstones lately, the one I grew up in and the one Shoshana lives in now. Brownstones are lovely, but not perfect. When they were built, they were a compromise, a way to achieve a certain level of beauty and craftsmanship with less money. Maybe her marriage was like that, for both of them, the protection of marriage but the understanding of freedom. Ultimately a compromise, however."

"Good. But the Fontaines don't compromise, do they? Neither father nor daughter. Not with your work, not with your life partner."

Wren smiled. "Marius Cadieux didn't compromise, certainly not in that house. That house, in a way I haven't yet figured out, is a monument to Rebecca, a gift to her. No compromise there."

"So they were lovers?"

Wren shook her head. "It doesn't seem so, although that's hardly my area of expertise. But I agree, there is something there, something in that house. Anyway, Shoshana went out of her way to brag about her relationship with Cadieux. She told us she had a child with him."

"Ooh, a mother-daughter love triangle. How wicked. That's where I was going, and I'm glad you found out that Cadieux then was, in fact, the father. Now, you have the advantage over me. You met Marius Cadieux, and I did not. Would he go as far as to seduce his client's barely adult daughter and have an unacknowledged child with her? Anyway, have a look." A moment later, Lavinia called up an image on the screen. That was definitely a younger Shoshana. And standing next to her was a young man in a cap and gown. Both were smiling. The caption was University of Pennsylvania, class of 1979, Shoshana Blaine and Raphael Rodriguez. "You can hide birth certificates and marriage licenses, but everyone puts everything online nowadays. I was looking for Blaines and Rodriguezes, and this popped up. Now, it's not a very good photo. But you can tell that he looks like a Rodriguez, no trace of a Blaine about him, or a Cadieux either. Female genes ran strong in this family."

"Well, you're not going to hear about him from the Blaines or Rodriguezes," said Wren. "The embarrassment of a child out of wedlock back then...but she was at least somewhat involved in his life, as she was at his graduation. At the end of the day, family is family, and I can see the Rodriguezes as being very tightly knit, and he'd be sent to grow up with cousins. That would be their great strength, keeping to their cultural and religious roots to maintain a family cohesiveness within a larger world."

"Yes—that's why he'd be called *Rodriguez*. More of a connection to them, or the Blaines. Or for that matter, Marius Cadieux. I wonder if he ever met his father? Anyway, it's easy enough to ask him. He lives on Long Island—not far from Cadieux House, interestingly."

"Rebecca's grandson," mused Wren. "He may know what his mother knows. And is more willing to discuss it. Maybe that's why she apparently is keeping him a secret. I might want to look him up at some point."

They were quiet for a while, and then Lavinia said, "You're thinking of the house, aren't you?"

Wren smiled. "Yes, of course. Busy little place, it seems it was. You know, I expect that of massive Victorian halls, but we're talking about a Cadieux, so open and yet...I am safe there. It's what I'm going for in the special writing studio I'm designing for Bronwyn, but I can't really perfect it until I understand the house—and that means understanding the people. But the deeper I look..."

"It's going to get more complicated. We're getting up to World War II. Dennis was past forty, but still young enough to serve. Not with a gun, but thanks to his good language skills and business connections, they made him a major and put him in some sort of economic warfare unit—I have a friend at the Defense Department who quietly shares records with me from time to time."

"And Rebecca? Shoshana was a little girl. So I guess Rebecca stayed at home with her and chaired war-related committees?"

Lavinia sighed and leaned back. "You'd think so, wouldn't you? The thing is, Rebecca just—disappeared. I have no idea what she was up to in the war years. There isn't one single record of her in New York, or anywhere else for that matter. I called everyone I know. This was a prominent and wealthy family. They were mentioned in the papers. The last mention was from mid-1942. Then she vanished. At first, I was annoyed. Then, I became obsessed. I went through every archive, called in favors from people who had access to various private sources. Nothing. Dennis was a visible figure in Washington and New York, but not his wife. Rebecca disappeared off the face of the earth and wasn't seen or heard of again until the war ended."

Chapter Fourteen

Wren knew Lavinia's reputation as the queen of historical research. If she couldn't find where Rebecca had gone, no one could.

"Cadieux was in England for the war," said Wren. "Was she with him? They had known each other before the war."

"I'd like to think so, but there's no trace she was in England. Now, you're the Cadieux expert. What was he up to—I didn't really focus on him."

"I do know he wanted to take up arms with the Free French, but even though he wasn't yet thirty, he was already clearly marked as a genius. So they put him to work behind the scenes. He designed some clever, easy-to-build troop housing—my father said they were a marvel, and they made D-Day possible. Cadieux even pioneered some camouflage techniques—he was a master of creating illusion with surfaces. A commendation later said it had saved thousands of lives."

She stopped. Something about that—but the thought came and flew away. Wren shook her head. "Anyway, that's what kept him busy. I heard De Gaulle personally thanked him after the war. My father said there was a bit of derring-do—he waited too long to leave and had to be smuggled across the Channel with the Germans on his heels. All I know for sure is that sometime after the war, he came to America to work with some top architects here and renewed his friendship with Dennis and Rebecca."

"And then they commissioned him to build Cadieux House. Was it always called that? You don't usually hear of houses named for their architects."

"I know," said Wren. "It was said that was Rebecca's idea. To honor him, perhaps. A less complimentary interpretation was that the Blaines wanted to piggyback on his growing fame. I'm finding I can't get away from Dennis's death—and now, the murder of his lawyer and Bronwyn's obsessive fan."

"And the house," said Lavinia.

"Of course—the house," responded Wren, but Lavinia could see her mind had wandered.

"You aren't going to like this," said Lavinia, bringing her back. "But there are some personality issues here. Rebecca is not easy to pigeonhole."

"Personalities are not my strong suit, but houses are. Cadieux put Rebecca's personality into that house. I may have to think some more about that residence, that connection."

"Very well. But give yourself a little more credit, my dear. You are nowhere near as bad as you think. Trust yourself a little more; you're not a shy undergrad, and you've worked successfully with some very demanding and difficult clients. I think you can build the connections. You can do them from both the architectural and personality ends."

* * *

"Yes. These doors work well," said Bobby. "You were right."

"Are you surprised?" said Wren with a smile. Bobby had given Wren her first lesson in how to hammer a nail straight.

"No—just admiring. And amused, seeing another generation of Fontaines working on a modernist home."

"Do you think my father would've come up with a better solution? Or would he have just insisted that Bronwyn not make a single change, not even the dish drain?"

"Oh, he might've tried to convince her, but in the end, realizing that he had to give her what she wanted, he'd do what she asked, even if it was with bad grace. I don't think I'm telling you something you don't know, but for all his original designs, Ezra Fontaine has always been a practical man. His homes are very livable. And this one wasn't entirely that way. Your father would've had a door here from day one."

CHAPTER FOURTEEN

Wren looked at the curved doors she had designed that completed the circle and gave some privacy to the master bedroom. As it had stood, the curved wall led into a dressing room, which led, though another bend in the wall, into the hallway, Wren had carefully designed a series of cunningly hidden doors that she felt maintained the look while creating a sense of privacy.

"I wonder if it was jealousy," said Wren. "It's not an emotion one normally sees as a driving force for architecture, but if he was jealous of Dennis, who got to share a bed with Rebecca every night, I could see him being amused that their privacy wasn't perfect. You couldn't just casually look into their bedroom, but there was no door either. Did Cadieux like the idea of reducing their privacy?"

Bobby laughed. "That would be insane, even by architect standards, but to be honest, I can't think of a better reason. Jesus Christ."

But was she just being fanciful? Shoshana was barely a woman when the house was built, probably only twenty when she became Cadieux's lover. Did he take the daughter when the mother was out of reach? That was so beyond what she could possibly understand…

"The one we've been calling the secondary bedroom—smaller but also with a good view. I'm sure they would've given that to Shoshana—probably even designed it with her in mind. Let's take another look."

Bobby was a head taller than Wren, but her stride was so full of purpose that he almost had to run to keep up with her. Cadieux House had no conventional floors, more like a series of levels, artfully served by a staircase that seemed to float in the middle of the house. Again, Wren felt the openness, even as the polished wood walls, accented with steel and copper, promised safety.

No—that was not quite the right word. *Security*. In any Cadieux home, you were *secure* in your place in the world. Maybe there were half a dozen architects in the history of the world who had achieved that.

Again, no door, but as with the master bedroom, a cunning series of curved halls that maintained privacy. Or was it just an illusion of privacy? No one was locked out, Wren thought, but the reverse was just as true: no one was locked in. It was a happy room either way, looking over an expanse of lawn and a small wood.

"Shoshana would've still been in her teens when they planned and built this house," said Wren. "I wonder…"

"Hmm?" asked Bobby.

"Nothing."

"Don't tell me 'nothing.' Your father has pulled that with me, too, and with the Fontaines, it's never 'nothing.' It's always something, young lady."

Wren gave Bobby a sly smile. He had always acted paternal with her, but unlike her actual father, he could be shocked.

"All right. I'm wondering if this is where Marius Cadieux seduced his client's daughter, who was more than two decades younger than he was and, as the saying goes, got her with child."

"Jesus, Wren," he said after a moment. "Is that what happened?"

"Apparently. Shoshana apparently has a son and says Cadieux was the father. Considering when the house was planned and built…I can't say when the two of them met or know when they took it to the next level, but she was pretty young. You say you know me, Bobby, so you know that for me, it comes back to the house. But…no."

"No, what?"

"I mean, I saw a picture of Shoshana's son. There's no telling for sure—it's said he got the Blaine genes. I really don't know anything about their relationship and even if you told me I probably wouldn't understand it. But I do know Cadieux wouldn't…*sully* this house with an affair like that. That happened somewhere else. This house is a temple to Rebecca. I know that much…but it's about the why that I'm coming to terms with."

"So this room has nothing to do with it?" asked Bobby.

"It has everything to do with it. Every room is important in a Cadieux house, even the broom closet."

Bobby laughed. "Now, that's your father talking!"

"Yes, it is. I happen to agree with him. There is a sense of family here. A very unusual family, I'm guessing, but Cadieux must've understood it. The homes…the way those rooms were designed. Cadieux understood that. It

CHAPTER FOURTEEN

was said he understood women, and I'm thinking he might've. I'm taking a fresh look at this room. Is it the size, the view of the woods rather than the sea? But Shoshana's room says 'closed' to me. It says 'separate' to me, where the master bedroom is more open. Perhaps it's just me? I wonder..." She thought of the elderly Cadieux, talking to her when she was ten. He told her...

"Well," said Bobby, clapping his hands, "Philosophy and psychology are your responsibility, Miss Fontaine. Mine is replacing a fuse box that belongs in a museum." He gave her a quick salute and left her alone.

* * *

Wren had carefully planned the home's changes. Although it needed fewer renovations than the 19th-century homes she usually worked on, for some reason, she worried over Cadieux House more than other houses. No, not for *some* reason, she admitted to herself. It was because it was designed by Cadieux, her father's greatest mentor, a man she had met herself. A house, she realized, she still didn't fully understand.

She heard the tritone doorbell. Had Cadieux picked that, too? No doubt. It was all of a part with him.

It was probably someone for her. Any delivery driver for Bobby would've just flagged down one of the workers. Still mulling over the house, she opened the door to Adam Fitzgerald, the state police detective.

"Senior Investigator Fitzgerald. How may I help you? Or are you just here to look at this house?" *Are you willing to share what you know with me?*

"Actually, viewing this house is reason enough to visit," he said. "Or do you think I have a more practical reason?"

"Either way, hosts at least as far back as the 18th century would say, 'welcome to liberty hall.' Their version of make-yourself-at-home."

She hoped that sounded welcoming, somewhat amusing, and not too pedantic.

"I like that. I like that a lot. Maybe I'll start using that at my home." He looked around the foyer, his hands thrust into his pockets. Wren was used to other people waiting for her to say something; here she was now, waiting for this detective to say why he came. He seemed in no hurry. Weren't police officers always shown as if in a rush?

"To be fair, though, I am here on business," he said.

"I am not surprised," said Wren. "Considering the connection to three murders," said Wren.

Fitzgerald raised an eyebrow. "Three? There has been another murder?"

Did I say something silly? "Tristan Archer, who was murdered here. Karen Weston, who was killed after stalking Bronwyn Merrick here. And Dennis Blaine, back in 1955."

"Yes—I forget Dennis. It was such a long time ago, and yet, it connects. Don't you think so?"

Wren wondered if he was teasing her. Hadley picked up on those things.

"I can tell you, as an architect, that I see all three events connected to the house. And…I think you agree. Here you are, back at the house. And I don't think you would be here if you knew who committed either the Archer or Weston murders."

"Technically, the Nassau County police are investigating those murders. But the state has a long interest in this case."

"In this house," said Wren. "Come, I want to show you something." She turned, not even looking to see if he was following her. She didn't know Sr. Investigator Fitzgerald all that well, but she did know no one could resist the Cadieux House.

"I don't know what they called this room," said Wren. "Living room, but it was so much more. I like to think of it as Rebecca's stage. It's a concept that goes at least as far back as the Renaissance. For some, a home is just a place to live. But for some people, for people like Dennis and Rebecca, it was a place…it was like a theater, I suppose. And this was the room, designed specifically for them by Marius Cadieux."

"I've seen this room, Ms. Fontaine," said Fitzgerald.

"I know you've *seen* it. But have you really *looked* at it? Note the way the ceiling soars to meet the tall windows reaching for the sky, the perfect curves giving it the illusion of infinite vertical space. This is a huge living

CHAPTER FOURTEEN

room, and if it were just a room, it would be too big. You would get lost in it and be uncomfortable. Fill it with people, and you're back in a college party. But not here—Cadieux tricks us again. I want you to look at the subtle variations in the levels that divide the room. So you are simultaneously free and secure...which makes it all the more startling what happened at their last party."

"Dennis Blaine was shot to death," said Fitzgerald. "Whether it was the waiter or someone else."

"Just off this room," said Wren. She looked closely at him, trying to see how he reacted. "I'm sure you knew it was in the master suite. You see how it flows and how easy it would be to slip out of here to kill Dennis Blaine? It's not like a typical house, where an exit might be obvious. Movement is so *easy*. But see it again now that you've really looked at this room. Separate groups existed here during parties—separate and yet together. Cadieux knew how to create a space for socializing. Not only was he a master of space, he was an avid partygoer. He knew how a room like this should work for socializing, for both forming groups and moving. People could come and go so easily, together and yet not trapped. Cadieux was not only a great architect, he was an extroverted partygoer. He knew how rooms like this should work."

"I never thought of that," said Fitzgerald. To Wren, he looked genuinely interested. "The concept of actually designing a place to facilitate a party."

"Every room, in every house, has a purpose, if an architect knows their business. The 19th-century houses I've specialized in—they were designed for people to show they ruled over the city." She looked at Fitzgerald—he didn't seem to be humoring her. She thought she had really intrigued him. *Don't go over the top now; get back to the subject.* "So you have this beautiful room, created specifically to facilitate a glamorous party. The lights are low—so everyone can appreciate the beauty of Long Island Sound by moonlight. You're the detective. Do you *see* this room now that you've really *looked* at it? Do you know what really happened to Dennis Blaine?"

"That is...very interesting, Ms. Fontaine. But does this discussion, these insights, tell us who killed him?" A faint smile. *Is he teasing me?*

"I wouldn't know about that," she said, hoping she didn't sound priggish. "I'm an architect, not a police detective. But I do know that no one was ever formally charged—I know that waiter was arrested, but on the thinnest pretexts, and he never went to trial. There was no real motive there anyway. All those police and all those journalists, and none of them ever found a reason for anyone to kill him. You walk through this house and go from room to room. So easy to socialize, to have an affair, even to kill someone. I believe the house contains the reason people keep getting killed. And perhaps…just perhaps…made it so hard to find someone who could legitimately be arrested for killing Dennis Blaine."

"So you haven't looked at the house and figured it out?"

"Very funny! But I don't really know who. It's more interesting to think about why."

Fitzgerald laughed. "Is this the way architects think? I like that. I like that a lot."

"Are you patronizing me, sir?" She felt her cheeks burn, trying to feel she wasn't back in high school.

"No. I'm not. I'm sorry. I meant it."

"All right then," she said. "I'm sorry, too. I don't always…"

Fitzgerald waved it away. "It's okay. I'm here about the house, and you didn't disappoint me. What does that tell you?"

Wren didn't answer right away, but he didn't rush her. "It tells me that you think it's somehow related to the house. Dennis Blaine, the master, and Tristan Archer, the family attorney. And Karen Weston, the obsessed fan."

"She would seem an outlier," said Fitzgerald.

"I don't think so," said Wren. "And I don't think you do either. As I said, I am not a police detective. But I don't believe in coincidences. Deaths so close to each other. And connected to this house."

"It always comes back to the house, doesn't it? For both of us? You've been helpful, Ms. Fontaine—and no, I'm not patronizing you. In fact, I'm going to share something with you, as a thanks for being so open with me. I don't know how much you know about Tristan Archer, but the firm has been running things for the family for a long time."

CHAPTER FOURTEEN

"For the Blaine family?" asked Wren.

"Actually, for the Rodriguez family. I get the impression the firm relationship was part of her dowry," he said, smiling. "A shrewd group of men tightly bound to the complex Rodriguez family businesses, for a very long time. I get the impression the firm knew about the house, that is, knew about it in more than just a purchase on a balance sheet."

"Because you've asked?"

"Ha! It's almost impossible for a police officer to get anything out of a law firm. They just keep talking about attorney-client privilege. And now Archer is dead…although…" he looked at Wren. "Archer had a son, also a lawyer. His name is Gareth."

"He wasn't involved in this house," said Wren. "We had legal dealings, and Tristan Archer was the only one involved—the only name on the papers."

"Gareth isn't with the firm. He's a big public interest lawyer for all kinds of leftwing causes. You know, Wren, it just occurred to me. He lives just north of the city, in Rockland County."

"Maybe he'd be interested in seeing this house, where his family has a major connection."

"Maybe," said Fitzgerald. Wren was pleased to see him look around the room again, feeling she had made him see the house as it truly was, appreciate it as planned by Cadieux. "Just one more thing, Ms. Fontaine. You talked about the purpose of a house earlier. As you said, the 19th century mansions were built for rulers, I think you put it. What was the purpose of this house?"

"I'm still trying to figure that out," said Wren. "But I am getting a sense it was very important to Rebecca Blaine, nee Rodriguez."

"A gift?"

"Yes, but more than that. Houses were parts of dowries for centuries, an important way of transferring wealth."

"Oh yes, wasn't that something in 'Pride and Prejudice,' Mr. Collins is going to get Longbourn because he's the closet male heir?" She must've looked surprised, because Fitzgerald said, "Yes, cops read Jane Austen too."

"I'm sorry…"

He waved it away. "Just kidding. You were being helpful, and I was being rude. Tell me about it being more than a gift?"

"Oh, okay. This is just my thought, but I think it was more than just, 'Hey, let me build a nice house for this woman I like.' I don't want to sound too fanciful, but he put her soul into this. I think the more I understand Rebecca, the more I understand this house and why things happened the way they did. The way they continue to do so."

"Because of a house? I'm not making fun of you—I'm genuinely asking."

"Not just a house, Investigator Fitzgerald. A Marius Cadieux House. Built for a woman whom I'm pretty sure he loved."

Chapter Fifteen

Hadley looked up the Hudson River from the George Washington Bridge. "I know we're supposed to like the Brooklyn Bridge best of all, but I've always appreciated the grandeur of the GW. Now, give me your professional opinion." She looked at Wren.

"The Queensboro Bridge. I like its Gothic look, and I find its use of the cantilever intriguing and impressive."

"When I was sixteen, I never would've guessed that someday I'd find myself in love with a woman who found cantilevers cool."

Wren took a hand off the wheel long enough to give Hadley a squeeze.

"And I never thought I'd find myself in love with someone who let me talk about cantilevers. And—using that to transition into my next subject—a cantilever is an element supported only at one end. That's what I'm feeling right now."

She had called Gareth Archer a few days before, wondering if she'd sound like an idiot. She had thought of bringing her father into it; he was so much better at things like that. But no. It was her project, her responsibility. And it wasn't just about her anymore. She couldn't figure out what Detective Fitzgerald was thinking, but he had given her the reference to Gareth Archer. He didn't mind her calling him. Indeed, he actually wanted her to—that was interesting itself.

"Mr. Archer? My name is Wren Fontaine. I'm the architect working on the renovation of Cadieux House on Long Island. I know the original owners, the Blaines, had a long connection to your family's firm, and I'm hoping you can help me with some research on the house."

She had half-expected him to hang up on her. Her request was a little over the top, and the man's father had been murdered in that very house just a few months ago.

He didn't hang up but didn't say anything for a while, either.

"Yes, your name is familiar. After my father's death, I thought I'd take a little peek into what was going on. My father and I weren't particularly close, but I was curious enough to wonder what the hell was going on. My God. If I had had even a small regret for not entering the family firm, getting a sense of that mess put an end to that quickly. If the Blaine-Rodriguez story was turned into a TV miniseries, there is no way I'd watch it. Can you imagine living it?"

Now, it was Wren's turn to be quiet. She had planned to say a few words about being sorry for Tristan Archer's death, but Gareth's little speech made that impossible. She had to…improvise.

"I understand," she said. "Still, you say you did have some curiosity. The Cadieux House is considered one of the finest modernist homes ever built. If you want to visit, I can give you a tour, and then perhaps we could talk a little about what you know of your family's history with the Blaine-Rodriguez family."

This is when he would say he knew nothing, which he had virtually admitted, and hang up. But all he said was, "Why? You're an architect, and I know nothing about the house. How could I possibly help you?"

"Houses absorb the personalities of the people who lived there and of those who even just had connections to the house. And vice-versa. It's an unusual house. It's an extraordinary house. The more I know, the better my work will be."

"Okay. To be honest, that sounds a little over the top, but then again, I'm a little over the top, too, so what the hell. I don't have an interest in Cadieux House, but if you're an architect, you may have an interest in seeing my house. Shall we fix a date?"

That took Wren by surprise. She had to think fast—she wanted Hadley by her side with this. She wanted a people person with Gareth, and if the meeting was going to be offsite, she couldn't just have Hadley there because

CHAPTER FIFTEEN

she was hanging around.

"Thank you. I would like to bring someone along. My friend, Hadley Vanderwerf, is an event planner and advises me on space issues. May I bring her too?"

"The more the merrier. Saturday for lunch, then…"

Hadley brought Wren back to the present. "So why do you think he passed up a chance to visit the legendary Cadieux House?"

"It could be what he said," said Wren. "That he doesn't want to be involved in the family business."

Hadley laughed. "'Family business.' It sounds like the mafia."

"Old, powerful families with lots of money and a strong sense of their own importance. Nothing changes. Anyway, I'm thinking it's something else. I wanted Gareth at Cadieux House, because that's where I'm comfortable. I'm betting he wants me at his house where he feels comfortable. And that makes me think about his house. I wonder what he's chosen for a home."

"All right, Little Bird. That's the way you look at the world. It took me a while, but I've gotten used to it. But what if he lives in a plain old average house? What would that say about him?"

Wren smiled. "It would say something. Houses always say something. The Biltmore Estate speaks loudly. Maybe Gareth Archer's house is quieter."

"And Cadieux House?" said Hadley.

"Oh, it speaks loudly." She smiled at her girlfriend. "But I'm only fluent in Victorian, still trying to get up to speed on Modernism."

The drive up the Hudson went quickly, and then the GPS directed them onto increasingly smaller roads, eventually sending them up a hill with no signs of habitation on either side and a wooden sign marked "private road—no trespassing."

"This is not a very welcoming entranceway," said Hadley as they bumped over the dirt road.

"I'm sure that's the point," said Wren.

At the top of the hill, they saw the log cabin, although Wren realized that "cabin" wasn't the right word. Although just a single story, it was long, with a wraparound porch, and perfectly situated for a grand view of the river. A Jeep Wrangler sat in a detached garage. Wren parked next to it, and she and Hadley stepped out. Hadley's eye quickly went to the view of the Hudson, but Wren turned to the house. It was a real log cabin, not a mock-up. The logs met neatly, with the notches created by someone who knew what they were doing. She didn't even notice the man standing there until the screen door slammed. He was in his forties, wearing jeans, a polo shirt, and docksiders. Gareth had his late father's height and lean build, but a more outdoor complexion and a wry smile that Wren couldn't imagine on Tristan's face. The joys of not having to work with the Rodriguez-Blaine clan!

"You found me," he said. "Not everyone does. But I expect an architect would have a good sense of direction. And I see you admiring my house. Again, not everyone does."

"It's impressive," she said. He was still smiling. *Gareth Archer is very proud of his house. He thinks it's...cool. That's why he wanted to meet here. It's important to him and who he is.*

"People may think it's trendy," she finally said, "but this style of building was already more than a thousand years old before Columbus landed in the New World."

Gareth thought that over for a moment, then nodded, apparently satisfied. "I'm being rude. I'm Gareth Archer. Welcome to my home." He approached them and shook Wren's hand.

"And this is Hadley Vanderwerf, a chef and event planner who advises me on space. She is also my co-vivant." Wren had practiced that introduction since they had moved in together, so she could say it without blushing.

"A pleasure," said Hadley.

"'Co-vivant.' I like that," said Gareth. "Once upon a time, we used the phrase 'common-law' husband or wife. Please, come on in. I have lunch, and I imagine you'd like to see my house."

With some amusement, Wren recognized the interior as what designers might have once called "traditionally masculine." The furniture was mostly wood, with a few oil paintings of Hudson River scenes. The chair and couch fabrics were earth tones. Handsome, but bare. There was nothing personal

CHAPTER FIFTEEN

about it.

"I love this," said Hadley. "I could charge a mint to stage a Super Bowl party in this room."

"I know—living the guy dream." But Wren didn't think he sounded entirely pleased with that. "I have everything here except a moose head. I'm a vegetarian." He showed them into a small dining room, where a table was already set, and came out a moment later with a cast iron pot. "Stew, with brown bread. I've already seen what the architect thinks of my house. What does the chef think of my stew?"

Hadley took a spoonful, closed her eyes, and smiled. "Very good, sir. I'm not a vegetarian myself, but I do spend a lot of time explaining that vegetarian food doesn't have to be boring." Wren added her agreement, but felt a little like she landed in Oz, wondering about the best way to get back to the reason they were here. Perhaps that's what Gareth was waiting for.

"I just wanted to say again how sorry I was about your father's death," she said. "I had only met him once, but I admired the diplomatic way he handled what I'm sure were challenging clients."

Gareth paused. And then he laughed. It wasn't a fond chuckle of fond remembrance, but a full-throated laugh, as if Wren had told a joke.

I'm never going to understand people, she thought. And then she looked at Hadley, who gave her a rueful look. *She understands. She doesn't approve, but she does understand.*

"'Challenging clients.' I like that. Yeah, Dad was good with that. That family has been the firm's most difficult—and lucrative—client for many years. My grandfather Percival pretty much started the firm with them. I spent one summer interning at the firm while in law school, and that was enough of them. Dad thought I'd come around, but he never forgave me after I said that not only did I have no interest in working with the Blaines and Rodriguezes, I wasn't even joining the firm. Thank you, Wren, for your well-meant thoughts, but he and I didn't talk a lot."

This is what I get for talking about people and not houses, Wren thought. Hadley just raised an eyebrow.

"You had King Arthur in common," said Wren after a silence. "I mean your names."

"Ah yes, a family quirk. Percival, Tristan, and Gareth. I think the idea was to lend a bit of grandness to a firm whose main role in life was cleaning up after spoiled rich people." He sighed. "All right, I'm being unfair. You didn't come here to hear me complain about my family's legacy. You want to know about the history of the family."

"The history of the *house*," said Wren, and she felt a little thrill to see Gareth surprised. He may have separated himself from his family, but a certain sangfroid remained.

"The house? Cadieux House? Ha! When you said 'house,' I thought you meant 'house' like they were the Medicis. You know, like a joke."

"Wren never jokes about houses," said Hadley.

"No, I don't suppose you do," he said, looking closely at Wren. "I hope then I haven't invited you here for no reason. I've never been in Cadieux House. I don't know anything about it. And I don't care to."

"Oh, but that tells me something all by itself," said Wren. "Cadieux House twists the mind of everyone who enters it. Its curves and angles constantly challenge you. You could spend your life there and find something new every day. And you choose to live in this log cabin, comfortable and warm. And predictable. That tells me something about you."

She thought she heard Hadley stifle a giggle.

"You're patronizing me because I don't appreciate modernist architecture, like my father and grandfather did with Cadieux House?"

Wren shook her head. "I'll be honest. Modernist architecture isn't my favorite. I would prefer to live in a late-Georgian mansion with perfect proportions. Now you know something about me. You wanted me and Hadley here because you are comfortable in your house, and you wouldn't be comfortable in Cadieux House. You may see yourself as the family rebel, leaving the firm and supporting fashionable causes, but perhaps you're the most conservative Archer of them all."

Wren saw Gareth study her as if she were an interesting archeological object. She had apparently insulted him and had gone way off where she wanted to be.

CHAPTER FIFTEEN

"That's...very interesting," he said slowly.

"But correct," said Hadley. "Wren is the 'house whisperer.' She connects people to the homes they live in."

"Does she?" asked Gareth. "All right then. Let's get back to Cadieux House. First, I lied to you, because I didn't want to find myself buried in an architectural discussion. But you seem to be interested in the family. And perhaps, in whoever killed my father, or that crazed fan who attempted to break into the house. Add that to whoever killed Dennis Blaine—no one was ever convicted there, either. The police aren't exactly batting a thousand."

"That's because they didn't attempt to understand the house," said Hadley.

"That's very possible. Anyway, as I said, I lied. I did visit Cadieux House once, when I was in college and was already set on becoming a lawyer. My father was thrilled, but wanted to make sure I joined the family firm afterward. He wanted to show me that because of the connection to our distinguished clients, that Cadieux House was part of our heritage, even if we didn't own it. It seemed strange to me. You know, I don't think even Dad much liked the family firm. He was in the army, served in the Judge Advocate General's office and was doing well, marked for high-level promotion. He always talked about it with fondness. Even though I liked my grandfather, I think he bullied my father to leave the army for the family firm in his early forties. Anyway, Dad asked me nicely to visit, and I figured one trip wouldn't hurt." Gareth stared into his bowl, and sighed, then looked up again. "I was wrong. It did hurt. Perhaps what I knew about the people involved tainted my appreciation of the house."

"And perhaps your dislike of the house made you think worse of the people," said Wren.

"An architect *and* a psychologist," said Gareth.

"You mistake me for my father," said Wren. "He reads people and knows what kind of house they want. I work backwards. I see houses and I know what kind of people they were."

"What kind of people lived in Cadieux House?" said Gareth.

"I admit I'm still working on that," said Wren.

"Perhaps I can help," said Gareth. He stood. "I'll be back." He left the room.

"Dear God," said Wren, slumping back in her chair.

"You're doing great, Little Bird," said Hadley.

"Am I? I keep thinking I'm in an amusement park hall of mirrors. That house…" she shook her head.

"Okay, I'm the people person here. And I'm on Team Rebecca. She must've been something with Dennis Blaine falling madly in love with her, according to Trey, and inspiring Cadieux. I want to learn more about her."

"Fair enough," said Wren, nodding. "The more we learn about Rebecca, the more we learn about Cadieux House. And vice-versa."

They heard some furniture being moved in the next room, and then Gareth came back. "Please join me in the living room."

Gareth had propped what seemed to be two framed pictures on the table, covered with sheets. "These are not my taste, but I keep them—they were willed to me. I was a particular favorite of my grandfather's, you see. I think he liked that I was a bit rebellious. My father was the rigid one. Anyway, he left me these two portraits." He pulled the sheet off the first one. "That's him." The artist had given him a resolute chin and piercing eyes, a lean body in a striped three-piece suit.

"You look like him," said Wren. Gareth smiled.

"And this is Rebecca." With a flourish, he flung the sheet off the second portrait. Wren gave Hadley's hand a squeeze and flashed her eyes to Gareth. *Watch him.*

Dennis loved her. Cadieux loved her. And this portrait artist probably did as well. He had posed her in vaguely Eastern robes and gave her a hint of cinnamon in her cheek. Dark hair, full lips, and almond eyes. Wren saw mischief in there. Rebecca was more than beautiful, Wren thought. She was *exotic*. She must've been a fascinating addition to the white bread world of the Blaines.

And yet, she wondered, had this been the best artist for the task? He had presented a Rebecca worthy of worship, a Rebecca of absolute classical perfection. Was that right for the woman who had inspired the decidedly unclassical Cadieux House?

"You're impressed with her," said Gareth. "You love her too. I can tell."

CHAPTER FIFTEEN

"She's got a real 'Helen of Troy' look about her," said Hadley,

"I am...charmed by her," said Wren. "The artist seems to have captured her personality, if it's true."

"Really? What does she say to you?"

"Even if I don't know people very well, I'm good with art," said Wren. "And this artist wanted everyone to know that Rebecca was something of a goddess."

Gareth laughed. "Bingo. That's how she was seen in her prime."

"You're showing me this portrait with your grandfather," said Wren.

"And where does that take you?" asked Gareth.

"It makes me wonder how such an obviously fine—and expensive—portrait ended up in the hands of the family lawyer," said Wren.

"Yeah, I don't think a woman would give something like that as a gift to a family retainer," said Hadley.

"'Retainer,'" said Gareth, laughing. "That's a word you don't hear much anymore. But you're named Vanderwerf. One of *the* Vanderwerfs, I assume?"

"Oh yes, and we're very democratic," said a grinning Hadley. "Whether a doctor or butler, a maid or a lawyer, they're all the same—they're retainers. All of them are here to serve us. Anyway, no Vanderwerf ever gave a portrait away like that."

"Can I ask," said Wren, "where your grandfather lived?"

Gareth blinked. "Oh—I don't...in Westchester, actually. We're originally New Yorkers, but we headed out to what was then the country. Granddad here built a huge pile in Larchmont. My folks took it over, and my mother is still there. But why—"

"Late 19th century, in the Tudor style, right?"

"How did you know...and what does that have to do with this portrait?" Wren flashed back to high school, those times when she could impress her more popular classmates, even her teacher.

"All right," she admitted. "It was partly a good guess. But in general, that's what big houses in Larchmont look like. That's where prosperous lawyers live. I can picture his house, so I think I know Granddad Percival. You told me your father took you to see Cadieux House. Was your grandfather still alive? He must've been very old, but if he was still around, I bet he came too, didn't he?"

Gareth sighed and gave Wren a close look. "Yes," he said heavily. "Granddad was ninety, a little slow, but mobile."

"I met your father. He didn't seem interested in the house beyond its value." *Oh, I just insulted his late father, didn't I?* "I'm sorry, that came out wrong. I didn't mean—"

"It's okay. You're right. He was the consummate man of business. He didn't think much of it one way or another beyond its dollar value."

"But not your grandfather. He had strong feelings about it." Wren looked up. Hadley winked at her. "He didn't understand it at all. He probably loathed it. A man like that would never appreciate Cadieux House." She paused, took a breath, and focused straight on Gareth. "But he loved Rebecca. He absolutely adored her. I doubt if he understood her. But he worshiped her."

Hadley flashed a thumbs up, and Gareth smiled broadly. "Do you want to tell me how you figured this out? I think, Wren, that you're better with people than you let on."

She shook her head. "Not really. It's all logic, not emotion, I'm afraid. Why did he have this portrait? He had it because he commissioned it himself. The houses I work on usually have fine old portraits, which meant something to the people who lived there. Your grandfather had this in his house, didn't he? Hadley said a woman like Rebecca would never have given a portrait like this as a present."

"Women like Rebecca don't give presents; they receive them," said Hadley.

"I'm sure," said Wren. "But more than that, look at this portrait. If Rebecca inspired, and loved Cadieux House, she wouldn't have commissioned something neoclassical like this for herself. Look how… this is. A prosperous, distinguished attorney with a loyal wife, a country club membership, and a closet full of good wool suits would ask for just this kind of portrait of the woman he secretly—or not so secretly—loved. Technically excellent. The beloved as an ideal. The beloved as a goddess."

"Wow, Wren…just wow," said Gareth.

CHAPTER FIFTEEN

Wren felt a little thrill, like when she closed a deal with a client. "Okay, then. Grandad had a crush on Rebecca. I don't know why we had to go through all this. I am just trying to get an idea of Rebecca and that extraordinary house. Why the game of twenty questions?"

"You're right. But hear me out. I know, I'm not in the family firm, and I live in a house in the middle of nowhere. Still, it's my family, and like it or not, we have a long connection to the Rodriguez-Blaine clan. And even if we didn't get along, he was my father, and now he's dead. I'm sorry I gave you what was essentially a test, but I wanted to see if you could understand us. And I see you do. Grandpa didn't have a crush on Rebecca. He had an obsession. Take a seat, and I'll tell you more."

Wren and Hadley took a seat on a wooden couch with earth-color cushions. Wren knew that its do-it-yourself look cost at least eight thousand dollars. Gareth picked up a manila envelope from the table and sat opposite them in a chair that matched the couch.

"I want you to understand my grandfather was insanely jealous of Marius Cadieux. That isn't my guess. He'd talk about him bitterly to me—we were pretty close. He lived until ninety-two and was clear of mind till the end, and I heard a lot about Cadieux. He even spoke more about him and Rebecca than he did about the War. He served—landed in the first wave on D-Day, won a Silver Star. He then got a spot on the prosecution team for the Nuremberg trials. He once told me that was the professional work he was most proud of. But still—it was that house that seemed to grab his attention. He called Cadieux a 'jumped up frog.' Said the house was the ugliest thing he had ever seen and sulked when he saw how deeply involved Rebecca was with Cadieux."

"But she wasn't even married to Cadieux," said Hadley. "Wouldn't he have been jealous of Dennis?"

"Dennis Blaine," said Gareth. "You know what my grandfather called him? The 'nonentity.'"

"He's beginning to sound like a real delight," said Wren.

"Oh, he was a piece of work. Keep in mind that the family firm was really tied to the Rodriguezes, not the Blaines. We owed our allegiance to them."

"Pardon the expression," said Wren, "but the Rodriguezes are Jewish, and Archer is an old-line, WASP firm. Why did the Rodriguezes engage them?"

"And why did Rebecca marry Dennis Blaine?" asked Gareth. "It wasn't for money—Rebecca had plenty. She didn't need Dennis Blaine to marry her or Percival Archer to manage her business. Maybe it amused her to have men falling over her? I don't pretend to understand her. But love her, they did. Anyway, according to Grandad, Marius Cadieux was the man to beat. Who knows, though? It was easy for Grandad to feel superior to someone as bland as Dennis, I'd imagine. But someone as accomplished, and as magnetic, as Cadieux—who had clearly captured Rebecca's imagination, and possibly her heart..."

Gareth shrugged and picked up the folder. "Grandad's diary made its way to me. He kept it for years, multiple volumes. For the most part, it is dull beyond belief—more of a journal than a diary. But when it came to Rebecca, he waxed poetic. When I leafed through them after he died, I found them amusing. I even bookmarked them, and I typed out some of the... more colorful descriptions. A bit of a prodigy was granddad—even clerked for Benjamin Cardozo on the Supreme Court. One of the greatest jurists this country has ever seen, but even he didn't get as many pages as Rebecca. Here you go—a printout of Percival Archer on Rebecca Blaine, nee Rodriguez. Enjoy it and take it with you. You might find something about Rebecca. And about the house."

Any maybe about who killed your father...there still hadn't been an arrest.

He handed the envelope to Wren.

"Thank you. I'm looking forward to seeing what I can do with it. But one more thing, if I could...what did you think of the house? Skip the people. What did you really think of the house?"

Gareth smiled. "If I understood you correctly, you can't understand a house without its people."

Wren shook her head. "Maybe you can't. But I can. My problem is understanding people without the house. Still, I'd like to hear if you are able to divorce your opinions about the Blaines and Rodriguezes—and your grandfather, for that matter. Think about the house—just the house. Do you

CHAPTER FIFTEEN

like it?"

"Fair enough. But I think you already know the answer to that. I live here, so I think you can assume that I don't like Cadieux House. And neither did my father. Neither of us ever understood it, I'm sorry to say."

"Did Grandad Percival like it? Did he at least understand it? He was the one who knew Rebecca."

"I'm sorry, Wren. We should've taken care of this a long time ago—any missteps my grandfather made and my father's response. All right, I've been a little hard on Dad. He wasn't as fun as Granddad, but he was a damn good lawyer, loyal to his clients, and devoted to the truth. I wonder…" Then he smiled shyly and stopped. *You wonder what—that your father, Tristan Archer, was killed because he knew something. No, not just because he knew something, but because with the change in ownership, he was going to reveal something…*

"But read the diary selections, Wren, and draw your own conclusions. Also, I left a business card in there from Rafael Rodriguez, Shoshana's son, Rebecca's grandson."

"Yes. I heard she had a son."

"Well, you might find it helpful to talk to him. We met a few times when I was young. He was generous in introducing me to helpful people early in my career, and we've kept in touch over the years. He's also a little different from the rest of the family." He gave her a look she couldn't quite interpret. "You can mention my name. Meanwhile, a pleasure meeting both of you."

"Likewise," said Wren. "Before I go, do you mind if I take a photo of this portrait?"

Chapter Sixteen

Hadley sat on the couch and deftly spread brie on a Carr's table water cracker, which she handed to Wren, resting her head on Hadley's thigh. Wren hadn't said much on the drive back to their apartment, but Hadley hadn't minded. It was just Wren being Wren, and she loved her for it. They happily ate cheese while listening to Dua Lipa.

"Gareth knows more, doesn't he?" asked Wren.

"Actually, he *suspects* something. I think it's not so much what he knows. It's what he *fears*."

"So he puts us onto Rafael. He wants us to find out what happened. He knows what I know—it's about the house, and he doesn't understand it."

"And this connects to Grandad Percival, apparently in love with Rebecca. After all, who wasn't? And did you get a look at Gareth when he unveiled the portrait of Rebecca?"

"Yup—got your signal. I think he was proud. Amused and proud that his beloved grandfather was in love with Rebecca. And who knows, maybe he had a fling with her? A bit of color in the grey history of the Archers."

"I can see that," said Wren. "Gareth lives in that log house as an escape. 'Look at me, escaping the central-hall colonials of my people.' But you can't escape, not really."

"Oh, Little Bird, I knew you understood people better than you thought." Hadley gave her hand a squeeze. "You knew I once was into emo rap. I dyed my hair blue and pink. Did I really think it would change who I am?"

Wren smiled. "Sorry I missed you like that. And I'm flattered you think I can understand what is going on. I really don't know anything about Gareth

CHAPTER SIXTEEN

Archer—but I did get a sense of Archer's house. It's a sign of something, because no one walks away from one of the most distinguished law firms in New York to live in a log house without a big reason."

"Disgust with the family firm?" asked Hadley.

"I'm thinking that maybe disgust with the Blaine-Rodriguezes. It's one thing to be amused thinking grandad had a glamorous affair, but quite another to work with a family like that. But you know what was the most interesting thing I learned? Percival clerked for a Supreme Court justice. And not just any justice—Benjamin Cardozo. He was of Sephardic Jewish background and a member of the Shearith Israel synagogue. Just like the Rodriguezes. Another interesting connection."

"Ohh...wow! Just a coincidence—or maybe this is how Percival got an entrée into the Sephardic community," said Hadley.

"We were thinking that Percival met Rebecca when he was already an older distinguished attorney. What if he met her when he was a young man, an 'ardent suitor,' as they say? Is 'suitor' even still a word? Anyway, suppose Percival was pining for Rebecca, this unusual woman a few years older than he was. No, not just unusual. Exotic, as I've said. Rebecca was no doubt familiar with his world but not part of it, and she'd know that. Now, a youthful crush, that would mean something different, wouldn't it?" Then Wren laughed. "Or would it? Is that the way straight people think?"

Hadley laughed, too. "Yes, my dear. You're making wonderful progress. So let's conclude, for now, that Percival Archer did not have a middle-age infatuation but a longstanding passion for dear Rebecca."

"Behind Dennis Blaine and Marius Cadieux," said Wren.

"Take a number," said Hadley.

Wren sat up. "It was the house. Rebecca was about the house, and the house was about Rebecca. If Percival didn't understand the house, he didn't really understand Rebecca. I'm sure of that." She picked up the manila envelope. "I'm going to have to dip into these diary entries."

"Trying to figure out why Rebecca inspired so much passion?"

"Perhaps. But I want to find out why the house did."

"Oh, Wren, that is so *you*." She gave her girlfriend a kiss. "You get the last piece of brie."

* * *

Wren returned to Cadieux House the next day. Bobby and his crew continued to implement the subtle changes Wren had planned based on Bronwyn's requests. She ran her eyes over the modified walls, the redesigned doors, changing the shape of the rooms.

"Checking my work, Miss Fontaine?" said Bobby, with a grin. Wren smiled back.

"No. Checking mine. It's one thing to update a 19th-century manor house, but another to change a Cadieux. It's one thing to see it on a computer screen, but to get a sense of the home's personality? Are we changing it?"

"And if we are, is that a problem?" He meant it as a joke, but Wren gave it some thought.

"If it were anyone but Cadieux. But you're right; even if we are, so what? The basic message of the house remains, and we're just making adjustments to suit our client. Still, that puts me on another track. If this indeed suits Rebecca Blaine, then why? What did that say about her?"

"Beyond my pay grade," said Bobby. "But come into the kitchen, and I'll show you some impressive things we're doing with stainless steel."

The previous evening, Wren had gone over the curious entries Gareth had shared with her. But she knew to truly appreciate them; she had to walk through the house.

At the top, Cadieux had placed what he called an "aerie," a room comfortable for no more than four or five occupants. The windows, a mix of curves and unusual angles, gave a three hundred and sixty-degree view. *If this were my house, I would spend so much time here. I would sit here with Hadley and watch the stars come out. But as much as he liked me, Marius Cadieux did not design it for me. It was for Rebecca. Did she bring anyone up here? Or did she come here by herself to smile triumphantly over her conquests? I keep thinking this is so different from the Gilded Age homes I so adore, but maybe Rebecca was just a new version of the chatelaines who had presided over great homes since the*

CHAPTER SIXTEEN

Middle Ages. The house was different, but the mistress still remained...

Then Wren laughed at herself. *I'm so over the top here! Maybe Rebecca was just a mean girl?* She realized she was casting Rebecca—a woman she had never met—as a Plantagenet princess, a Victorian grandame, or one of the popular girls who made her life hell in high school.

Her eye caught a car coming along the road. Bronwyn had said she was coming by at some point, but although she could see it was a Mercedes, it wasn't Bronwyn's SUV, but a more sedate sedan. Curious, she watched it pull into the driveway, and then a man quickly got out.

Woody Blaine.

Wren knew enough about human behavior to know that anyone walking that quickly was not happy. But there was nothing to worry about. No one would get by Bobby and his crew. Then she realized that was cowardly: her father wouldn't cower behind his workers. She'd go down and tell him he wasn't her client, she had done enough favors for him, and her worksite was sacred.

Then she felt the envelope in her hand—insights into Rebecca and the house. And here was a Blaine, who may be able to help. What would be truly brave would be to work with him to find out more about Rebecca and Cadieux—and the house.

Her phone buzzed—a text from Bronwyn. "Be there in ten." Wren steeled herself and headed back down, finding Woody squared off with Bobby.

"I need to speak with Ms. Fontaine at once."

"You will need to wait in your car. No one is allowed in here without Ms. Fontaine's authorization," said Bobby.

"For God's sake, my family built this place, and you're hardly tearing it apart. I just need a few minutes…"

Wren appeared. "Mr. Blaine? This is a surprise. But Mr. Fiore is right. For practical and legal reasons, access to the worksite is strictly limited."

Woody sighed dramatically. "Fine. But I do need a few minutes with you, if you can spare them. We can sit in my car, or take a walk, but it is urgent, and it involves you, too."

"Is this about our discussion regarding the privacy around this house? I have kept to my end but can't speak for my client or anyone else."

Another dramatic sigh. Wren was finding him increasingly annoying.

"Ms. Fontaine. This house, the family that owned it—my family. The history. It's about a lot more than putting in a new boiler and making sure the roof doesn't leak. There are major privacy concerns, and I need some reassurance."

Wren was about to respond, but stopped. She needed his help but couldn't possibly reveal that. As satisfying as it would be to throw him out, it wouldn't help in the long run.

"Mr. Blaine. In a few minutes, my client, Bronwyn Merrick, will be here. If it's okay with her, I have some items to share about the house, and we can address any concerns you have. I can't tell you anything without her permission anyway."

Wren watched him consider his options and master himself.

"All right then. It's just that…all right. I understand about your worksite. If it is all right with you, I will have a look at the immediate grounds until Ms. Merrick arrives."

But Wren was saved from deciding that by Bronwyn's arrival. Darren got out first, looked around, and then opened the door for Bronwyn. He walked her into the house.

"Bronwyn, Darren—good to see you again. Bronwyn, you know Woody Blaine, of course."

"Of course," she held out her hand, then turned to Darren. "Woody represented the family when I bought the house, and we have met since. Woody—giving the house a final visit on behalf of the family?" He stiffened.

Wren organized her thoughts. "Mr. Blaine has some issues to discuss. Bronwyn—you want to see the progress. And I have some new insights into this house that may be of help to all of us. I'd like to do a walkthrough. Bronwyn—this is your house. It is your decision, if Mr. Blaine is allowed to join us."

Bronwyn looked a little amused. "The more the merrier. Maybe he has some items to share."

Woody looked unhappy, but seemed to realize that he was there on

CHAPTER SIXTEEN

sufferance and had nothing to gain by making demands.

"Thank you," he said. "I just want to remind you that you promised to remain discreet. I have business plans. And I am hearing things. Gareth Archer, who's not even in the family firm, has been asking things. Someone told him. Someone has been…looking into the past."

Wren didn't even think. It just came out. "The past isn't dead; it isn't even past." Woody looked confused, but Bronwyn laughed. "Faulkner! I love it. I know, I know, I write crap, but I majored in English at Ohio State."

"I'm sorry…?" said Woody.

"You don't get away from the past, Mr. Blaine. I have worked on many old homes, most of them much older than Cadieux House. A home's history will come out, no matter how discreet we are."

"But—"

"Mr. Blaine, I have some information here."

"Which you got where?" asked Woody.

"I reassemble century-old homes, Mr. Blaine. Finding out about them is my job. And I'm very good at it."

Wren got a double jolt of pleasure—Woody started speaking a couple of times but said nothing, and Bronwyn, a step behind him, smirked.

"There are some stories here. I think of them as a precis of the house. If you agree, we'll address some of them now. It will help us understand this house. And Mr. Blaine—you may find out something too. Or even be in a position to help us."

And without waiting for a response from them, she turned and headed to her first stop.

"I don't know what they called this room—I think of it as the main parlor. This is where they had the parties. Their very famous parties. Percival Archer would come—he was the father of the late Tristan Archer and the family attorney." Wren pulled a page from the folder. "And Mr. Archer made some interesting comments."

"May I ask…" started Woody. "That is, can you tell me where you got this?"

"I was given some Archer family papers from someone who had the right to give them to me," said Wren. "That is all I can tell you. Now, Percival was very interesting. I think to a certain extent, he understood this house. He didn't like it, but he knew something about it, even if it was subconscious. He was rather shrewd and may have known about the Sephardic culture that nurtured Rebecca. He understood her, I'm guessing, and I imagine she appreciated it. He may have been in love with her, although I don't think it was reciprocated. So there's a party. Everyone has arrived, I imagine, much like the Gatsby parties some thirty years earlier." Wren looked up. "I was going to grab some of the workers to act this out, but I'd have to pay them, and you will do it for free. Bronwyn, how would you like to be Rebecca?"

"Super!" said Bronwyn. "Let me guess—you were a theater club director in college?"

"Set design, actually," said Wren. "Please stand by that window—in profile, half staring out at the night sky, half keeping an eye on the party." Bronwyn walked briskly to her assigned spot and posed dramatically.

"And you, Darren. You can be Dennis Blaine. You stand in the far corner there. You are looking at Rebecca from the opposite side of the room." He wasn't quite as enthused as Bronwyn, but dutifully stood where instructed.

"Dennis Blaine was my cousin—okay, second cousin, once removed, but still," said Woody. "Shouldn't I be him?" Wren braced herself to argue with him again, but this time, he wore an amused smile. All right, he was a difficult man, but probably a practical one, and figured, at least for now, if you can't beat 'em, join 'em.

"Oh, but I have a much more interesting role for you, Mr. Blaine. You are going to be Marius Cadieux. You have sought her out. Please stand by Bronwyn-as-Rebecca. You are talking to each other." He nodded and stood by Bronwyn, who was looking expectedly at Wren. "Remember, it is night. You are looking over the dark Sound. Lights are low. There's a quartet playing cool jazz, and this room is full."

"Do we act?" asked Bronwyn.

"No need to. Just stand there. Now, I'm going to be Percival Archer." Did Woody stiffen at that? "I'm going to read from his memories of that evening. 'The house truly represents everything I detest about modernism, and I wonder if I am the only one who realizes how soulless it is. The

CHAPTER SIXTEEN

conundrum is that no one has a deeper soul than Rebecca. Perhaps that is enough. Perhaps she lends her home her own soul, and that is enough. Is that what Marius Cadieux understood? I watched them tete-a-tete during the evening, looking at each other. No, that isn't fair. Looking at the house together.'" Wren looked up from the page. "As an architect, I find that very interesting: a soulless house that comes alive thanks only to its mistress. And not just any house, one designed by Marius Cadieux."

"So was Cadieux just lucky?" asked Bronwyn, grinning. "He wasn't a great architect but was fortunate that he built homes for astonishing people, and they made it work?"

"That would be a fascinating theory," said Wren. "But I'm not going to take Percival at his word. He may have adored Rebecca. He may have been jealous of Cadieux. Still, this wasn't his last thought on the house. But first, Darren—what do you see from where you are?"

He was a bodyguard, and had been a police officer, a detective. Wren knew little about him or those professions, but assumed they were rooted deeply in observable facts. He was a couple with Bronwyn, however, very much rooted in imagination.

"Oh! Hadn't really thought about it. I'm Dennis Blaine—Rebecca's husband, right? I see my 'wife' talking to the architect, the man who designed our house."

"It isn't the man who's sleeping with your wife?" teased Bronwyn. "They spent an awful lot of time together."

"As the A.D.A.'s used to say, 'that assumes facts not in evidence,'" he replied, and she laughed.

"Mr. Blaine," continued Wren. "You are playing Marius Cadieux. Also, as a Blaine, you're the only family member here."

"Yes, a Blaine, but Rebecca was only a relation to me by marriage, not blood. But all right, I know the stories. I suppose...I suppose, from what I heard, that Cadieux would be looking at Rebecca, not at the house, whatever Percival said. Maybe Percival was in love with her, but so was Cadieux."

"That is...very insightful," said Wren. Did Woody look confused or upset? *Does he think I am mocking or patronizing him?* "All right then. I'd like to do one more scene. This one is outside. Cadieux House is equally as magnificent on the outside looking in. We can leave through the door by the pool." Wren glanced at the participants. Were they annoyed? Curious? Amused? Bronwyn seemed to be having fun—perhaps she was filing away this little game for her next novel? But she couldn't read the men.

Wren walked to the edge, where the ground fell away deeply to the shore. She turned and contemplated the house from that angle. The others did the same thing, and Wren gave a small smile of triumph. She didn't read people well, but by this point, she could recognize when a house truly amazed someone. Bobby's crew was working here, so Wren had kept people away, but she was glad she had brought them here for this splendid view, even better than the one from the road. Cadieux had done that purposefully, she decided. This is where people would be congregating in the good weather. Cadieux knew how people viewed, reacted to a house...a thought crossed her mind, but disappeared a second later.

She gave her guests a few moments to take in the house, the exciting way the curves and angles blended into each other, both exhilarating and yet satisfying. It was as if Cadieux knew how human minds worked. He did, of course.

"All right, same cast as before. This time, all three of you get to be together. In fact, you hardly have to move. You are all talking. It's a summer afternoon, and people are having fun in and around the pool. A bartender in a white jacket is serving drinks. Percival is here again, as an observer—"

"For a busy lawyer, he seems to have had plenty of time to go to parties," said Woody.

"When a man is in love, he makes time," said Bronwyn, with the firmness of a teacher correcting a slow student. Everyone turned to her. "Look, I'm no Emily Bronte. But my books end up on the bestseller lists because I know what I'm talking about. I know how people behave. I know that Marius Cadieux would wear trunks and a linen shirt but not go swimming because he didn't want to look less than perfect even for a few minutes, and our Rebecca was pushing fifty by this point. She was no fool and would be wearing a custom suit that covered her neck, where women first show their

CHAPTER SIXTEEN

age, and a wide-brimmed hat to shade her face. But she never lost her model figure or great legs, and the suit would show those off. She would know this, be aware of what worked from her teen years to the day she died."

Bronwyn stopped, aware she had amazed her audience, and was a little embarrassed.

"Thank you," said Wren. "That helps me, helps all of us, picture the scene even more accurately. All right then. The three of you are talking."

"Are we, I guess, *recognizing* the house while we do this?" asked Darren.

"Yes—of course. You can *never* get away from a Cadieux residence. Whether you're inside it or next to it, you are always aware of it, even if it's subconscious. That's the point of his houses, the reason why he's considered one of the greatest architects of all time." She suddenly realized she had echoed Bronwyn's tone. She had done this before, many times, getting so caught up. She could hear her father say, "Wren, read the room." She fancied she saw the two men exchange a knowing look.

"All right then. The three of you are talking about—I don't know—the weather—"

"Probably music," said Bronwyn. "Rebecca loved all kinds of music, and Dennis dabbled in record producing."

"All right," said Wren. "You're talking about 1950s music. And I'm once again Percival Archer, watching from the bar." The old bar cabana had fallen into ruin, but Wren had already designed a new one for Bobby to build. She placed herself where it had stood.

"All right then—here I go. 'It seems when you reach a certain level of sophistication, you can all talk together. Maybe that ridiculous house makes it possible. I still don't like it, but I suppose one could say I appreciate it. It's as complex as Rebecca, and in a way I cannot understand, it seems to satisfy her, if that is the right word. It makes Rebecca's world possible. It makes Rebecca possible. And so I must in some way accept the house as I accept Rebecca.'" Wren saw she had their complete attention, and then their eyes flashed to the house. Yes, it was the same as the first time she had read it. Percival knew in some way that Rebecca had a connection to the house.

"There's another interesting bit," she continued. "'I don't know if it's just my imagination, but watching the three of them together, I see she favors Marius so much and wonder that Dennis doesn't see it. He was never the smartest man, but I would think he'd see that. Everyone else has. Or does he just not care? I was a fool to hope for her. I could never give her what Marius did. For reasons I will never understand, I will never bond with her the way Marius does, never give her a present like that house, and he will take that secret to his grave.'"

Wren looked up. "There's some jealousy here. I wonder how far it extended? The men were envious that they couldn't give the astonished Rebecca a present nearly as good. But were the women also upset that no man would ever give them anything like that?"

Wren let the silence hang for a while. It wasn't simply a rhetorical question; Wren literally had no idea how to answer it. Even the talkative Bronwyn said nothing. Wren wondered who would speak first and what they would say, but then realized there was nothing to say about Percival's comments: Words weren't always necessary. She knew that better than anyone. Meanwhile, she had learned something. Even if she couldn't always read reactions, she knew the house had gotten under their skin, and something may come of that later. It was no different from when her father presented a new design to his clients and seeing the way it affected them.

Eventually, she spoke. "I wanted all of you to understand the house better. I think you do now. I know reading Percival's comments in the setting he observed helped me become a better architect."

"Yes," said Bronwyn. "You're absolutely right." Darren took her hand and nodded, still looking at the house.

"Now, I know that you wanted some more information on what we're doing. I will do that now. Mr. Blaine, do you have any further questions?"

Woody roused himself. "Oh, ah. Thank you. You have given me…thank you. I realize you are busy, but if I could just have a word with you on the way out? A brief word?"

"Of course."

Bronwyn said, "If we may, Darren and I would like to spend a few more minutes here, if it doesn't get in anyone's way?"

CHAPTER SIXTEEN

"I'll see you here shortly."

Wren and Woody walked in silence to the foyer. He gave another one of his sighs.

"I owe you an apology," he said. "It hasn't been easy, but that doesn't excuse my behavior. I have family responsibilities, I'm the family ant in a world of grasshoppers, if you know the Aesop fable…" she nodded. "The family rolls along, but someone has to take care of the hard work of being rich." He gave her a wry smile, and Wren liked him better for that. "I thank you for today's demonstration."

"Did you learn more about the house?"

"Actually, I learned more about *you*," he said. Wren blushed despite herself and didn't know if she had been complimented or insulted. "You care very much about this house, which pleases me, but more than that, I think you care very much about the family that lived here, a family that is still around."

"This is newer than most of the houses I work on, but often, I work with families with close connections going back a century or more."

"It shows. I was worried that you wouldn't understand that, that you would put the house before all else, with no thought given to the people who lived here."

"Houses, especially homes, are about people. Not walls. My father taught me that."

"I see that now. You know, I don't just manage the family's money. I'm a money manager for many wealthy families. Your partner, I hear, is a Vanderwerf. They go back to the 17th century. So do the Blaines and many of the families I work with. I wouldn't be surprised if somewhere in the past, the Vanderwerf and the Blaine family trees crossed." *Oh, but not the Rodriguezes! That was special for Dennis.*

The connection, Wren figured, was Woody's attempt to ingratiate himself with her. But, otherwise, she was feeling lost. Maybe her face showed that.

"I guess what I'm trying to say," he continued, "is that I feel confident now that you won't do anything to embarrass the family. It would hurt the deal I'm working on, but the Blaines and Rodriguez clans are widespread—I have a lot of people to answer to. Indeed, I still act for Shoshana and her son.

It must've been clear to you at the meeting how much she dislikes me, but she doesn't much like anyone anymore, and I'm trusted to take care of the business. No one wants the apple cart upset."

Wren nodded. She guessed this was a matter of "I guess I can trust you not to embarrass the family, and I'm sure you won't want to disappoint me."

What are you worried about? I already gave you my professional assurance and didn't violate it. What has you so frightened? It's the house, isn't it? Percival knew it. And now Percival's son was dead.

Wren wondered how her father would respond to this. He'd suggest the KISS principle: Keep It Simple, Stupid.

"Thank you, Mr. Blaine. I appreciate that."

"I knew him—Percival Archer. He lived to a ripe old age, and as a young man, I met him once. He was a charmer, but professional through and through, a grey-flannel suit guy. You have no idea how surprised I was to hear about his passion for Rebecca. I mean, she had something, caught every man's interest. But that she roped in Percival Archer…that should tell you something. Anyway, one small piece of advice before I go. Speaking of Shoshana. She is truly crazy. Not just rich-person-eccentric, but certifiable."

"At our meeting at the Archer law firm, I got the impression you and Shoshana had a longstanding disagreement?" *Is this…okay? Am I pushing too hard?*

But he didn't seem upset with Wren. He just shook his head. "I don't want you to think too badly of me. You may have noticed she mentioned my father, Woodrow Senior. His father—my grandfather—was Dennis's younger brother. My father lost both his parents at a young age, and Dennis stepped up. Looked after him as if he were his own. I know Rebecca got all the attention, her and that delightful daughter of hers. They were Rodiguezes. Dennis was ignored and even half-blamed over the years for his own death while he indulged his wife in building…this." He waved his arm. "I'm sorry. This is your bailiwick. But I don't like this house. I'm wondering—do you?" He gave her a shrewd look.

"Let's just say my specialty is the 19th century. But that doesn't stop me from appreciating the genius of Marius Cadieux."

CHAPTER SIXTEEN

"Marius Cadieux. You say he's a genius, and you're the expert. But my father always said he was a smug bastard, patronizing to Dennis, and revolved his clientele around the wives he could seduce."

"Oh!" said Wren. "Well, he did have a reputation as a womanizer, but you have no idea how widely he was regarded in the profession."

"I appreciate your tour, and I admit now that, thanks to you, I can see why this house is so special."

"Thank you," said Wren.

"But I still despise Cadieux." *For seducing Rebecca, Dennis's wife. Or no—Rebecca might have seduced Cadieux?* "My father detested him for the way Cadieux treated Dennis, and my father's word was good enough for me. My father admired no one more than Dennis Blaine, the finest man he knew. And that whole smug, Rebecca-centered coterie…" His voice got louder, he clenched his fists…and then took a breath and conquered himself. "Again, I am sorry. I am dumping my family history on you, and that isn't fair. Shoshana is completely her mother's daughter. Now, I know you're thinking, what could a woman of her age do? But you haven't met Rafe Rodriguez—he's one of that group, son of Shoshana and grandson of Rebecca. I daresay you'll find him no better. Anyway, thank you so much."

"For what?" She was genuinely confused.

"For understanding that, as an architect, you know homes are important, but that at the end of the day, it's the people who live there who really matter. Good day, Ms. Fontaine."

Chapter Seventeen

Wren walked Bronwyn and Darren through the changes, and although she was on autopilot, they seemed happy with it. *Just one more thing, and I can be alone.*

"Thank you so much, Wren," said Bronwyn as she was seeing them out. "I can't wait until we can move in."

"I'm so pleased," said Wren. She gathered her courage. "This is a special house, as I'm sure you know. And this is a special situation."

"The murders, you mean," said Bronwyn.

"Yes, of course, that's the key part. But we are involved in a very unusual family situation. I need to know what is happening, because I am the architect renovating one of the greatest 20th-century homes built in the U.S., I need to know because I am responsible for the safety of the workers here. You have a connection with the family much deeper than I realized, and I need you to share it with me."

She hoped Bronwyn and her detective partner could not see her heartbeat under her blouse.

Bronwyn remained impassive—at least as far as Wren could tell. She saw Darren squeeze her hand, and Bronwyn turned to him. He nodded.

"Fair enough, Wren," she said. "I could make a case that it's not your business, but as you said, this is not a usual situation. I may have indicated that my interest in Rebecca and Dennis came about as a result of this house. Actually, that came first. I've been fascinated about them, for several years. I got in touch with Shoshana Blaine. She is obsessed with getting the 'real story' out there. I am writing a book, and we already have a miniseries in

CHAPTER SEVENTEEN

the works."

"This book…is it going to be a novel? True crime?"

"The idea is a mix of history and, I guess you'd say, 'speculative fiction.'"

"The lawyers are putting in their two cents," said Darren.

"So Shoshana is behind this? What about the late Tristan, her lawyer?"

"I think so. I didn't work with him myself, but she talked about him. She trusted him. Look, I'm sorry I wasn't completely forthcoming with you. Normally, it wouldn't have mattered. I don't think any of what happened could possibly have anything to do with my deal. This is going to be huge—no one from the family has ever cooperated on this story, and Shoshana is Rebecca's daughter. I own the house—we can film in here."

Wren took a breath. "Thank you. It helps me to know about this."

"I'm very sorry."

"There is no need to apologize. But it's best for this house, for all of us, to know the whole story."

"That's more than reasonable. Can I ask what gave me away?"

"You knew too much, and that was especially clear today."

Bronwyn nodded. "Yeah. When I get interested in something, I just can't contain myself. Anyway, I'm sorry again, and frankly, I'm glad you found me out. I don't like keeping secrets, especially from someone like you, whom I like."

"I'll keep your secrets, of course, but with the police digging into everything, they may come out anyway."

"I'm afraid you're right," said Darren.

"Oh well. The publisher and the TV folks will just have to deal with it," said Bronwyn. "Meanwhile, thanks for those little plays today. It was fun, and my head is buzzing with ideas as a result."

"Mine too," said Wren.

"Ha! Well, we creative types have to stick together. We'll get out of your hair now." She surprised Wren with a kiss on the cheek.

Darren smiled and shook her hand. "Thank you for keeping Bronwyn safe," he said.

"I want my client to remain safe, of course, but I can't take credit for doing anything."

"Oh, I think you have, Wren. I am good at reading people—it was necessary in my job as a police detective. I think you know people well, too. Better than you think. What you are doing with this house, will keep Bronwyn safe. So again, thank you."

And they were gone.

Wren felt like her legs wouldn't support her. How did both Woody and Darren seem to understand her better than she understood herself? Was she working toward an end she didn't even realize? *But maybe I'm just doing what I should have been doing all along, working on a house for people. Maybe Lavinia was right—I do understand people better than I realize. And, they are understanding it. Or maybe they are making unfair assumptions that I am somehow on their side? Am I overthinking this?*

Dealing with so many people! Her father loved this part of the job almost as much as he did designing houses, but she didn't and found herself exhausted. She remembered her father had told her she had to do the whole job, not just the parts she liked. That was life.

But she was going to give herself a present.

She headed directly to Dennis and Rebecca's bedroom. The old mattress was covered only with a plastic tarp. She tore it off and flopped down, looking at the ceiling with its artful use of recessed lighting. Cadieux again. She could see him with his trademark smirk. "Of course, the lighting, mademoiselle. What is the point of designing a house with absolutely perfect proportions if it isn't lit well enough to see it?"

All right, but everything worked out well. Her father would be so pleased, and Hadley would be proud of her. She had learned more about the house and the people who lived there, soothed Woody, told the necessary information about the house and continued to bond with her client.

That was fascinating, actually, the merging of the house into a book and miniseries. A lot of room for drama there! Wren then remembered it was about more than just the family—there was Karen Weston, the dead fan of Bronwyn's books. Bronwyn had admitted she was chatty. So, presumably, Karen had gotten hints about the big picture. She did show up at Bronwyn's

CHAPTER SEVENTEEN

new house, after all. What if this wasn't entirely about the Blaine-Rodriguez clan, but about Hollywood issues? Still, either way, it centered on the house.

And Darren, of course. Wren rather liked him, but she knew he was committed to Bronwyn, and unlike everyone else connected, he was probably cool enough to kill and knowledgeable enough to know how to do it. Was what he said to her a compliment? Advice? A warning?

She continued to look again through the diary entries Gareth had given her. She had read enough lines about Percival mooning over Rebecca, but other people came up as well. Shoshana made a few guest appearances, just becoming an adult. This must have been the time she met Cadieux and apparently had an affair with him. Percival certainly noted that: "Shoshana blessed her parents with her presence, still young enough to be dissatisfied with everything, except when she was smirking. She is entirely Rodriguez, as beautiful as her mother, but nowhere near as sophisticated yet—or anywhere near as charming. She is unpredictable, even wild. Marius has certainly noticed. Is he trying to get her on his side in that sordid love triangle?"

Wren knew she could spend forever trying to figure out Shoshana's mind. *But maybe I have more in common than I think with Shoshana, both of us feeling we have to live up to a famous parent!* That was an interesting path, actually. What would it be like to be the daughter of a renowned personality like Rebecca? Would you want to be like her? Wren wanted to be like her father, but sometimes she admitted she liked the idea of surpassing him, as when she bonded particularly well with a client. Or…was able to work on a house he treasured even before he stepped foot in it!

All right—she thought she was getting a sense of Shoshana, but overall, it was a mess. She went back and forth on Percival. He was of his time and place; there was no doubt about that. Although, he didn't have a prayer of understanding Rebecca or that house, he did have a sense of just how important that house was. The real love triangle was Cadieux, Rebecca, and the house.

On the other hand, Percival misunderstood what was happening with Cadieux. Although thinking the worst of him, Percival didn't seem to realize just how awful he was, making a play for both mother and daughter. Well, that was disgusting, but given Cadieux's reputation, not entirely unexpected.

It felt wonderful to be alone again, and not just alone, but cradled in this room. She'd rather be in something more Jane Austen but working on this house made her realize there might be a place for modernism. Yes, Cadieux knew his stuff. He had seduced many women over his long life, and Wren's last thought was that he had seduced her, too.

It was the last thing she remembered for two hours when an amused Bobby roused her.

"You're lucky I like you," he told the embarrassed Wren. "So I won't tell your father you're sleeping on the job."

"In all fairness, I had to take on some especially arduous tasks," she said with as much dignity as she could muster.

"Really? I thought it was my crew that was hauling a ton of equipment and supplies from the trucks into the house."

"I had it worse. I had to deal with *people*," she said. "I spent a summer working on your crew when I was eighteen—remember?"

"You did a good job, I'll admit that."

"I'd rather haul ten wheelbarrows of cement than deal with people. I was under the impression that being an architect meant I'd only have to deal with blueprints, not people. They didn't teach us about how to work with people at architecture school."

"Wren, was I shy about telling you when you made a mistake when you were working for me?"

"Not at all."

"Then believe me when I tell you that I've seen you working with people. You may not like it, while your father does. Maybe you won't find it so hard if I tell you, in all honesty, that you're better than you think."

* * *

Wren called her father from the car on the way home and gave him the update. Yes, she had promised discretion, but she was speaking for the firm, and her father was the head of the firm.

CHAPTER SEVENTEEN

"So basically," said Wren, "we have clients as strange as the house I'm working on."

"Wren. Cadieux House isn't strange. It happens to be—"

"Father, I'm on the road. Let's save the modernism lecture for another time."

"Very well. And by the way, our clients aren't strange either. They're eccentric."

"What's the difference?"

"About five million dollars."

"Very funny. I'll drop 'strange' for Cadieux, but there's definitely a secret in that house."

"You don't mean a trap door in a hidden basement? That's more in line with the Victorian homes you adore."

"Yes, Marius Cadieux would never do anything that trite. No, something about the style, shape, and proportions tells me about the idiosyncratic Rebecca. And something about the idiosyncratic Rebecca tells me about the style, shape, and proportions of Cadieux House."

"Wren, you're absolutely right. You get Cadieux. I'm so pleased."

"Don't overthink it. I'd still rather be in the Carson Mansion in California. Those incomparable Italianate touches—"

"I don't want a lecture either, my daughter. Meanwhile, do be careful. They still haven't made any arrests in those murders. Something is going to have to happen. People are asking questions."

"I stay around Bobbie and his crew." She paused. "And our eccentric clients and their equally eccentric associates."

"Thank you," he said, drily. "I will give you a tip on Cadieux, meanwhile. His work may be abstract. Esoteric. But it is always honest."

"Isn't the work of any decent architect honest?"

"If you were older and knew more about Cadieux, you wouldn't ask that."

"Oooh, you offer me obscure advice *and* patronize me. Or are you simply mansplaining? I'm almost home. I'll keep you posted."

But she knew he was right. And he knew it, too. That was an interesting statement about Cadieux being honest. Yes, he was a genius, but in the lingo of another age, he was also a cad. Still, he was honest about it. "You couldn't say he ever cheated on a woman," her father had once said, "because he never promised fidelity in the first place." What did he promise, or not promise, with Cadieux House?

It was experiment night at their apartment. Although Hadley rented a commercial kitchen, she liked trying out new ideas at home and used Wren as a test subject, which she always enjoyed. Even Hadley's second-rate trials were delicious.

"One of the advantages of being a Vanderwerf is I have the inside track for Episcopal events. I have a confirmation party coming, and I'm trying to lead my people away from the long, sad history of protestant cuisine. It's an afternoon event, and I'm doing my damnedest to avoid potato salad in any form. You have to draw a line somewhere. I'm thinking Mediterranean, and I have you to thank for that, all this talk about the Sephardic Jews. Maybe I can branch out into bar mitzvahs."

They delighted in the Spanish, Italian, and North African food while Wren updated Hadley. *I can tell her—what do lawyers call it—the spousal privilege? Did she have that right? Did that count? Should they get married?* Hadley had always been in the "we don't need a piece of paper to prove our love" camp, but hadn't said she wouldn't, effectively leaving it up to Wren. *She should think about it...but where was she?*

"Wow, and I thought I worked with some strange people. So the starched shirt Percival Archer was hot and heavy for the lovely Rebecca. Middle-aged to elderly men are always inappropriately falling for some young woman. But Rebecca wasn't younger, was she? She was actually older than him. She must've been something, still turning heads as she pushed fifty."

"Yes, you can help me with that," said Wren as she helped herself to another sambusak, a sort of Mediterranean empanada with cheese. ("You like them?" asked Hadley. "The key is the semolina flour.") "Maybe you have a better idea than I do about why straight men went crazy for her. I know she was beautiful. I've seen paintings and photographs. But still...am I missing something here?"

"You've come to the right place," said Hadley. "Straight men have always

CHAPTER SEVENTEEN

seen me as a nonpartisan consultant in their romances. I probably could've started an advice column. So let me tell you about a girl I once knew, in my early twenties. On the short side, a bit plump, somewhat blotchy complexion, lank mousy-brown hair. But she dated some of the coolest, most popular, best-looking men. Again and again."

"She was…good in bed?" asked Wren.

"I have no idea. She wasn't promiscuous. And you had to buy her expensive dinners to get her favors. No, I'll tell you what her secret was, with men or women. When you were talking to her one-on-one, you were the only person in the world. You were the most important person she had ever met. You can't develop an attitude like that—you are born with it. Now, I'm guessing that Rebecca was like that. She was gorgeous, yes, which no doubt helped a lot. But that wouldn't have been enough. There are lots of beautiful women in the world. She had something else. Anyway, that's my two cents. Try the black-eyed pea hummus. It's quite a surprise."

Wren savored the unusual hummus while she thought. "Absolutely. I wouldn't object, if you made more here. But about Rebecca. That makes a certain amount of sense—Marius Cadieux, Dennis Blaine, and Percival Archer. Of course, it comes back to the house."

Hadley laughed. "It always does. Clue me in."

"Cadieux built that for her. She inspired him. Something about who she was inspired him. And none of us know what it is. And you pointed out something interesting—something about Rebecca, and we can't know that if we haven't met her." She paused. "I'm going to need to talk to Shoshana again and to her son, Rafe." She took out Rafe's business card, which Gareth had given her earlier.

"Rafael Rodriguez, Facilities Manager, the Balmoral Club. That's very fancy, isn't it?" asked Wren.

"Oh yeah! It's supposed to have one of the greatest golf courses in the northeast. I'm sure I have a cousin or two who belong. It costs a mint, and there's a waiting list to join. The word is that the restaurant is good, and they can put together an elegant event, if not an exciting one."

"No North African delicacies?"

"Heaven forbid. But no doubt, a well-stocked bar. Also, they're supposed to have great tennis courts. Rafe would certainly have the right pedigree for a spot there."

"You seem to know something about that scene."

Hadley raised an eyebrow. "So you want me to come?"

"I would, if I were going to see him there. It was one thing to see Gareth Archer in that log cabin of his, but we're getting close to the bone here. If I have a Rodriguez, I want him in the house his mother and grandmother lived in."

"All right," said Hadley. "And you know, you do better than you think."

"People have been telling me that."

"Maybe you should listen to them. Anyway, you don't need me there, although I'm always there if you want me. Now, I'm going to say something very heavy here, so brace yourself." Wren laughed. "Maybe the line you keep drawing between being good at houses and being good with people is artificial, or at the very least, a lot fuzzier than you think."

"Thank you—I mean that. Part of me knows that, but then I think of my father—"

"And if you compare yourself to him again, I won't make sambusaks for you anymore."

"That's enough of a motivation. I'll call him from the house and invite him over. I bet he'll come, if for no other reason than curiosity. And Shoshana, too, eventually. I wonder why she hasn't called me herself. Or Bronwyn. They're working on the miniseries together."

"There's no practical reason for her to avoid a visit," said Hadley. "But maybe there's an emotional one. Or maybe she doesn't want to be questioned again by the shrewd Wren Fontaine."

Wren laughed. "I didn't get that vibe from her, but there's a lot going on here. She was a young, beautiful woman who went to bed with him and had his child, I assume in that house. But who knows?"

Hadley picked up her phone and opened Google Maps. "I wonder if the police have spoken to Rafe. I'm just looking at the country club where he works and Cadieux House. I'm thinking about what Lavinia mentioned:

CHAPTER SEVENTEEN

They're not far from each other. Not far at all."

Chapter Eighteen

An essential part of her job was research, so Wren decided she'd know as much as possible about Rafe Rodriguez before calling him. His parents were apparently unmarried, so it wouldn't be unusual for him to have his mother's name. But actually, Shoshana had given him her own mother's maiden name. A way to emphasize the Sephardic side of the family?

His picture appeared on the club's website, much clearer and more current than the graduation photo Lavinia had found. He was in his late sixties, but he could pass for younger. Just a touch of silver at the temples, and it was clear he had a masculine version of that lovely Rodriguez face. Wren knew little about golf or tennis, but all kinds of organizations indicated he was a top amateur player in both sports. He had been a country club pro around the country, with stints as a college coach.

Could she find anything else about him? Google was a little tricky—there were a lot of men named "Rafael Rodriguez"—but eventually, she found a number of sports references and various trophies as a player and coach. Nothing personal, no mention of connections to the Rodriguez-Blaine clan. After all that family had been involved in, his life seemed almost bland. Maybe he liked that! He was born after Dennis's death, and the family had abandoned their famous house. There were other scandals and other mysteries to fill the gossip pages, and Rafe may have been happy to leave them to it.

She did a check in with Bobby in the morning and took another look at her plans for Bronwyn's special writing house. She hadn't started on it yet—at

CHAPTER EIGHTEEN

first, she wasn't happy with the way it reflected the house, but then she realized that wasn't it. She wasn't secure in building it until she understood the main house. Both had to have the same *psychology*, for want of a better word.

Wren had established a makeshift office in one of the guest bedrooms. She went over her script, got as comfortable as possible in a folding chair, and put her feet up on the table. She reached a secretary, a personal touch in the era of voicemail. But Balmoral Club members were not the kind of people who wanted to communicate with a robot.

"Hello. My name is Wren Fontaine. I'm an architect renovating a house that once belonged to Mr. Rodriguez's family, and I want to speak to him about it, if he has some time." A moment's pause—not the usual kind of request. "One moment, please." She put Wren on a musical hold, and a cheerful voice connected a moment later.

"Ms. Fontaine? Or Wren, if I may. Yes, my mother mentioned you. You're the architect handling the Cadieux House. Good for you! Quite a pile. So how can I help you?"

All right, sound clear and firm, but not like a schoolmarm. "As a specialist in historic home renovation, I find it helpful to speak with family members, or anyone who has a connection to the house, and I was hoping you could help me. In fact, I'd be happy to show you around the house, which has been closed for nearly seventy years."

"Oh, that's something! Mom said there was a lot going on. Thanks so much for inviting me, but I've never been in the house. I drove by it a few times, but that's about it. I heard there was a recent death connected with it, and of course, my grandfather died there—killed, they say. But I grew up in California. This is all secondhand for me. You want my mother."

"Oh yes, I met her."

The laughter poured through the phone. "I can hear your tone loud and clear. You met mom. She's a piece of work, isn't she? And I knew Rebecca—yes, my grandmother. But she never let me call her grandmother. She was—Rebecca. She was something else, too."

"I also want to host your mother here. But she didn't seem as curious about it as I expected."

"I know, right? She was born there, I mean that literally, and it wasn't because Rebecca went into labor quickly. My grandmother wanted to give birth in her bedroom." *What would Cadieux have said about that, someone so close to him delivering a child in the house he built? Had "childbirth" been part of the plan?* "Anyway, it was owned by the family trust all those years. With some minor arrangements, I think she could've visited at any time. But I don't believe she ever did. Or Rebecca either, after they left for good, shortly before I was born. I just assumed that they didn't want to return to where their husband and father died. I don't know about your family Wren, but with Mom and Grandma—I didn't want to ask a lot of questions. You understand." Yes, she did. But wouldn't the upcoming book and miniseries have intrigued her? It wasn't the past Shoshana was afraid of, not the house itself. Unless, of course, Shoshana had a different version?

And was Rafe even in the loop on the big plans? That would be interesting to know.

"Okay, I'll keep an open invitation for your mother, but meanwhile, would you like to see the house?"

"Well, yes. I've heard enough about it over the years. Like Mom, I could've made arrangements with the family trust, but I didn't think she'd support it. But if I can, I'm actually curious…I know it is going to sound silly, but Mom is getting old, and I don't want her upset if she hears I'm visiting the family homestead. I can even come today, if that works for you? But I'm afraid it's going to be one-sided. As I said, I don't know much about the history of the house, or the family's part of it."

"I'm just happy to introduce the house to the grandson of the woman who inspired it."

"Oh…ah, okay then. Looking forward to it."

Wren rang off. Then she leaned back in the chair and closed her eyes. *Look at me, taking a risk on people.* Rebecca. Shoshana. They were tied to the house. Perhaps Rafe was lying when he said he didn't know anything. Maybe even just lying to himself. She realized she might be getting a little romantic about the house, but didn't think the descendant of those two women could

CHAPTER EIGHTEEN

possibly be that ignorant.

"We're having another guest," she told Bobby. "Rafe Rodriguez, whose grandmother was the famous Rebecca."

"I suppose he wasn't old enough to even live here," said Bobby.

"No. But I think that he may have a connection to the house anyway, given his pedigree."

"That's a little, I guess, *psychological* for you."

"I hope so," said Wren. "I don't see how I'll get anywhere with this house otherwise."

"Whoa! That's quite an emotional step forward for our Wren. The next thing you know, you'll be saying the house is haunted."

"Oh no," said Wren, with a grin. "It's a well-established fact that a house needs to be at least one hundred and fifty years old to have ghosts."

"Okay, I'll buy that. I don't want to imagine modernist ghosts anyway."

"Cadieux House has the opposite problem. Actually, it's the house that's doing the haunting of the people who lived here. Even those who only lived here briefly." Bobby just nodded. "Even me," she added. "Don't tell my father."

* * *

Wren got the door herself when she heard the bell. She opened it and was amused to see that Rafe had taken a few steps back and was contemplating the house.

"Everyone has the same reaction," said Wren. Rafe smiled.

"And I can see why. You must be Wren Fontaine." He stepped forward with an outstretched hand. "Rafael Rodriguez. Everyone calls me Rafe. Pleased to meet you."

"Wren Fontaine. I'm glad you were interested. Please come in."

He gave a low whistle as he contemplated the foyer, with its soaring ceiling. While he looked over the house, Wren looked over him: He was wearing chinos, neatly pressed, and a well-cut light blue jacket over a contrasting shirt. Wren knew he was pushing seventy, but he could've passed for a decade younger—the online photo hadn't been retouched. He sported a lean figure, and in person, it was even clearer he had his grandmother's face. Wren looked for signs of Cadieux but couldn't immediately see him in Rafe.

"This is...something," he said. "Mom talked about it, but I had no idea."

"You didn't see pictures?" asked Wren.

"A few. But pictures can't really capture something like this, can it?"

Wren had braced herself—Woody had hinted that Rafe was as eccentric as other family members, but there was something pleasant and open about him. It made sense—the Balmoral Club was not a place for the offbeat. Had Woody tried to frighten her from talking to Rafe, wanting to keep control of the Blaine-Rodriguez saga? Or had she just not seen Rafe's full personality yet?

"That Cadieux must've been something," he said. *Yes, your father. But how can I casually bring up a man's parentage in casual conversation?*

"Come—I'll give you the full tour." She had to work on that, realizing that not everyone had the same obsessive interest in every architectural feature that she did.

"Note the shape of the staircase—it flows, giving the sense of infinite space. That's pure Cadieux. He was also fascinated with shapes, interesting angles, and curves. Individually, they may seem odd, but together, there's a sense of completeness...."

They went room by room. Wren could discuss the home by rote by now, and she could afford to focus on Rafe. Although reading facial expressions remained difficult for her, by this point, she could tell when someone was truly interested in a home as opposed to just humoring her. Rafe was genuinely absorbed. She ended at the master bedroom.

"So this was Dennis and Rebecca's room? Nice view. Mom always said Rebecca worked closely with Cadieux on this house. I guess she chose this bedroom?"

"More than that," said Wren. "Cadieux specifically designed this room, indeed, the whole house, with her in mind. I'm wondering if she ever talked to you about it. You must've been almost thirty when she passed."

"Rebecca had an interest in a lot of things. She was curious and forward-

CHAPTER EIGHTEEN

looking. But she never thought much about the past, at least that's what I gathered. There was a line she quoted from a book—I can't remember the title anymore. She'd say, 'The past is a foreign country: they do things differently there.'"

"'The Go-Between.' A novel by L.P. Hartley. It came out shortly before you were born."

"Yeah, that was it. Rebecca was a big reader. Me, less so." He gave her an amused look. "Look, Wren. I'm pretty good at reading people. It's necessary at my job. I not only run all the athletic facilities, I'm one of the partners. I deal with a lot of demanding rich people. I'm sure that's something you've had to do, too, over the years. Hell, you've met my mother."

"Yes, working with the wealthy has its challenges."

"I should know—I'm one of them. I drifted around after college. I was an indifferent student but a good athlete. Not quite professional, but I found a niche as a college coach, tennis pro, golf pro."

"You came back to Long Island in the end, though? You work, and I assume live, just a few miles from where your grandmother had lived, where your mother had been born."

"You sound like my mother. Yeah, I may consider myself a Californian, but she always said I'd come back to my East Coast roots. Mom was getting very old, and I knew the Balmoral people. They knew I'd fit in for that position, and a year later, I put some of my money into it. But you're still fishing for family lore—"

"I'm sorry..." *I really put my foot into it. I should've known I was over my head here.*

Rafe waved away her apology. "It's okay. I came to terms long ago, that I was born into a well-known family, even a slightly notorious one. A lot of that has faded over the years, but from time to time...anyway, I suppose the home's sale and those two deaths have raised the profile again. You asked about visiting. I was spending part of a college vacation visiting a friend who had a summer place in the Hamptons. As a long-time Hampton resident, he was fascinated with the story and was a huge fan of Cadieux's work. I asked Rebecca if I could arrange to visit. 'Oh my dear,' she said, 'don't do it. It will drive you mad.' I can see that now. I really can."

Wren didn't know what to say.

"You judge people by their homes, don't you?" he asked.

"I—I wouldn't say *judge* as much as *draw conclusions*. Given choices, people always gravitate to the homes that suit them. Even if they don't immediately realize it."

"And where do I live, Wren?"

"I don't know you well enough."

"Give it a shot."

Wren looked him over. His clothes were neat but with little individuality. He held a job that was responsible but not glamorous. He was not a family man. As an athlete, he had a focus on the physical.

"Although wealthy, you live in a small ranch-style house. You keep it very neat. It is at the end of a cul-de-sac. I watched you watch this house. You find its openness overwhelming. You find the proportions disturbing. There is no comfort for you in its curves and angles."

Rafe raised an eyebrow at her, stuck his hands in his pants pockets, and looked around the room.

"Maybe it's me," he said after a while. "I always felt that my mother and Rebecca were members of a special club, and I wasn't invited. I figured it was because I was a boy. There was a past, and it was centered on this house. I got that much. That I wasn't strong enough, somehow, to understand and appreciate this house. You know what my mother said? She said it was a house for women and that that men couldn't cope with it. But Rebecca was a little, I don't know…kinder? More open? She once stopped my mother and told me she thought if I ever got to see it, I would get it. As I said, she liked me." He shrugged.

"That is…something," said Wren. "I've never heard of anyone gendering a house like that. Oh, we talk about kitchens for women and home offices for men—we did that once, and some homeowners still think that way. Not Cadieux, but others. Of course, it's their house—they can do what they want. But the way you tell it…" She shook her head.

"I agree," said Rafe. "I always put it down to my grandmother, who liked

CHAPTER EIGHTEEN

to make a special entrance everywhere she went. Look, my mother was beautiful and is still striking now in her old age. But there was something about Rebecca. She wasn't just beautiful; she was *entrancing*. Men were taking her out to the best places, photographers snapping her pictures for gossip magazines, even as she aged. I had school friends who developed crushes on my grandmother, for God's sake. She loved it. She wasn't stupid, she didn't get lost in the attention, if you know what I mean, but until the day she died, she loved being in a group. She was entertaining and gossiping with the nurses in her final hospital stay. But maybe you think I'm crazy."

"I've seen pictures," said Wren. "And I don't think you're crazy or exaggerating. She was very attractive. Now, to be even nosier—Rebecca was Jewish, Sephardic Jewish, and you were even given her maiden name as your own. Can you give me some insight into why she didn't marry into her own community? To be blunt, why marry Dennis Blaine? Wealth and position were hers anyway, and nothing I've heard indicates she was passionate for him."

"You're not the first to ask that," said Rafe. "You want my thought, for what it's worth? She didn't marry my grandfather despite him being a gentile, but because of it. It would create a separation, a gulf, between them, and she liked that. She may have wanted the security, in a social sense, that came from being a married woman. I think she liked the space that would prevent her from giving herself fully to her husband—the ethnic and religious differences that separated them. I don't think she gave herself fully to any man. It was a reason, an excuse."

"That's telling. I appreciate your insights."

"You're welcome. It's part of the big picture. I grew up in a glamorous world, raised by a glamorous mother and a glamorous grandmother with a wide circle of friends. I saw the way the world worked, at least our world—the men were strong and the women good-looking." He gave a self-deprecating laugh. "I'm getting off track, but here's the point I want to make: My mother was attractive. But Rebecca was entrancing. She was alluring. When you were with her, you knew you were the only person in the world."

"Oh!" said Wren. "That's so interesting. I was talking about Rebecca with my girlfriend, and she guessed that was her secret. She said the same thing. Hadley is a bit…worldlier than I am."

"She can pat herself on the back for her intuition," he said with a laugh. "But where was I? I keep getting lost. Right—this all leads back to understanding the house. My father couldn't, apparently. And not Percival Archer—the family lawyer. Mom and Rebecca would snicker and call him the *consigliere*. He clearly had developed a longstanding passion for Rebecca, even though he couldn't understand the house, or at least that's what they said. Mom said even Cadieux couldn't cope with the results of his own creation. She said the house had a feminine energy. Whatever the hell that means."

"Intuition. Feminine energy embraces intuition, among other things. This is an intuitive house, Rafe. I'll give them that."

"But it was designed by a man. Unless you're giving credit to Rebecca."

"No. Rebecca was an influence, but Marius Cadieux designed it. Still, he was known for working with women. Some said it was because he was progressive and recognized women as equals. Others said it was just because he wanted to get them into bed."

"And your thought?" he asked.

"Something in the middle, actually," said Wren. "We can go back centuries to great mansions, palaces, and castles. They were built by men and for men, but women ran them, provisioned them, made guests feel welcome in them. I may be exaggerating this a bit, but I don't think a lot of men gave that a thought. Marius Cadieux did. And I think he knew it working with Rebecca. But in the end, although I'm a woman, this is still not my favorite house, feminine energy aside. But slowly, I'm understanding it. Because I am beginning to understand your family."

"I wish I could help you more," he said.

"You might be able to. Your grandfather Dennis," said Wren. "He died in this house. He was shot here. Because of the family energy? Are you telling me your mother and grandmother never discussed that?"

Rafe gave her a dubious look. "Why are you even involving yourself?"

"It's my house," said Wren, putting more strength into it than she felt. "As

CHAPTER EIGHTEEN

long as I am working on it, it is my house. I need to understand it."

Rafe spent so much time looking out the window, Wren thought he wouldn't answer at all, and that he'd eventually just leave. But after more than a minute, he turned to her.

"I made a mistake coming here."

"I'm sorry. I shouldn't have pushed you."

"No. I don't mean that. I had wanted to stay away from this, but my curiosity got the better of me. Anyway, Rebecca and my mother shared secrets about what happened here. I was a quiet boy. I heard things when they thought I wasn't around. We lived in a large house in San Diego—Rebecca had her own suite when she wanted privacy, but she and my mother spoke a lot together. They were quiet about the family history. My requested visit was denied, as I said, but that wasn't the first time I ran into the family wall. When I was sixteen, I finally put it all together—you're too young to remember life before Google, but it once was harder to do research."

"So my father reminds me," said Wren.

"It took some time in the library. I found out my grandfather died—was killed—in the family home. I found the newspaper accounts. I asked my mother and grandmother. I'll never forget what Rebecca said to me. She said she had no details beyond what was in the papers. She didn't know who killed Dennis Blaine. But that I should know it was inevitable. That's what she said. That was her exact word. 'Inevitable.' My God. But you're an architect. I looked you up. I looked up your father. It took only a few clicks to find out your father is considered Cadieux's finest disciple. You wanted to meet Cadieux's son. Christ."

Wren didn't trust herself to speak for a long time. "When did your mother tell you?" she asked.

"She always told me I didn't need to know. She said I was a Rodriguez, and that was better than being a Blaine, which is why she gave me that name."

"That's unusual," said Wren. "And progressive for its time."

"I suppose. I thought it a little odd, but my mother and Rebecca were very much wrapped in the culture and history of the Rodriguezes. If it's not too elaborate, I'd say the *mythology* of the family. It was exciting to be a

Rodriguez, and that was all I needed to know. My mother was always vague about my father. But when I turned twenty-one, I came into certain funds from the family trust. I told my mother that I'd hire a lawyer to find it out. With bad grace, my mother told me it was Marius Cadieux."

"I would've thought she'd be proud of that?" asked Wren.

"You'd think so, right? Among family and the close friends, she'd talk about it, after she had told me, but maybe she felt I'd…mess it up somehow. Or create legal problems. Anyway, this may be clearer in a moment," he said with a sigh. "But at the time, she told me they had a brief but passionate affair. Then she also told me—full of smugness—that her mother, that Rebecca, had been in love with him but that Cadieux had loved her. She seemed very proud of that. My mother was barely twenty. This is why I wanted to see this house. I remember what she had said to me. She said Marius Cadieux may have given Rebecca a house, but she had inspired it. And she was the only woman he gave a child to—me. That's it. I was set to balance the books. A gift even greater than this—ridiculous funhouse."

"That sounds—horrible," said Wren, "being told you were essentially a trophy of your mother's conquest."

"Oh yeah. It was great. But it got worse. I asked if he knew, and she said yes, but he didn't care. I said I understood that—even at that young age, I understood the way things worked sometimes. But I said maybe now he would want to meet me. I said I wanted to meet him."

Rafe sat on the bed. To her horror, Wren thought he was on the verge of tears. She wished she hadn't started on this. She wished she could fall through the floor.

"They say every generation gets a little more accepting, but that's not really true. Rebecca lived her life honestly. My mother did not. I was going to be the trophy. I was going to be put on display as the offspring of the great Marius Cadieux. But she found out how damaged I was pretty early, when I was in high school. She talked a good game, but when she was faced with dealing with it…Rebecca knew, even before my mother did, and was fine with it. But mom said Cadieux would be disgusted with me. She said she hadn't even told him about me."

CHAPTER EIGHTEEN

"I'm afraid I'm being very stupid," said Wren. And it wasn't a lie. She was missing something very big.

"You referred to your *girlfriend*. In fact, I found a picture online of you two at some housewarming for a house you refurbished," said Rafe. "So I thought you'd understand. That's what convinced me to meet with you." He gave her a smile she couldn't interpret. Was he looking superior to her, patronizing this idiotic woman who couldn't figure out what he was talking about?

"'Not the marrying kind,'" he finally said. "That's how they used to refer to men like me, gay before it was fashionable. My mother may have led an unconventional life, but it was for straight people only. Rebecca was true—I want you to know that, Wren. She knew who I was before I knew myself and accepted and loved me until the day she died. My mother came around eventually, but it was too late. You can't fix that, can you? Being told as a fatherless boy, while being raised by two women who had had a succession of lovers, that I was a freak."

Wren struggled to figure out what she should say. Fortunately, Rafe took care of that.

"You're a generation younger than I am. Was it hard for you to come out?"

"I never did, actually. My mother died when I was nineteen. She was sharp, and we were close. She knew. As with you and Rebecca, I think she knew even before I knew myself. We never spoke of it—I didn't have a big social life anyway. And my father—I never had an explicit talk with him either." She smiled. "He's always been a practical man, and I think that he was so pleased at finding that I was actually capable of maintaining an intimate relationship, the gender was immaterial."

Rafe laughed. "That's wonderful. I wish…" He shook his head. "You look at my mom, and you think about the sophistication. But it wasn't. It was about selfishness, about doing what you want. It was pretty obvious by my teens who I was. Her long-term plan was to parade me as proof of her consummate skill in bearing Marius Cadieux's child. Never mind the intellect, I was not going to fit the masculine template of the renowned womanizer Marius Cadieux."

"I am so sorry. I never heard this or imagined. You must have heard that the rumors were always that Cadieux was having an affair with Rebecca."

"We're some family, aren't we? I couldn't say. They loved each other, I know that. The women in my family are competitive. My mother wanted to prove Cadieux loved her more than he loved Rebecca. What did I know? What do I even do with that?" He laughed. "Now, this is something funny—two people with no insights into straight women discussing the romantic history of two straight women."

"A lovely bit of irony," said Wren, smiling back at him. "From what I've learned about Rebecca, I think she might've appreciated that." And Rafe nodded. "I am very sorry for causing you pain," continued Wren. "That wasn't my intention. I am a very private person, and I respect the privacy of others."

"It actually feels good, in a funny way. I've been running away from my family, from this house, for a long time. I have many friends, but I don't discuss my past with them. Congratulations, Wren. You've brought the past and present together for me." Wren just looked at him. "That's a bit of a joke; you can laugh," he said.

"Thank you. I often have trouble figuring that out," she said solemnly. "I do better with houses than with people." Hadley had said if she could deliver that line straight, with her chin up, people would think she was a brilliant eccentric rather than a social incompetent.

"Something else we have in common—we both went into professions that suit us well."

"Indeed. And that brings me back to this house. You called it a 'ridiculous funhouse.' So you don't like it, even apart from your family interest?"

"I'm sorry. I didn't mean to insult you or your work."

"Cadieux remains controversial. He reveled in that. To be honest, I'm more at home in another century. I guess I'm asking if you could look at it just as a house, now that you've had a tour."

He looked around. "It's too twisty for me. I guess that says I'm a barbarian?"

"It says you are honest," said Wren. "I do appreciate your coming and I am sorry it was so upsetting for you. I try to make people happy with my work."

CHAPTER EIGHTEEN

"I'm the one who's sorry. I dump my family unhappiness on you, but don't help you at all."

"You've helped me a lot," said Wren. "The more I understand the family, the more I understand the house. And there's something else I may be able to help you with, although I'd understand if you wouldn't want to. As far as we know, Marius Cadieux didn't have any other children and never married. But he came from a big family and had many nieces and nephews. My father has kept up with some of them. I'm sure he'd be happy to introduce you to them."

"I'll think about that. Thank you. I guess I was afraid that without any concrete proof, they wouldn't accept me, would think I was just after a connection to his fame."

"My job has made me somewhat knowledgeable about family relationships. If they were willing to cooperate, you could get a DNA test. That is, even a test with a cousin or aunt or uncle could establish your relationship."

"I didn't know that. I'd have nothing against such a test, and I'd be willing to sign a paper disclaiming any interest in my father's estate to show it was just about family history, not money."

"You think about it. And with your permission, I'll mention this to my father."

"That would be fine. Thank you, Wren. 'You can't go home again.' See, I can make literary references too. But can I say something more about the house?"

"Of course. Now, or a week from now, anytime."

"As I said, it isn't to my taste. But thinking about Rebecca, I can see how it could've been to her taste. It is as unusual and unpredictable as she was. And as…"

"Alluring?" asked Wren. Rafe laughed.

"Yes. The house and its mistress…both alluring." He was ready to go, and Wren debated whether she could discuss one more thing with him to show how hard she was trying to understand the house.

"I am going to be rude again," said Wren, "with another question."

"At this point, considering what we've been discussing, it would be ridiculous to take anything off the table," said Rafe, spreading out his arms.

"Okay then—Rebecca's religion. I know the Sephardim varied a lot, and even the most open of them could still be religious in private. What was Rebecca's attitude toward her Jewishness?"

Rafe leaned back. "Now that is a good question," he said. "A good one and a funny one. Here she was married to an Episcopalian, but occasionally attended Sabbath services and always on the High Holy Days—Rosh Hashanah and Yom Kippur. We always had a menorah by the Christmas tree. Were we American or what?"

"Did she love your grandfather Dennis very much? I'm not trying to be nosy. I'm trying to get a sense of how their relationship affected this house."

"Oh gosh. I really don't know. She never talked about Dennis to me. I was a grown man, and I asked her why she hadn't settled down with a nice Jewish boy. She laughed and said she could ask the same thing of me. I loved that! But she didn't really answer me. Do you want my opinion? I think Rebecca was an actress. One role was Mrs. Dennis Blaine. Another was the scion of the magnificent Rodriguez family. Then you had the mysterious friend of Marius Cadieux and the renowned society hostess."

Wren nodded. "Thank you. That makes a lot of sense. Do you think anyone else understood that? Is that what Cadieux put into this house, a 'home of many parts?'"

"I don't really get this house, and what I told you about my grandmother was just a theory, my way of understanding her. I wish you luck in connecting it with this house. I'd suggest you ask my mother, but even if she decided to tell you the truth about her mother, she couldn't. She's lied so many times, I doubt if she even knows what the truth is anymore."

"I am sorry for how your mother has behaved," Wren said. "And I won't insult you by saying I understand what you're going through. But I may have an explanation. I think your mother was obsessed with Marius Cadieux, which is very different from loving him, and it had a lot to do with Rebecca—and this beautiful, maddening house he built for her. I am not absolving anyone. I am just trying to explain, because I am sure it had a lot to do with this house. I think your mother knew it would never be long-term with

CHAPTER EIGHTEEN

Cadieux—even at her most self-delusional. But she would have you. She wanted you to be a version of him in every way, to look like him, to behave like him. And when you weren't? The irony is that I watched you take in this house. That is something I have a lot of experience with. And I think you understand Cadieux House in a way your mother never did. In a sense, even more than Cadieux did. You and Rebecca—you understand it. You *get* it." She hesitated over the final bit. "I may be very bad at giving personal advice, but I will tell you to spend more time thinking about Rebecca and less about Cadieux. I think that will help you."

"Are you a psychologist, Wren?" he asked, smiling sadly.

"Just an architect. But in the long run, I think you will find my advice useful, because it is about this house."

She showed him out the door, and Wren was pleased to see that he stopped and continued to stare at the house. She knew she was right about him and Shoshana—and Rebecca.

Chapter Nineteen

After dinner, Hadley made a recipe list for an upcoming job while Wren leafed through her plans for Bronwyn's writing room.

"Too much pain," said Hadley, after Wren told her about Rafe. "I know your father is president-for-life of the Marius Cadieux Fan Club, but it seems there's a lot of unhappiness in that house."

"Yes, there is," said Wren. "I don't like it. I know any house must've had its share of good and bad times, but in a one-hundred-and-fifty-year-old house, I just sense the beauty and grandness. Why am I seeing so much unhappiness here? Is it because it's still relatively new, or did Cadieux hide something there I'm not yet seeing? Yes, my first instinct was to blame Cadieux, but it doesn't seem fair to blame him for what appears to be a dysfunctional family."

"You shock me, Little Bird! Doesn't the house influence the family?"

"It can. But it does more than that. It can *reflect* the family, too. Not all was glamorous at Cadieux House, and if that family was damaged—there could be a thin line between mind-bending and just plain overwhelming. It's making this special writing cabin all the more difficult. I'm getting more information on what was going on in Cadieux House, more of a sense of what he was trying to achieve for Rebecca."

"She sounds like a woman of many parts," said Hadley.

"And so is that house. Comforting and yet freeing. It's a complicated design, but, yet does a very good job of providing both a setting for parties and privacy for its residents. I want the same for this writing room. I have initial drawings Bronwyn liked, but I don't want it good, I want it great."

CHAPTER NINETEEN

Hadley leaned over and kissed Wren on her head. "My darling perfectionist. Don't be discouraged. Do you know how long it took me to create the world's greatest bechamel sauce?"

"Well said!" Wren spread her arms dramatically. "We're tortured artists—I'll create the perfect kitchen for your perfect bechamel, my love."

The doorbell ring at eight took them by surprise.

"Unlike your clients, mine might be crazy enough to visit me at home, although I do try to keep our address private. How did they even get through the downstairs door?"

"Who's there?" asked Hadley.

"FBI, ma'am."

"It's too late for prank calls."

"Ma'am. It's the FBI. We will show you our badges."

"Is this some kind of joke?" asked Wren quietly.

"Don't worry. My misspent youth made me an expert on law enforcement badges," said Hadley. She looked through the peephole, gave Wren a thumbs up, and opened the door. Two men in perfect suits entered. Wren reflected you didn't see many men in suits anymore. They held out their IDs again for their inspection.

"I'm William Esterhaus, and this is Arthur Jackson," said the older man. "We know both of you have had recent contact with members of the Rodriguez and Blaine families. There are some issues that we'd like to discuss with you."

Wren blinked. Her work was heavily regulated, and she was used to dealing with a variety of government agencies. But not the FBI. She glanced at Hadley, who shrugged and said, "There's no plumbing the mind of the law enforcement community."

"What do you want to discuss?" asked Wren.

"Not here," said Esterhaus. "Some people would like to speak with you downtown."

"The Javits office building?" asked Wren.

Agent Jackson looked surprised. "You know about it, Ms. Fontaine?"

"I know it's the tallest federal building in the United States. I'm an architect."

"And do you like it?" asked Jackson, showing a little amusement.

"Wren is going to take the Fifth on that," said Hadley.

"I'm happy to cooperate," said Wren. "When would you like me to visit?"

"Now," said Esterhaus. "It has to be now."

"I'm sorry—" said Wren. "Do you mean *right now?*"

"I'm afraid so," said Esterhaus.

"Are you arresting us?" asked Wren. "Are we being charged with something?"

"No," said Jackson. "Neither of you are being charged with anything. But this will be a lot simpler if we can settle this now, quietly. You're in the middle of a complicated job. Your firm is involved in multiple projects. And you, Ms. Vanderwerf, also work with wealthy and well-known people. Settling this now, and quietly, is in everyone's best interest. We can explain more downtown."

Wren looked at Hadley, then back at the agents.

"If nothing else, I'm curious," she said. They grabbed keys and phones and followed the agents to their car outside.

***

Wren and Hadley looked at each other but didn't say anything in the presence of the agents. It was a quick ride downtown. They followed the agents into an elevator upstairs. Even at that hour, agents milled around the office, but no one gave them a special look.

Esterhaus and Jackson ushered them into a conference room, with a table that could sit about ten people.

"Where should we sit?" asked Hadley.

"Anywhere except the head or the foot," said Esterhaus.

"In Japan," said Wren. "It's very important for people to be seated at a conference table according to their rank, their level of importance."

"No kidding?" said Jackson.

Wren pointed them to the middle, on the side away from the door. They'd

CHAPTER NINETEEN

be well-positioned to see anyone and at a good discussion distance from anyone who'd be talking to them. The agents sat in the middle opposite them but said nothing. Another minute later, a woman walked in, also in a good suit. She looked about forty and walked briskly to the head of the table, sat, and clasped her hands on the table.

"You gentlemen can go," she said to the agents. They looked at each other, then slowly got up and left the room, closing the door behind them. The woman watched them until they were gone.

"Ms. Fontaine. Ms. Vanderwerf. Sorry for the night call. I'm afraid we work twenty-four/seven and I thought it would be best for all of us if this were done quietly. My name is Ann Eichelberg, and I am an officer with the Central Intelligence Agency."

"Wow," said Hadley.

"But this is the FBI office…" said Wren, realizing a moment later how lame that sounded.

"The CIA cannot arrest citizens. The FBI can," said Eichelberg.

"So we were going to be arrested?" asked Wren.

Eichelberg smiled thinly. "No need to hash out jurisdictional rules. It's late. Let me get to the point. Ms. Fontaine, you've been very closely engaged with the Rodriguez and Blaine families in the course of renovating Cadieux House. Ms. Vanderwerf, I know you've been involved peripherally, too. You have been digging diligently into the history of the family. I'm going to ask you, for the sake of national security, to not do that anymore."

"You want me to stop working on the house?"

"Oh no. I wouldn't dream of interfering."

"A certain amount of research is essential to work on the house."

"Of course. I'll be more detailed. I'd like you to stop focusing on Rebecca Blaine, nee Rodriguez."

"She died nearly forty years ago. I just don't understand."

Eichelberg bestowed another smile on them. "I bet you annoyed the hell out of your professors."

"Wren's professors loved her. We socialize with some of them," said Hadley.

"Yeah, but she still annoyed them. Ms. Fontaine, World War II is not as far back as we'd like to think."

"Oh—1942. Rebecca disappeared in 1942."

"Good for you, Ms. Fontaine."

Wren felt herself tense up. "It's late. Can we dispense with the patronization," she said. She heard Hadley stifle a snicker. She knew how her girlfriend hated being treated like that.

"Fair enough. My apologies. Let's just say that there are some aspects of Rebecca Blaine's work that, even after all this time, would embarrass some people. She was well known. Her family was well known."

"So this is about avoiding embarrassment for an old, wealthy family?" asked Hadley. "I wouldn't have thought that the CIA had to get involved."

"Ah, you're a Vanderwerf," said Eichelberg. "You know all about that, don't you? Your ancestors came over on the Mayflower, didn't they?"

"Yeah. Centuries of getting away with all kinds of things. But we usually got around things by bribing congressmen, not by calling in Jason Bourne."

"That's very funny," said Eichelberg. "But you have a bit of history dealing with law enforcement, so you've gotten good at it."

"Practice makes perfect. But I've been on the straight and narrow for some years now."

"I'm sure," said Eichelberg dryly.

"I don't suppose you can tell us who reported us?" asked Wren. "I don't see the FBI or CIA monitoring architects renovating modernist homes."

"It's not a matter of 'reporting,'" said Eichelberg. "And no, I can't tell you anymore except to say this could cause some embarrassment for us. All I'm saying is that there are some aspects of Rebecca Blaine's life that would cause some problems for this country if they were publicized. I'm going to request you not look into her past. That's all. Since I cannot see how further investigation into her history could profit your work on the house, can I have your assurance you will not dig more deeply into Rebecca?"

Wren looked around the room. She was once again amidst people who knew the value of working in their space: the long, plain room. No decoration. Probably soundproofed. Eichelberger sat at the head from a position of strength.

CHAPTER NINETEEN

"You have my assurance that Hadley and I will do nothing to put this country in peril. I know more than enough about Rebecca to work on the house already," said Wren. She glanced at Hadley, who probably wanted to argue it more. There was no point, though.

Even Eichelberg seemed a little taken aback by Wren's quick agreement.

"Okay then. Thank you. This is much appreciated."

"Can we get a ride back home?" said Wren.

"Of course. One of the FBI staff will drive you. Sorry for the whole cloak-and-dagger thing. Thanks again for your help." They all stood, and Eichelberg led the way out the door. Wren gave Hadley's hand a quick squeeze. *It's going to be okay.*

Eichelberg walked them to the reception area. "Oh, and one more thing, Ms. Fontaine. I once got to visit the Paxson house your father designed in Westchester. Absolutely amazed me."

"Thank you," said Wren. "I'd tell him if this wasn't a top-secret situation." Eichelberg laughed.

Again, they didn't speak in the car and waited until they got upstairs. Hadley knew that personal interactions like that exhausted Wren—but not that evening. She watched her girlfriend pace.

Wren felt wired. A hundred thoughts ran through her head. None of it seemed to make any sense, but she felt she could start seeing a path forward. Hadley watched Wren pace in the small living room while she brewed the herbal tea they both liked in the evening.

"Sit," said Hadley. "Sit with me on the couch and drink your tea."

Wren took a deep sip and closed her eyes. It was Hadley's own recipe, and it never failed to calm.

"Someone reported us," said Wren. "Someone with a lot of connections. I know nothing of the intelligence community, but I am used to working with wealthy, powerful people. They were rather clever, putting the CIA on to us. Rebecca's missing years. Cadieux, from France. The family's French deal—all those connections. The thing is, those were hardly secrets. It didn't have to be the family. The real question is why someone doesn't want us to find out something about Rebecca."

"Okay...that's possible," said Hadley. "Someone may be gaming the CIA here, although it would take a lot to do that."

"I hate to say it, because I rather like them, but Darren might have government connections from his years on the force."

"Government agencies are inclined to paranoia. The thing is, it couldn't be completely made up. There would have to be something, and as you said, she mentioned Rebecca's missing years. What was she up to?"

"Rebecca spoke perfect French, according to her daughter. Let's consider Bronwyn, buying the family home, researching the family. She actually tested me when we first met, seeing how much I knew about Rebecca. Maybe I know too much."

"Yes—and I could see her doing that," said Hadley. "It's not just Darren with connections. She could have lots of contacts in all kinds of places, thanks to her past books. She tells an insider at the CIA that she's come across something in Rebecca's past that could still embarrass some people. They know Bronwyn. I've done plenty of work with media superstars: There's a lot of favor trading, and if Bronwyn is making the FBI or CIA look good in one of those sweeping sagas—who knows?"

Wren laughed. "Sounds plausible. Or are we being the paranoids now? But there is one legitimate connection here with Rebecca's missing years. So, let's say it's Bronwyn trying to throw us off. Maybe she promised Shoshana she'd be quiet about something Shoshana wanted to be kept private. And Bronwyn is trying to stop us because she doesn't want Shoshana upset."

"Or...this is Shoshana herself doing it," said Hadley. "Maybe she and Rafe are messing with us, never mind Bronwyn."

"And Shoshana, as Rebecca's daughter, may have some juice. The Blaines and Rodriguezes knew all kinds of people, and the CIA long had a reputation as a gentlemen's club. Okay—we could do this all night. For that matter, this may be an Archer situation. A lawyer in a firm like his would have powerful connections—I imagine there are lawyers at the Agency. You know..." Hadley watched Wren's eyes lose their focus and stay quiet. "Okay...the OSS, the Office of Strategic Services. It was the wartime predecessor to the CIA. Percival Archer—well-connected lawyer. I'm guessing he'd be just the kind

CHAPTER NINETEEN

of guy they'd welcome onboard. His son Tristan is killed—for something he knew? Something about Rebecca?"

"Ooh, I like that one a lot," said Hadley.

"All right. When it comes down to it, it's about Rebecca's lost years. That's what we have to uncover."

"I knew it, Little Bird! Even the CIA is not going to put you off your goals."

"Of course not. But we will have to bring in the big guns. If we're looking at something that happened back in the 1940s, we're going to need some major research help. I'm calling Lavinia tomorrow—she'll have some insights here."

"All right then!" said Hadley. Then she gave Wren a sly look. "So are you telling me this might be about some wartime shenanigans and not about the house after all?" She meant to tease, but Wren was serious, even solemn.

"Oh no. It's definitely about the house. I'm more sure of that than ever. It's always been about the house."

Chapter Twenty

"All right," said Lavinia as she walked into Cadieux House. "All right. You say it's all about the house, my dear Wren. And even at first glance, I might even agree it's worth killing over. But you'd disagree, wouldn't you?" She gave her professorial "look" at Wren.

"I'd disagree because I am too moral to kill for just a house?" said Wren, grinning back at her.

"Oh, no. You'd happily kill for a house, but it would have to be more Gilded Age. You wouldn't kill for modernist. But something with decorative gables? No question. However, your father would kill for Cadieux."

Wren and Hadley laughed. Wren had called Lavinia the morning after the CIA meeting, and she went to work immediately.

"I've run into a lot of issues looking into history. There are plenty of hidden corners that too many people wish would stay hidden. But I've never run into the intelligence community. Good for you! I'm guessing we need to delve into Rebecca Blaine's dark past."

"If you could find the time…"

"Just try to stop me. I'm raring to go on this. But I'm going to have to take a page from the Wren Fontaine playbook. I want to see the house—let's pick a time this week. Hadley, too. We're going to have to brainstorm on this. I've found a few things in the last few days, and we'll all want to discuss our next steps."

After she got over the astonishment of the entranceway, Wren gave her the house tour. It was interesting, seeing how differently Lavinia took the tour compared with Rafe, someone looking at it as a historic monument, as

CHAPTER TWENTY

opposed to a family legacy.

A family legacy indeed! Considering my father's connection to Cadieux, am I really seeing it through his eyes? Now, that would make Cadieux laugh!

"Thank you, Wren. Nothing like a sense of being at a place to put it all in perspective. I remember when I finally got a chance to visit Ellis Island—it put my immigration studies on a whole new plane. If this is Rebecca's special place, as you say, what I have to show you may make a lot more sense. Now, I don't want you to think that this was just a Google search. I had to speak to a lot of people who normally don't like to talk."

"Oh! I didn't want you to expend too much intellectual capital on my problem." Wren, Hadley, and Lavinia took seats in the office.

"Wren—no need to be so self-effacing. I've told you about that before. Anyway, it's been quite a bit of fun. Now, here is the story on our dear Rebecca." She took a notebook out of her voluminous leather bag. "As I'm sure you know, Rebecca spoke very good French."

"Her daughter Shoshana bragged about how well she and her mother spoke French."

"As you can imagine, as the war proceeded, the OSS had a need for those who could speak French, to help support the underground. Now, as I said, I couldn't find anything about Rebecca. But I approached it from the other side now, to get a sense of what the OSS was doing, and seeing if we could meet in the middle. In 1942, the OSS recruited a group of women—surprised to hear about our secret agent women all the way back then?"

"I'm not!" said Hadley. "One of my heroes served—Julia Child."

"Very good—the oft-unsung war heroes," continued Lavinia. "I don't have their names in the information I found, but I do have some descriptions." She leafed through her notebook. "I found a reference to five women, at least one of whom has a particularly good Parisian accent, and a notation that she already knew C."

"C—Cadieux. I know he was still in France then," said Wren. "The story was that he didn't get out until the last minute. And Shoshana said her mother had a perfect Parisian accent."

"Let's not move too quickly," said Lavinia. "There could be other women—

Cadieux knew plenty of women, I've heard. Even if it's him—he wasn't the only C."

"Oh, but it would explain a lot," said Hadley. "Everyone said they loved each other—Rebecca and Cadieux—but no one could figure it out. What if it was because she saved his life."

"The love that comes from overwhelming gratitude," said Wren. "He built this house for her as a thank you."

"Wren, I've had to talk to you as an undergraduate about jumping to conclusions. It was all right then—you were only twenty. But I should hope for better from you now."

Wren felt a little abashed. Lavinia was right, but she and Hadley had been caught up in the enthusiasm, and it just seemed too perfect.

"My apologies," said Wren, flashing back to Modern American History. "Of course. It just adds up so neatly. Is there any more? Oh yes..." She should've remembered: Lavinia was a bit of a showman. Of course, she'd have something else up her sleeve.

"This is where it gets fun. Now, France seems to be a black hole, as far as this story goes. At the start, we have five women, one of whom may have been Rebecca."

"She knew Marius Cadieux," said Wren. "She knew him from before the war. I know it's still an 'if,' but I could see her volunteering if they wanted to get Cadieux out of France. They had a relationship—"

"Ah, but what kind of relationship," said Lavinia. "Wouldn't that be some kind of Hallmark Channel story: heroic American woman rescues her French lover from Nazi clutches."

"We just don't know," said Wren.

"Oh, but I've got the whole scenario," said Hadley. "They meet before the war. They fall in love, but Rebecca must be loyal to her husband, Dennis. They separate. And then she has a chance to save him."

"Sweetie, that's lovely," said Lavinia. "But it's also the plot of 'Casablanca.' Now, as I said, we don't know what happened. Let's say the heroic Rebecca saves Cadieux in France. We don't have any additional details right now. We do know that at one point, Cadieux made it to England and then America.

CHAPTER TWENTY

And that's it." Lavinia gave a dramatic pause. "Except for one note. A letter, a confidential memo, from the OSS case officer in New York to his boss in D.C. Now, these items should've been destroyed. But someone found this funny, I'm guessing, and it was saved in someone's desk. Eventually, it was scanned with a pile of other miscellaneous papers from the war. No names mentioned, for safety. Standard protocol, I imagine. I'll do the honors." She pulled a folded page from her notebook and read.

> C and the lady landed fine. Getting the details and will forward by usual courier. Got two rooms in hotel, but I don't know why. The lady's got a husband and daughter (I thought they were all supposed to be single!), and we let them board. We all found C and the lady curled up in the back. For warmth, they said. Red faces all around, but everyone happy. Lady awaiting new assignment. C passed to the colonel.

"So ladies, what do we think now?" asked Lavinia.

Wren had nothing to immediately say. Hadley eventually started to snicker. "It's kind of funny, actually," she said. "Getting some action in a World War II transport plane."

"Let's be fair," said Wren. "That was a long, and no doubt uncomfortable, flight with two tired people, who were already friends. So they 'crashed' together."

"Wren—I know you don't want to believe Cadieux would do that—" started Hadley.

"Oh, come on. Remember college," said Wren. "You finish studying, hanging out together, you have a couple of beers, and then you all half fall asleep together. Maybe that's what this was." She looked at Hadley and Lavinia for support. "Stress and relief, that's all."

"You know," said Hadley, "you keep saying you don't understand people, but as I've said, maybe you're better than you think."

"I'm thinking of a cramped airplane," said Wren.

"I think," said Lavinia, "that we have more pressing issues to discuss other than whether Marius Cadieux got to second base with Rebecca Blaine—"

"Please, professor—not in front of Wren," said Hadley.

"Very funny," said Wren.

"As I was saying," said Lavinia. "If we can get our minds out of the gutter, the issue is that this unnamed lady was an unusual wife and mother in this position. So it's probably fair to say she was, indeed, Rebecca. And that means Dennis saw his wife curled up with Marius Cadieux when they entered the plane after it landed."

"Even more important," said Wren, "so did a seven-year-old Shoshana."

* * *

Hadley had mentioned a French restaurant she wanted to try, which Wren had said was appropriate, considering the story. She said lunch would be courtesy of Fontaine Partners. They discussed the case over Coquilles Saint-Jacques, which Hadley pronounced "inspired."

"Thank you," said Lavinia. "And speaking of Fontaine Partners, how did the senior partner, AKA your father, take the news about his daughter's late-night interrogation by the CIA? Angela and I have a bet on it. I said the cool and aloof Ezra Fontaine would instantly break down and insist on calling lawyers and staging guards on the worksite. He may have won a Pulitzer for sarcasm, but when it comes to his little girl…"

"All right," said Wren. "You win the bet. Yes, I may be his little girl, but he does not like anyone interfering with the firm. Not difficult clients and not government agencies, not even the FBI or the CIA. I managed to hold him off on making a big deal about it, and he agreed no lawyers."

"Really? Not up to pushing back?" challenged Lavinia.

"Not that. I just think we're on the right track, and I don't want lawyers to derail it."

"And what track is that?" asked Lavinia.

"This has finally given me a solid connection between Rebecca and Cadieux. I can't say I know what their relationship truly was. I don't think we'll ever know. But at least I've found a significant, perhaps *the* significant,

CHAPTER TWENTY

event in their lives that bonded them. She risked everything to save him, left husband and daughter to slip into occupied France to save Marius Cadieux. And he built that house to thank her."

"And do you think Dennis liked living in the house Cadieux built for her a few years after he found them wrapped up in the back of an army transport plane?" asked Hadley.

"All right," said Wren. "That's a case for why Dennis might shoot Cadieux, but that's not what happened. Someone shot Dennis. There are still pieces missing—"

"But don't you now have what you need to fully understand the house?" asked Lavinia.

"Why was Dennis killed?" asked Wren.

"Ah—you want the whole deal," said Lavinia.

"Yes. And then there are the practical situations—two people killed on my worksite. There's a sense of incompleteness here..." Wren frowned. "Dennis. We keep forgetting about him, right?"

"You said *why*," said Lavinia. "*Why* Dennis died."

"I think even if I knew who killed him, it wouldn't mean much if I didn't know why. You know who we need to bring in? Erik."

Erik Leopold was one of the foremost pathologists in the country, a frequent consultant on major cases. Wren had met him because he was a member of the 19th-century cosplay club she and Lavinia belonged to. His specialty was well-heeled gentlemen out of Dickens.

"Ah—a fresh look at Dennis," said Hadley. "Are you going to dig him up after all this time? Wouldn't you need someone's permission?"

"Shoshana is the next of kin," said Lavinia. "I don't see how you'd approach her about this. I don't see her agreeing to a disinterment."

"That may not be necessary," said Wren. "There would've been a report at the time—this was a murder, after all. But we're talking about powerful, rich people. Maybe Erik could find—I don't know—an anomaly of some kind. The conclusion was murder by person or persons unknown. Maybe there was a fact someone ignored or misinterpreted."

"A longshot," said Lavinia. "But if he can help, I could see that providing an answer. Not just who, but why the change was made."

"And then there's Shoshana," said Wren. "God, I don't want to face her again, but I'm going to have to. I can't say she's guilty of anything, but she's tough and wily, and getting something out of her isn't going to be easy. But she knows something. She knows a lot."

"I have a feeling she's a master liar," said Hadley. "People like that lie so much they even forget what the truth is. They've started to lie to themselves. Look, I was an addict. I was a *spectacular* liar."

Wren gave Hadley a squeeze around her shoulders. "I don't entirely know what her game is, but her love of Cadieux was a driving force. That's going to color everything. It's funny, though. Born in the house, grew up there—but now doesn't want anything to do with it. Even pushed to sell it. But I'm going to need all the information I have to get it out of her. I wonder…I hope I can tempt her to come back to Cadieux House."

"But isn't that giving Shoshana the home-field advantage?" asked Lavinia.

"It was once hers," said Wren. "But that was nearly seventy years ago. Now—now it's mine."

They finished lunch. As Lavinia got back into her car, Wren said, "You said you and Angela bet on how my father would react. What did Angela bet?"

"Oh, she bet you wouldn't tell him at all. But I know my Wren. You'd hate to do it, but you're no shirker. You never were. Thanks, dear. Keep me posted."

Chapter Twenty-One

Wren called Erik Leopold when she got back to Cadieux House.

"My dear Wren! So good to hear from you. I'll see you and Hadley next month, of course. I can't wait to see what costumes you're coming up with."

"I'll give you a hint. Hadley has always had a Gothic bent, so we're doing something from the Castle of Otranto."

"That book invented Gothic literature. I can't wait. I'll be taking a page out of 'A Tale of Two Cities.' So, what can I help you with? I've heard what was happening at Cadieux House. With apologies to your father, modernism was never my thing—or yours either—but good luck. I wasn't called in on those deaths, but they sound pretty straightforward."

"Right house, wrong people," said Wren. "I'm going back a few years to the first Cadieux House murder, Dennis Blaine, the original owner with his wife Rebecca. He was killed by a single gunshot in 1955."

"Yes, I remember that, well before my time, of course, but it got a lot of attention because it was never solved. I read about it. You want me to look into that? Dear lord. Even if we were able to get the body disinterred, it's just bones now."

"That wouldn't be a problem for you," said Wren. "You've worked miracles on old cases just by looking at a skeleton."

"Oh, I just love it when young women flatter me. It's becoming a rarer situation every year, unfortunately. Yes, there's a lot you can tell from a skeleton, but from what I remember about that, it was pretty straightforward, a single gunshot at close range."

"Actually, I'm thinking that because it was a murder, there must've been an extensive autopsy, a detailed investigation. Could you find it? Could you have a look at it? Maybe there was something wrong there?"

"Oh, wow, Wren. What the hell is going on?"

"You know me and old houses. There is something dark there, like there is with many old homes. And it starts with Dennis Blaine's murder."

"Do I want to know the details? Or am I better off not," he said.

"I can tell you that I have Lavinia heavily involved in this."

"Oh my. A full-court press. Well, if you roped in Lavinia, I have to do my part. Dennis Blaine, 1955. It'll have to be back-channel, but I know a lot of people. Just a quiet look, something I need, just for background, of course, for a paper I'm writing. Give me a few days, and I'll get back to you. But everything may be in perfect order. I can't promise to pull a rabbit out of my hat."

"I have complete faith in you," said Wren.

"There it is again, a young woman flattering me. All right, I'll get on it. I'll start making some phone calls, and I'll let you know. As a payment, can you get me a tour someday? As I said, modernism is not my thing, but now I'm curious."

"I'm sure there will be an opening reception, and I'll get you on the list. Thank you!"

Wren clicked off. She was hoping that he'd be able to find something. She'd need every lever possible. Shoshana would know what happened.

Meanwhile, Wren had fresh ideas for Bronwyn's writing cabin. Wren knew there was love there now. But there was something more, of course, and she needed it all. She looked at her initial designs for the ADU. Was it up to Cadieux's level? Would he approve of what she had done? Bronwyn had said she liked how bright Cadieux House was but said she needed more privacy. That was interesting—Cadieux didn't need to provide a deep level of privacy, but he had been clever about it. Maybe Rebecca didn't need deep privacy. Wren thought with some amusement about Rebecca and Cadieux cuddled in the back of an army transport plane.

But Bronwyn wasn't Rebecca—even though she had been carrying on

CHAPTER TWENTY-ONE

her own secret romance with her bodyguard. What did Bronwyn want—a refuge? Was that the right word? Is that what Rebecca had wanted, a refuge from the world, from the danger she had endured as an OSS agent? But on the other hand, it was a little too open to be properly called a refuge. Had Rebecca's life overseas been a little too claustrophobic? Was that what it was about?

Or was she being naïve? Were they having an illicit relationship after all?

There was a way of fixing the ADU, some windows up high, bright and open but still private. She was still unhappy with the Murphy bed solution. Would Bronwyn accept a quick loft at the top, a neat little staircase? Bronwyn might not like that for the long term. A cunning spiral staircase wasn't practical once the knees started to go.

But a few changes, and she could have a sleep nook, all on one floor, while keeping the main writing area clean. It may not be what Bronwyn demanded, but it's what she wanted. It's what her father would do, smoothly guiding his clients away from their own worst instincts. She could do it, too.

Did Cadieux have to do that? From all Wren knew about him, he would have no problem. His smooth and charming demeanor, that sophisticated French accent, his movie-star face.

The little girl with the Lego house hoped for his approval twenty years later.

***

Two days later, Erik Leopold called her in the evening at home and asked if Wren could meet him at his office.

"I'm happy to, but I don't want to put you out. If you've found something, you can tell me on the phone or send me an email." She felt almost giddy—if there wasn't anything, Erik could've just said, "Sorry, everything is squeaky clean. Better luck next time, and see you at next month's party." He must have discovered something.

"Let's just say there are some things I don't want to put down on paper. Or even on the phone. I don't know what you've landed in, but there is something here rather serious, I should say. I'm only going to discuss this in person. We're going to have to be quiet about it."

"Ohh...I hope I didn't cause you a problem?" asked Wren.

"This is going to cause *someone* a problem," said Erik. "Eight tomorrow morning? It's nice and quiet here."

"I'll be there."

"It sounds like Erik has come through," said Hadley.

"Maybe more than expected. This is a man who has seen a lot, been called in for all kinds of major crimes, and yet he sounded almost spooked—about a murder decades ago."

"So since he didn't have a body, I'm guessing he found something in the file, something that would collect dust in a government building basement. Who would do this?"

"And why," added Wren.

They went to bed early, but Wren had trouble falling asleep. Had she started too many things—a World War II covert operation and a con job in the medical examiner's office?

Excited about what Erik might have for her, Wren woke up early and slipped quietly out of bed. She let Hadley sleep—her chef girlfriend was more of a night owl and had a big event to handle that night. Coffee, orange juice, and French bread with hummus, and she was on her way to Erik's midtown office. She was early, there by 7:45, but Erik had already arrived.

He had always chosen well for their costume evenings; his tall, portly frame was perfect for well-heeled Victorian gentlemen. He usually looked cheerful, and a sunny disposition over even the most ghastly deaths made him something of a law enforcement legend. But this morning, he was frowning as he let her into the suite. His office was a monument to the Victorian era he so loved, the heavy wooden furniture and some 19th century prints Wren could tell were valuable. He even had leather-bound 19th-century medical tomes on his shelf.

Erik sat behind his desk, and Wren took one of the visitor's chairs, walnut and green leather.

"You've given me something new, Wren, and at this point in my career,

CHAPTER TWENTY-ONE

that doesn't happen very often. I managed to dig up the report—friends and friends of friends. Understand that this is very under-the-radar. We can't do anything with this. Officially, it's still sitting in the basement of some county building—and I have to return it fairly soon. But I did get the M.E. report and much of the police report, too." He pointed to a pile on his desk. Wren wanted to rush him to the conclusion, but Erik was very methodical, and Wren, who worked the same way, appreciated that.

"As you probably already know, a waiter who worked at Cadieux House parties was arrested for killing Dennis Blaine. Now, I'm not a cop, but I can read the reports. A handgun was found next to Dennis—it was Dennis's gun, and it was covered with Dennis' fingerprints. No surprise there, as he had a firing range on the property. There were no other fingerprints. The waiter was said to have shot him and dropped it there so they wouldn't find it on him. No indications he fired it, however. He had been dismissed earlier for stealing, but apparently sneaked back unseen, grabbed Dennis's gun, shot him, and slipped out again."

"That doesn't sound very likely," said Wren.

"It's unheard of. No witnesses, and no forensic evidence, even by 1955 standards. He supposedly came back, bent on revenge, and went to the trouble of getting Dennis's gun from a hidden place in the bedroom? If the poor guy hadn't been killed in jail, the whole thing would've been thrown out. The police had to arrest someone, I imagine, for something this big, but it was for show to quiet the family while they looked for the real culprit. There wasn't enough here to even go to trial, let alone achieve a conviction."

"The family," said Wren. "Are you saying they pushed for an arrest of someone, anyone, as part of a cover-up?"

"Wren, the fact that they arrested someone whom it would be impossible to convict is nowhere close to the interesting part of this. I wish I could put this into my memoirs." Wren almost stopped breathing. Erik had never been this emphatic before. He picked a bound report from the pile. "The investigation at that time concluded someone shot Dennis at point-blank range—just an inch or two from his body."

"Wait," said Wren. "You said no fingerprints from the waiter. But it had

Dennis's fingerprints. He couldn't have wiped his own fingerprints off and left Dennis's." Erik flashed her his usual grin and slammed his hand on his desk.

"Very good! That would've been impossible. I want to see if you can uncover what the authorities missed in 1955. Missed or covered up. Keep going."

"He could've had gloves," said Wren. "Did the waiters have gloves?"

"Good, good! They looked for gloves—but this was the 1950s, not the 1850s. The waiters wore white dinner jackets—but no gloves. The police checked. Of course, he could've brought gloves with him."

"That makes no sense," said Wren. "He had to scrounge for a gun but remembered to bring gloves to protect his identity? Okay, so it wasn't the waiter."

"So if it wasn't the waiter, then who?" asked Wren. "After all that, did Marius Cadieux kill him? No—Rebecca. It was a formal party in 1955. She'd be wearing white gloves. It would be among a lot of people, but she just had to get him alone for a few minutes; easy for a wife to do, especially for a trained OSS agent. So Rebecca killed her husband? Is that what you found out?" She looked at him. He was still smiling.

"You don't want it to be Rebecca, do you?"

"I may not be a forensics expert," said Wren, feeling defensive. "But I can't find a motive. It wasn't money. It wasn't…I guess you could say, 'respectability.' But if she wanted another man, I don't think she'd kill to avoid a divorce. Or do I have the wrong end of it. There were other ladies there—the young Shoshana…?" But would she have killed her own father? That seemed impossible…

Erik was still smiling. "Wren, in a couple of minutes, you got further than the Long Island cops did, who were happy to send the waiter to Sing Sing. It's that logical architect mind you have. But as you said, you're not a forensic expert. I kept going back and forth between thinking they were criminal or merely incompetent., I don't like either option. However, I'm thinking it's 1955, and you're dealing with some wealthy and powerful people. Maybe they thought it was Rebecca and didn't want to stick their necks out. Who

CHAPTER TWENTY-ONE

knows after all this time? But I'll tell you this. There was a very good reason: only Dennis Blaine's fingerprints were on that gun. He was the only one who used it."

"Oh, you don't mean…"

"Yes, I do. It was a suicide. I've seen enough of them. In the U.S., about half of all suicides are with a firearm. Usually, they're in the head, but it's not unheard of to shoot oneself in the chest. I'm not a psychologist, but I understand Dennis was handsome. Maybe he wanted to leave a good-looking corpse. But it isn't easy to hold a handgun to shoot yourself in the chest. The angle is awkward, and the bullet trajectory is distinctive. Even the way the gun falls after a suicide is clear. Apparently, no one disturbed the body or the gun, and we have photos that show the gun is where it should be if he dropped it after shooting himself. They collected all the crime scene and ballistic details, but never drew the conclusions. Dennis Blaine committed suicide. And that's what I meant when I said you showed me something new. I've seen plenty of murders designed to look like suicides. But, a suicide assumed to be murder? That's almost unheard of."

"Oh, but we have heard of it," said Wren. "Sherlock Holmes, 'The Problem of Thor Bridge.' A suicide set up to look like murder."

"Yes, of course!" said Erik. "And it's believed Conan Doyle based it on an actual case. But that was deliberate—she committed suicide with the intent of framing an innocent person for her murder. Do you think Dennis did that?"

"I'm still trying to get used to the idea that he killed himself," said Wren. "That changes everything. No one has told me or even speculated that's what happened. But the question remains: Was Rebecca having an affair, and is that why he killed himself?"

"A broken heart is a hell of a reason for suicide. We're not talking about a moody teenager here," said Erik.

"And we still don't know if they were having an affair. Oh, I'm not talking about some lingering kisses after too much champagne," said Wren, "but a full-blown affair? After his death, Rebecca and Shoshana moved to California. Cadieux went back and forth between New York and Paris for the rest of his life. My father said they kept in touch, but they were never a couple. If they spent time together, it was brief, and the newspapers would've brought up the story again if they had become a couple. I can't figure it out."

"And you need to figure it out because…"

"Because I think Cadieux knew, and I want to know everything about him to figure out that house of his. But you said that this would be a problem for someone—surely the investigators are all gone now. That was nearly seventy years ago."

"You're right. But let's say someone did know, and they passed it down. A lawyer knew, a doctor knew, and it was passed down. A memo remains. These things happen." Yes, like a couple cuddling in the back of a military transport. "Someone may know. And they won't want anyone else to. Be careful, Wren. I can be fairly certain no one will find out that I saw these documents, because no one will want to admit they gave them to me. But if someone finds out, they could be unhappy. Lavinia would hand my head to me if anything happened to you because of something I did," he said.

"And she'd get away with it, because you wouldn't be around to solve your own murder," said Wren, and Erik laughed.

"One more thing, on a different subject," said Wren. "DNA tests. Can you get them from a corpse?"

"We have a lot of cheery questions today, don't we?"

"You are hardly in a cheery profession," said Wren. Erik nodded.

"Fair enough. In general, you should get it quickly. All kinds of things can degrade it. Is this more Cadieux House investigations?"

"I was thinking about comparing a recently deceased person, but it's probably too late. Tristan Archer, the lawyer who was murdered."

"Was there some confusion about who he was?"

"No. But about DNA tests, it doesn't have to be direct, does it? That is, you can compare siblings, cousins, nieces and nephews, right?"

"Yes…" said Erik cautiously. "It depends, what exactly you're trying to show. Wren, what is this about—"

She sighed. "I guess it doesn't matter, if someone has been dead for a while."

CHAPTER TWENTY-ONE

"Not unless, for some reason, he already had a DNA test filed somewhere. But that isn't common, unless he did one of those commercial tests. The military has been keeping track for years."

"Really?" said Wren. "The army has a database of anyone who served?"

"Yes, since the early 1990s. It's called the Armed Forces Repository of Specimen Samples for the Identification of Remains—AFRSSIR. The idea is to make sure there are no more unknown soldiers. But it's strictly confidential. Wren, where are we going with this?"

"If you had it, you could compare it with someone living who'd happily give."

"That's a pretty big 'if' Wren. So okay, yes, *provisionally* yes. But my dear, it's one thing to pull a few strings for an ancient case cataloged in a small-town municipal building and quite another to pull a fast one with the Department of Defense."

"But if the next of kin were okay with it? Maybe you could offer your services to the case pro bono, to help out. That would give you nexus, as they say?"

"What case? The Tristan Archer death, or the Karen Weston death? They were both pretty clear-cut."

"No. The Dennis Blaine death."

"Which we just decided was a suicide. So, I'll offer my services to settle a non-murder to get the DNA of Tristan Archer, who wasn't even born when Dennis was killed. Do I have that correct?"

"My father has upbraided me in the past for posing difficulties in a negative light. He says it makes a bad impression on clients." She watched him carefully. If she could pull this off—it was beginning to come together.

Erik sighed. "No promises. But get me the name of Tristan's next of kin and I'll see what I can do."

"You're the best," said Wren. "You have no idea what this means."

"You're going to solve some murders?"

"That may happen. But I'm very close to deciphering the finest modernist home ever."

She said her goodbyes, and outside, realized that she was forgetting to breathe. She took in gasps of air and felt lightheaded. She couldn't believe what she was doing. Only her desire for the house gave her the courage.

Wren knew she had to find a quiet place to make three phone calls while she still had the courage. Still high from her meeting with Erik, she felt somewhat confident, but knew it wouldn't last. She walked down to Bryant Park and found a bench.

First, Rafe Rodriguez. She thought he'd agree, but without his buy-in, nothing would work. She gave her name to the Balmoral Club secretary and was soon on the phone with him.

"Wren! Good hearing from you. I just want to say sorry for how emotional I was. You were very kind."

"It's I who should apologize. I sprang this all on you. I tend to focus on houses, not people, and that becomes a problem sometimes."

"Well, all-in-all, I'm glad I visited. Anyway, what can I do for you?"

"I think I can help with some family issues, and you might welcome that. I just need a little help from you."

Rafe was a little bewildered, but when he said he'd be happy to help, she felt the tension quickly drain away.

"You'll share the results?" he asked.

"Absolutely." But she felt she had to be completely transparent. "I can't promise you'll like what we find."

"That's very fair of you to say, but anything, good or bad, will be welcome."

Okay, next Gareth Archer. He also answered quickly.

"Wren, a pleasure. Is this professional? Your firm is now going to design log cabins?"

"Not a bad idea," said Wren, wondering what her father would say about that. Probably turn it over to her. "But in my research for the house, I came across some unusual connections. They will help not only with your house, but with who killed your father. I can't promise anything, but there are some records I'll need that may be hard to get. Maybe even impossible. Your permission may make it easier."

"Ha! What kind of records? When you say 'records' to lawyers, they think police records. I had a run-in with local cops while in college, but other than

CHAPTER TWENTY-ONE

that, I've been a good boy."

"Nothing like that," said Wren, trying to match his light tone. "As an architect specializing in historic homes, I'm also a bit of a historian, and I have an interest, or hobby, you could say, in genealogy. I thought you might too..."

Being a lawyer, he was more cautious than Rafe.

"What exactly are you trying to prove?" he asked.

"I will assure you that it has nothing to do with anything your father did. But there are questions. It's about the house. Your father and grandfather thought it was important. I am hoping you might, too."

"Jesus, Wren, you're asking a lot. I don't even know it's possible. You can't tell me more?"

"Other people are involved. But everyone involved will get the details when the results are ready. If I'm wrong, no harm. But I'm not. And you're a lawyer. You should want the truth." She heard nothing on the phone for a few moments.

"All right. This is very strange, and normally I'd say no, but I was impressed by you, Wren. I trust you. If there's anything I can do to grease the skids, that doesn't involve outright bribery, okay. The family, our name, still has connections, so let me know. And good luck."

All right. Two down. It might work. Now came the hardest of all—Shoshana. Wren didn't need her permission for anything, but it would be easier for her if she cooperated. Should she wait until she got to the house? Would she feel more in tune, calling Shoshana from the house built for her mother? *You're looking for an excuse to procrastinate.*

She called her and got Millie, the *factotum*.

"Hello. This is Wren Fontaine, the architect restoring Ms. Blaine's old home, Cadieux House."

"Oh yes, I remember you. And so does Shoshana. You got her very...you put her in a spirited mood."

"I don't think she's been in that house since she was a young woman. It may have stirred up old memories."

"You might be right. So you want to speak with her?" She made it sound like a challenge.

"If she's available."

"When is she not? I'll get her."

Oh my.

"Wren? Need some insights into the house, like where we kept the canned goods in the pantry?"

"I wouldn't have thought you would know that," said Wren.

"Good one! In truth, I barely know how a stove works, but I liked eating there back then. I don't even go into the kitchen here, however. So what do you want now?"

"I know we had some, I guess you could say, different views about how we look at the house and the history of the people who lived there. But I think we both love the house and at the end of the day, we'd want what is best for it. So, to get going on the right foot, I'd like to invite you to visit Cadieux House." She forced herself to make it as simple as possible. She had been there before, inviting clients and prospects to visit various homes to help her plan the renovations. Her father invited them to see modern houses. Business as usual.

"Excuse me," said Shoshana.

"I'll be honest," said Wren, thinking humble might work with Shoshana. "It's a bit of a challenge working on this house. I'm used to old homes, but Cadieux House is in a class by itself. You're the only one left who has actually lived in it. You would be of enormous help to me—and ultimately to Bronwyn—if you would help me by coming for a visit. Your reactions and thoughts would guide me." Bronwyn had said she was working with Shoshana, even if that was secret. Maybe she'd do that to oblige a business partner.

What would her father do now? She had seen him show a starting design to a client who might find it a little too outré for them. But of course, Ezra Fontaine knew best. He always knew best. "I understand," he'd say with a smile. "No need to apologize. Not everyone can appreciate a modern idea like this. It's no bother, I'll pull together something, a little more *old fashioned* for you."

CHAPTER TWENTY-ONE

The wealthy people who could afford Ezra Fontaine occasionally might accept that they're traditional, but never "old fashioned." They would take a second look at the plans. "You know, Ezra, giving it another thought, I find it growing on me. I think we can go with it…"

"As you know, Wren, my last days there were tragic. My father died violently. My mother and I left shortly thereafter."

"I understand," said Wren. "And I apologize for putting you in an awkward position. I should've considered that your great age and infirmity meant such a visit would be…unwise. I won't bother you again." She waited a moment, and Shoshana responded, strong and clipped.

"It is not my age or infirmities that prevent a visit. I choose not to visit a place of such unhappiness."

"But there must've been happiness, too, in a house of such magnificence."

"You seem a lot more focused on the house than on the people who lived there," said Shoshana.

"My father has frequently criticized me for that. I'm trying to improve." Wren was amused to hear Shoshana laugh.

"Tell me why, Wren. Tell me what you'll get out of my visit to Cadieux House."

"Your memories, thoughts, and insights into the people who lived in that house and reacted to its extraordinary design. I wouldn't ask this normally, but this is not an ordinary house. People reacted to it in singular ways, I'm sure. So, with all due respect, you're wrong about me. I am trying to change. I badly want to know about how the people lived in the house. You're the only one who can help me." *A challenge, with a humility chaser.*

"I will give you back to Millie. She is in charge of my schedule. I have always detested loud noises so I expect your work crew will be on a break when I arrive. Good day, Wren."

A few moments later, Millie came back on the line.

"I'm afraid of making your life difficult," said Wren.

"Driving any distance with Shoshana can be difficult."

"I can imagine. I know the elderly often get anxious driving faster than fifty."

"No, Shoshana gets anxious if I drive under eighty. We can do the day after tomorrow. How about eleven, so we can miss the rush hour traffic? To be honest, I'm a little curious myself."

Wren ended the third call and found herself deep in a funk. Three tense phone calls in a row, thoughts flying in a dozen directions. If she was wrong, it would be embarrassing. But she wasn't wrong. She knew, and nothing was going to be the same ever again. It wasn't about people, after all. Once again, it came back to the house. Even with all these people, it came back to the house. And to Marius Cadieux.

"Excuse me, miss, are you okay?" Two beat cops were looking at her. They appeared concerned. No…amused.

"I am sorry…just lost in thought…about a business deal."

"It's a little quiet here, miss. You might be a little safer thinking about business in your office."

Her office, in a seventy-year-old crime scene.

"Thank you," she said and, without looking back, walked toward the avenue.

Chapter Twenty-Two

That night was a business meeting with the managing partner—her father. Family events including Hadley were typically held at their apartment. Business events were at her father's favorite steakhouse, with just the two of them.

"On schedule? On budget?" he asked.

"Schedule, yes. Budget—well, Bronwyn can always write more checks." His fork came down on his plate.

"I assume that's your attempt at humor. No one is more tightfisted than a rich person."

"Oh, Father, you know I'm far too OCD to be late or overpriced. We're well within the estimate. Although Bobby and I continue to uncover surprises. Marius Cadieux was not predictable."

"No, he wasn't. You're getting a lesson. Meanwhile, no more trouble from the FBI, CIA et al? One more visit and we're calling the lawyers."

"No. I think it was just that we touched a nerve. Rebecca did some kind of war work during World War II, and maybe we triggered something."

"After all this time?"

"Who knows? Someone is paranoid. Anyway, we're done with the research, so we should be okay."

"Just a lot of oddities. Murders—and still no arrest. And then the CIA."

"It made me think about Cadieux, though. Now, he got out of France by the skin of his teeth, I've heard. But I never learned the details."

"You think the CIA was concerned about an architect who escaped from the Nazis eighty years ago?"

"It doesn't make sense, I know. But aside from that, I want to know about the house, and I can't do that until I know more about Cadieux. And no one alive knew him better than you."

"Nicely said. You're trying to flatter me into revealing secrets about my mentor. And you say you're not good with people."

"All right, I was transparent."

"That's okay. I like to be flattered." Wren laughed. All right, he was in a good mood. Porterhouse and baked potato tended to do that. "Yes, I knew him very well, and he was actually not a private man. He liked telling stories, and next to his houses, he was his own favorite subject. Which made it all the odder that his escape from France was off-limits. He always slid over it, said it was secret, gave a wink, and was off and running on another amusing anecdote. Now tell me, what is this all about? This isn't just idle curiosity." He knew her too well. There would be no manipulating her father.

"I convinced Shoshana Blaine to visit later this week. She wasn't happy about it. I basically challenged her. She's the last person alive who lived there, and I want to hear about how people lived in the house."

"All right," said Ezra cautiously. "This wouldn't have anything to do with Marius Cadieux being there the night Shoshana's father was killed? Is that why you want to know about him?" He drank some wine, but his eye never left her.

"When have I been interested in parties?"

"Don't answer a question with a question. Rebecca and Cadieux were close. He was the most important mentor I ever had. The most important mentor any architect ever had. I flatter myself that he was my friend. I won't see him embarrassed."

"Embarrassed how? Every building he built was a masterpiece. His personal life was…imperfect."

"Wren. I won't see my friend humiliated. What have you been doing? You and your partner-in-crime, Lavinia. There's nothing she can't research. Are you saying Cadieux was involved in the Dennis Blaine murder?"

Wren forced her voice to remain even and fought down her fear. She was not a child. And she knew things her father did not.

CHAPTER TWENTY-TWO

"You once told me it was impossible to separate any great architect from his work. And you also told me there was no calculating the number of women he took to bed. What does that tell you about that odd and twisty house I'm trying to put back together?"

"You're in charge of the project. The real question is what it tells you."

"You just told me not to answer a question with a question."

"I get a pass because I'm the senior partner." She should've known he would make this as difficult as possible.

"Do you remember his memorial service in New York?" she asked.

"I spoke at it. You were there."

"So was Mom. I was eighteen. She was already showing signs of her illness. After the service, you were gathered, all of you, the friends and acolytes of Marius Cadieux. I asked Mom if she didn't want to join the group. She said she had only come to watch you speak, that she had no interest in Marius Cadieux. Then and there, she told me about the first time she had met him, in Paris, shortly after you and Mom were married. She told me the four of you went out to dinner. You, Mom, Cadieux, and his—girlfriend? Mistress? Cadieux was about fifty years older than you, and his girlfriend was younger than Mom. She said she couldn't square the man who had designed buildings of such magnificence with a personality that required the adulation from a girl barely old enough to drink. I can't either."

She wondered if he had heard her. He had more steak, more potato with sour cream and chives, more burgundy.

"Your mother was old-fashioned. You are, too."

"Don't slander Mom. She was not a puritan. It wasn't the fact that he liked keeping company with young women. I know that's a big trend in the heterosexual world." Ezra laughed. "It was that a man of such accomplishment and brilliance felt a need to keep company with a giggling schoolgirl. It wasn't even about the sex, Mom said. It was about a girl who would worship him unconditionally. That's what bothered her about him. It made her think less of him."

Ezra nodded. "And what about you?"

"I agree with her."

"Your mother had an unparalleled shrewdness about people, but she wasn't an architect. You want to know what Cadieux's behavior says about him as an architect? I'll tell you. He poured everything he was into the buildings he designed. I knew him, and I knew his buildings, and that's what I'm telling you. No architect has ever done that, nowhere near to that extent."

"That is very helpful," said Wren. "So if his personality was that flawed—and it was, very deeply—that would lead to flaws in the house. Which I've found. Cadieux's failures are the home's flaws."

"Nicely reasoned. You say you found flaws—or, I should say, what you *think* are flaws—" Now, Wren laughed. "And you have been fixing them. I think it is very likely that what you don't like in the house dovetails with the parts of Marius you don't like. But can you match them? You have a perfect eye for houses. For people—" he smiled wryly—"less so."

"Fair enough. But I can make up for it. I am looking at Cadieux more clearly than you. And I am looking at the Blaines more clearly than Cadieux did."

"I might give you the first might. I might. But what do you mean about Cadieux?"

"He was too close to his clients."

"There's no such thing as too close to clients. The better you understand them, the better you are able to work with them. The better you are able to realize their needs."

"But that's what led to the flaws. I am going to dare say that Cadieux lost perspective. Oh yes, that house is a masterpiece. But I am sure that Cadieux overdid it. He made it perfect, too perfect, too *personal*. Cadieux knew it himself by the end. I'm sure Rebecca did, too. What's worse is that everyone else figured it out, one way or another, even if they couldn't put it in those terms. That's what led to…everything."

"Wren," he said after a few moments. "I don't know what to say."

"Wow. An Ezra Fontaine first." He didn't smile. Wren cleared her throat and continued. "Talking to you has clarified this for me. I'm hoping Shoshana Blaine will be able to fill in a few blanks for me. Dear father, you're not the only one around who was side-by-side with Marius Cadieux. So was

CHAPTER TWENTY-TWO

Shoshana."

***

Hadley made her herbal tea iced for Wren and told her she had to take them in bottles to the worksite.

"You are wired, Little Bird. You're always wired when in the middle of a big job, but especially so now."

"I'm seeing Shoshana soon. It's funny, really. She has spent the last seventy years away from the house but has never managed to leave it."

"Is that because she's insane? Or because the house is so special?"

"A little of both, actually."

With her iced tea, she drove to Cadieux House. Everything was proceeding well—compared with the 19th century homes she usually worked on, there wasn't much that needed changing. But what needed to be done had to be perfect. She could leave the heating and air conditioning to Bobby, but she personally checked the new doors, the redivisions. She had gone over the proportions a dozen times on screens, but needed to see everything in place to make sure she wasn't changing what made a Cadieux—a Cadieux. What would Shoshana say? Would she even remember?

Wren laughed at herself. She was used to caring about what the client would think, but Bronwyn hadn't shown a great deal of interest in what was happening. She signed off on everything. She liked the idea of the house, but for Bronwyn, it wasn't about owning a Cadieux; it was about the family and the story. It was all going to come together soon. It was the opposite of Shoshana. She was too close to it, which is why she didn't want to come at all.

She hadn't heard from Erik about how the genealogical research was going, but it was early days yet, and she knew he would call when he had something.

"So we're getting Shoshana Blaine tomorrow?" asked Bobby.

"Yes. And her ladyship wants to make sure your people keep the volume low on their machines."

"Of course, of course. Anyway, this is going to be something new. We work on old houses, so we rarely get to meet an original resident. What do you think she'll want to see first."

"I don't know. Maybe her bedroom, where I believe she lost her virginity." Bobby didn't laugh at that. Just nodded.

"Yeah, I could see that."

The next day, Wren dressed more carefully than usual.

"What look are you going for?" asked Hadley.

"Powerful. I was going to go with the grey pantsuit, white blouse, with my mother's cameo at the neck."

"Yes. It has a strong sense of control. But a white blouse is a little too... matronly. Black blouse with a silver necklace." It wasn't her usual look, but Wren admitted it made her look a little edgier than usual. Good.

"You'll be great," said Hadley.

Wren arrived early and kept an ear and eye open for Shoshana, and she was right on time. Maybe Millie had resisted the pressure to drive eighty mph. Millie opened the back door and let her boss out. More bohemian clothing. She had probably been on the cutting edge since they had walked away from the house for the West Coast.

Wren watched her from an upstairs window. Shoshana was no different; she stopped and looked at the façade. Cadieux would've loved that. After all those years, it was still attention-grabbing.

Wren was there to greet them when they rang the bell.

"Shoshana, Millie. I'm so glad you could come. Please come in." Millie was unabashedly curious, but it was a little harder to gauge Shoshana's look. Was she excited about seeing her childhood home? Or was she still worried about old memories? She saw a gentle smile on her face, but Shoshana had a long history of disguise.

"It looks very good—have you fixed it?" she asked.

"It didn't need much work. Your cousin, Woody Blaine, saw to it that a management company took good care of it. But this was a Cadieux building. This house was made to last for a long time."

"I would be happy to take you through the house," said Wren.

"Perhaps..." said Shoshana, with a smile. "Perhaps I should take you

CHAPTER TWENTY-TWO

through the house."

"You remember?"

She didn't answer. Just looked around in wonder.

"I would be happy to have you walk me through it," said Wren. "It's why I have you here."

"Parties," said Shoshana. "My parents loved parties. That's what you want to know, isn't it? How people used this place. I mean, bedrooms are all the same, aren't they? You want to know how people really used this house, don't you?"

Shoshana turned to Millie. "Maybe there is a place you can wait."

"There's food and coffee in the kitchen, right down there. Just tell anyone you're with me."

"Thank you," said Millie. She gave Wren a pitying look and headed off for a well-deserved break. Shoshana waited until she was out of earshot.

"You want to know about that night? I'm not quite senile yet. I have no wish to relive those years and especially that night. But I see what's happening here. With the house open again, there will be a lot of interest. Everyone has a personal interest, a selfish interest, in what happened in Cadieux House. But I've watched you, Wren. You're interested only in this house, and therefore I agreed to come here. So I'm thinking if I told you, you could see how it played out here, you, who knows this house. And that would mean something."

"I appreciate that. I really do. But if there are any legal or estate issues, I have no standing."

"For God's sake, I know that. But you will be interviewed. Maybe you'll write an article about this famous house. And you'll be able to say it all makes sense. You'll be in my corner."

Yes, that's the way it worked in her world. Who was on your side, in your coterie? And Wren was the house expert, worth something.

"Everyone was here," said Shoshana. "It was thirty years after the F. Scott Fitzgerald era, but still as glittering, in its own way."

"Where were you that evening?" asked Wren.

"Where wasn't I? I saw lots of people. Everyone wanted to meet me. We had a band. It was right there. And a dance floor. All the men wanted to dance with me. I was very beautiful. I had a beautiful dress."

"I know about some of the people that were there that night. Marius Cadieux, of course."

"Of course. A chance for a party with pretty girls, where he was able to show off his triumph." Wren had thought she was wistful at first, but not anymore.

"He was close with your mother, I believe."

Not bitter now. Smug. "So everyone said. But as I told you, I was the one he loved. I was the one he gave a child to. His only child. We danced. He was a great dancer. We danced a lot that night."

"There's a beautiful view. You can see the stars at night from here, over the Sound. Did you and Marius go for a walk?"

"That wasn't really Marius' type of activity. Except when he was working, he liked to be with people. He was very extroverted. You aren't, though?"

"No," said Wren. "I prefer small groups of close friends and family."

"That lovely girlfriend of yours. I don't blame you. Would you have liked one of our parties here?"

"Probably not," said Wren. "But Hadley would've. She would've danced with the beautiful people here. She was more like you. I would have been content to be in a corner."

Shoshana laughed. "Oh, I was never content to be in the corner. I liked being the center of attention. You know, everyone said my mother inspired this house. But it was me. For God's sake, Wren, my mother, was nearly fifty when Marius designed this. I was the one who inspired it."

She looked to Wren for confirmation.

"The family lawyer, Percival Archer, was also here."

"Percival," said Shoshana. "Now, if you're looking for my mother's affair, look there. Percival loved my mother. He was around her all evening."

"Were they having an affair?" asked Wren.

"I doubt it. I mean, he cut a good figure, to use an old-fashioned phrase. He wasn't very amusing, though. I think my mother liked having him around. She liked having men fascinated with her. I guess it was becoming even more important to her as she aged."

Wren paused to contemplate the cruelty of that comment.

"My mother was beautiful," said Wren. "I always thought she was beautiful."

"Did she like it when men were attracted to her?"

"Just my father."

"But what about when she was younger? When she was in college?"

"I think she was popular," said Wren, dreading what was coming.

"But you weren't?" Wren didn't say anything. Shoshana slipped her arm through Wren's. But it didn't make Wren feel warm. It made her feel trapped. "Come on, Wren, just us girls. You can't expect me to give you the story of my life without getting the story of yours." Shoshana would give her what she wanted to know, but she'd make her pay for it. Anything for a chance to brag about her mother, about herself.

"I was quieter," said Wren. "If we're using old-fashioned phrases, you could say I kept myself to myself."

"Because of who you were?"

"Of course," said Wren. "What other possible reason could there be?"

Shoshana just stared at her. "Are you fencing with me? Or is it actually possible you don't know what I'm talking about?"

Wren tried not to blink. Shoshana moved on. She'd share the story but would make sure just how impressed Wren was with her family. With her.

"Where were you? I am sure you saw everyone, but probably spent most of the event with Marius Cadieux. After all, he was your…" Wren stopped. "Boyfriend" seemed ludicrous in the situation.

"Lover," said Shoshana. "The word you are looking for is 'lover.' And yes, I spent a lot of time with him that evening."

"What did your parents think? He was probably more than twenty years older than you. And you were only about twenty yourself."

Shoshana smiled smugly again. "My father never cared about things like that. As for my mother—she was jealous of me. She wanted him for herself. But he made this house for me. We would've stayed if my father hadn't been killed here. We moved to California. By the time my mother died, it was no longer practical to move back here."

"Come with me, please," said Wren, forcing her voice to remain steady. "I want to see your parents' bedroom with you." Shoshana raised an eyebrow but followed Wren. For someone that old, she still walked steadily, if a bit slowly.

"You're adding a door here," said Shoshana.

"Bronwyn wants more privacy than your parents apparently did."

"My mother liked a sense of openness."

"She suffered from claustrophobia?"

"I wouldn't go that far. In fact, I wouldn't say my mother *suffered* from anything." She laughed at her own wit. "But she liked openness. As I got older, I realized the importance of the windows, those grand vistas."

Wren nodded. "I can understand that. Cadieux was especially good at that. He even made bedrooms large, with great views."

"What do you mean by 'even?'" asked Shoshana.

"Big bedrooms are essential for the wealthy now, but that's a fairly recent development. They were seen as just a place for sleeping. But Cadieux felt differently. He saw them as a place to live, not just sleep."

"Well, considering his reputation, that isn't surprising," said Shoshana. "What do you think, Wren? Do you judge a man for his reputation?"

"I judge architects by the work, not their personal behavior."

"Good girl. So you don't think less of a man in his forties seducing a woman barely out of her teens?"

"I always assumed that you seduced him," said Wren, and was pleased to see Shoshana discomforted by that. *Is she trying to figure out if she was flattered or insulted?* Wren didn't know herself.

"I'll lay my cards on the table, Wren. You're not a celebrity watcher. You're not an idle gossip. You only care about Cadieux for his house and only tolerate me for what I can tell you. You don't even like this discussion. I wanted to see that. I wanted to see what you really wanted."

"I want to understand this house," said Wren. "And I can't understand that without understanding Cadieux. And I don't think I can do that without understanding your part."

Now, she definitely liked that! Shoshana bestowed a smile on Wren. "What

CHAPTER TWENTY-TWO

an unusual young woman you are."

"He was killed here. Your father," said Wren. "In this room." She couldn't read Shoshana. "I didn't know if you were aware of that. I am sorry if that brings up painful memories."

"They said it was a waiter, but he was never brought to trial."

"You may know that some people thought it was Cadieux, who may have felt your mother would never have given herself to him fully as long as she was married. She alibied him that night. Were you together? I thought the two of you would be together. For what it's worth, I never thought Cadieux would've done that. But I am now wondering why your mother was Cadieux's alibi and not you."

"Why would that make a difference in your understanding of the house? You only would trust one of us?"

Wren shook her head. "No. I told you I don't think he did it. I met him when I was a little girl, and he was attending a dinner party at our house. Whether he was making love to you or your mother or both, he didn't kill your father."

"As a little girl, you could draw a conclusion about that man's morality?"

"No. I drew a conclusion that all he deeply cared about were houses. He wouldn't have killed Dennis because no lover would be worth it to him. Still, he was with your mother, not you. You said you were on the beach with the rest of the young set. Why weren't you with Marius Cadieux, the love of your life?"

Wren wondered if Shoshana could see how fast her heart was beating. Would she just walk away? But no, she sat in one of the room's two chairs. Shoshana was very old. Wren had to remind herself. Wren grabbed the other one and sat opposite her, and looked at her closely. Was she imagining it—or did she see doubt?

"Your father was here, in this room. A few moments in the ensuite bathroom? Changing a broken cufflink? Fetching a business card? It was a crowded room—maybe he just wanted a few minutes by himself. But he was here. And someone killed him. I don't think it was that waiter. A lawyer I know said there was so little evidence that it probably wouldn't have even come to trial, let alone lead to a conviction."

"Percival Archer," said Shoshana, eventually. "He was in love with my mother."

"Are you saying he might've killed your father out of jealousy? In the hope she would turn to him in time? Percival was married. He'd have to divorce his wife, a terrible scandal back then. Unless he was planning to kill his wife, too."

Dennis had been a suicide, but that possibility didn't seem to occur to Shoshana. Unless she just didn't want to face that her mother and Cadieux were having an affair, and Dennis had killed himself in response.

"We had to be discreet," said Shoshana. "He had designed a house for my parents. It was the 1950s, and even in our sophisticated set, if it had been known he and I were having an affair. He was more than twenty years older than I was." She flashed Wren a nasty smile. "At the same time, he was seven years younger than my mother. She was fifty when my father died. Do you really think she inspired this house? Have you seen pictures of how beautiful I was back then? Is it beyond your imagination? I wonder if you have looked at this house, really looked at it, not as an architect, but as anyone seeing it for the first time. There is such beauty here, such tremendous beauty. My mother knew that—she always did. That's why we left after my father died. It was to punish me, to save her from the humiliation that the grand house she presided over was really her daughter's. Especially after she knew I was having Cadieux's child. In addition, I was the one who inspired this house. I was the mother of that house, too, in a way. So my mother took me away so I would never live with him, and he would never know his son. Then she ruined my son and came close to ruining me."

Ah. The story comes out, at last. A jealous woman in a love triangle with her own daughter, then the ludicrous story of turning her grandson gay in revenge. Oh, Shoshana, you're not as progressive as you'd like us to think!

Wren looked around the room. Even this one small area spoke of the house's perfection, and if she knew anything, it was that it wasn't inspired by a teenaged girl. Had Marius Cadieux taken her to bed? Possibly. Even probably. Wren didn't know people very well, but she knew homes, and

CHAPTER TWENTY-TWO

Cadieux hadn't built this for the lovesick young Shoshana.

Wren almost wanted to call Erik Leopold and tell him to forget the rest of the tests. It didn't matter anymore. But no, might as well see it through to the end. She owed the details to everyone, especially to Bronwyn. She was her client, after all, the mistress of the house. She was next in line, but no one could've foreseen that Bronwyn would've been protected by an armed bodyguard.

"Thank you," said Wren, eventually. "Thank you for being so frank with me. I am glad you came. Do you want to see your old bedroom? Or any other parts of the house?"

Shoshana looked closely at Wren. Did she wonder if she had convinced Wren, or was she afraid Wren was just humoring her? Wren wondered about self-delusion. How long could you tell yourself a lie before you started believing it was the truth?

"Thank you," she said. "I think I'm done." She looked tired—that last emotional upheaval had taken it all out of her.

"We can find Millie in the kitchen. Or I can have her come here."

"I can make it to the kitchen. Actually, I liked the kitchen here. We had a cook a long time ago, and she would make tea for me."

They walked slowly and didn't speak anymore. Even after all she had done, Wren still found her story sad. She had been set up for happiness, but threw it away, and even though Wren hated to think so, she knew the house was largely to blame.

But at least I finally know how to design Bronwyn's writer's retreat. It was going to be perfect.

Chapter Twenty-Three

Wren went to work on Bronwyn's ADU with a fury. She tried doing it in the firm's midtown office, but it didn't work. She needed to work *on* a home *in* a home. Her father just shook his head and wished her luck.

She called Bobby and told him he was on his own for a few days. "We have our marching orders, Chief," he said. Wren set up her laptop in a corner of her living room and went to work. Hadley came and went at odd hours because of her jobs, made Wren strong coffee, and provided plates of carrots and celery with her own yogurt dip.

After three days, Wren collapsed in the chair and just stared at the screen. She had it. It would give Bronwyn what she wanted and needed for a writer's retreat, and it would make Cadieux happy. She imagined him content that his house had a—child—that would live up to his house, match it without overwhelming it. And yet, Wren thought with some pride, it was hers. It would complement Cadieux's design, but it wasn't what he would've done himself. It wasn't what her father would've done either. But it was right. Cadieux would agree; Wren was sure of it.

"It really is smashing, Little Bird," said Hadley. "Now, maybe I've gone crazy hanging around with you, but am I seeing a touch of Victorian in this supposedly modern house?"

"Glad you see it! Yes. You know, for all their supposed sophistication, these were actually some very old-fashioned people. Shoshana especially has a lot to answer for, conceiving her son on a whim and then turning away when he failed to materialize into what she wanted. And Rebecca—I doubt

CHAPTER TWENTY-THREE

if she was mother of the year, but was probably honest, at least with herself. And I know, we have two modern-day dead people. I might've stopped this earlier, if it weren't for them, but it's my house, too, my workspace, and they deserve a resolution. And they shouldn't have to wait for it for more than half a century like poor Dennis Blaine. As the Prince says in Romeo and Juliet, 'all are punished.'"

That night, before she went to bed for her first good sleep in several days, she saw she had two important emails. The first was from her father. "Thanks for sending the design. Let's talk." Okay, that was all she could've expected at this point. The second from Erik. "Rafe and everyone cooperated. I have the results. You're going to owe a lot of people a lot of explanations."

* * *

Wren was going to give state police investigator Adam Fitzgerald a chance for another visit to Cadieux House. "I have some interesting…insights to give you." That's what she would tell him. She knew she had to be careful with her words and her explanations. What she had discovered was unofficial, but there was no way she could wrap this up without his cooperation. How flexible was he willing to be?

"You could let me talk to him," offered Hadley. "Once upon a time, I had a reputation for delivering very plausible explanations to the police."

Wren laughed. "I'm sure. But the fewer people involved in this, the better. Fitzgerald is likely to be more cooperative if he thinks it's just me. Does he want to find out the answer so badly that he'll take some procedural shortcuts?"

"At the end of the day, he has to bring people to court with real evidence."

"For the current murders, yes. But Dennis was a suicide. We know that now. The two later murders lead from that, and Fitzgerald can take of that. It's only fair. But the rest of the story? There's no crime there. Misbehavior, but no crime. As for the killer, I can't even prove who it is. But I think they'll tell me."

"You'll beat it out of them?" asked Hadley.

"Yes, I'd make a perfect Inspector Javert," said Wren, referring to the grim antagonist of "Les Misérables." "Basically, there are two groups here: People who understand the house and people who don't. And to be fair, there are two other groups: people who understand the characters here and people who don't. I don't think I understand them all, but I do understand the house. They're all pretty emotional and I think everyone is willing to implicate themselves just to prove a point. They just need a push. When I was a girl, Bobby let me try our thirty-six inch bolt cutter. It was almost as long as I was, but its length made it so powerful even I could snap a half-inch cable in half. I felt like Supergirl. I think I can give Fitzgerald that bolt cutter, if he's smart enough to listen."

Wren got him on the first try.

"Investigator Fitzgerald? It's Wren Fontaine, from Cadieux House."

"Yes, Ms. Fontaine. Always good hearing from you. Unless there's another murder?"

"No, but perhaps the solution to one. I have some insights. And I think we can both get what we want if we can bring everyone together at Cadieux House, including you."

He was quiet for a while. "Ms. Fontaine, you're framing this as a deal. The police don't work that way. You tell me what you know. Period."

"I'm sorry. I phrased that badly." Yes, she had. Behind her, Hadley squeezed her shoulder for reassurance. "What I meant was, I got what I need. I've found out what I need about the house. I already know what I need to know. I meant I can and will tell you everything—a mix of what I've found and what I think. But I don't think you'll have any of it in a useful format unless we bring everyone together. It's going to require some finesse."

"Finesse," he said, treating it like a foreign word. "You mean, I can't just take out rubber hoses and beat it out of them? Pity."

"I'm trying to help. Look, for one thing, Dennis Blaine was not murdered. He was a suicide."

"And you know this because…"

"Because if you can get a warrant to release Dennis Blaine's postmortem and turn over the results to a pathologist, you will see it's a suicide." No

CHAPTER TWENTY-THREE

doubt Erik had already returned the documents—she knew he didn't want to be caught with them in hand.

"Why does that make me think you've somehow already done that?" he asked. Wren said nothing. "I asked you a question," he continued.

"I'm sorry. I thought that was rhetorical."

"Wow. First 'finesse' and now 'rhetorical.' Did you get a thesaurus for Christmas?"

"Very funny. The point is that you don't have to take my word for anything. I'm not a lawyer, but it can't be too difficult for you to get those documents. I don't know if it was incompetence or someone was bribed to cover up a potential scandal, but Dennis Blaine killed himself."

"All right. I will need to check myself, but I'll take your word for it for now. But that still leaves us with Tristan Archer and Karen Weston. Presumably, they were not suicides, too?"

"No, of course not…oh! You're making fun of me. I am really doing my best here." She felt the heat rise to her face, as it always did when she felt she had lost track of a conversation.

"Occupational habit. My apologies. Please continue."

"All right then." She took a breath. "I have absolutely no evidence whatsoever about who killed Archer and Weston. You said it was the same gun. And so, it was the same person. It's about the house. It's about people who didn't understand, and who still don't understand, the point and purpose of Cadieux House, and if they did, there wouldn't be any tragedy, two people would be alive today, and Dennis would likely have lived to a ripe old age with his wife, Rebecca. So, if you want to know for your own amusement, I'll tell you, but unless we can get the whole clan together in Cadieux House, you'll never be able to prove it."

"You do know—and I'm not joking now—that there is an actual crime of wasting police time."

"So I've heard. But the penalty won't be nearly as bad as what my boss—my father—will do to me if I don't pull this off."

Now, Fitzgerald gave a genuine laugh. "Okay! I guess we're both putting something on the line here. So you want me to…encourage people to come to Cadieux House. What do we call it?"

"A history of Cadieux House. I'll try to bring everyone there myself, and I think that will work, because, at the end of the day, no one is going to want to be left out. I need you to be there, of course, with some of your colleagues. Discreetly. Let me pick a date." She put the phone on mute and turned to Hadley.

"Next Monday—can you do a lunch for a murder reveal?"

"I've never catered an event like that before, but I'm free."

Wren got back on with Fitzgerald. "Let's try for Monday. We'll bring the food."

"You're feeding us? Wow."

"People have called Cadieux House many things, but never inhospitable."

Chapter Twenty-Four

Hadley had decided a murder revelation was best handled buffet style. "It's not the kind of thing you really want to do a seating chart for," she said, and Wren agreed. They dug up some old tables and folding chairs in the garage, and Hadley had brought tablecloths and seat cushions.

"I didn't know what kind of palates we might be dealing with, so I kept it simple—sliced turkey, scalloped potatoes, green beans, and finally, an apple crumble for those who have finished their green beans."

"No one has to be bribed to finish vegetables you cooked," said Wren.

"You're sweet. But I have a feeling this is going to be a tough crowd."

Wren and Hadley had arrived early in Hadley's business van. Her father came next in the family car.

"You were rather vague," said Ezra. "Before we get started, do you think you could give your father—your partner—more details on why we're here today?"

"I don't need to tell you that no one put more of himself, or his clients' personalities, into any house than Cadieux. Those who lived here, visited here, or who are going to live here, should understand this house, why it is the way it is, and the connection between the people, the house, and Marius Cadieux."

"If you say so," said Ezra, not looking entirely convinced. "You got our client's permission, I assume."

"I told her this is what I was doing, and she said she would come. As you said, the house may belong to the client, but the workspace is the architect's.

I need this to finish the house properly. Oh, and we have a few minutes now to review our client's private writing house—her ADU, if you're interested. I've hooked up a large screen in the site office, so you can really get a look at it."

Wren had it all ready. She just flicked on her laptop, and there was the picture on the screen. Ezra didn't say anything right away, but Wren didn't expect him to. She was determined to let him speak first, though, and not start defending herself out of anxiety.

"It doesn't match Cadieux House," he finally said, and Wren couldn't immediately tell if that was a criticism or just an observation.

"No. Not in physical detail. Cadieux's designs don't scale. But it complements the house, and that is what's important."

"It is modernist. But you did sneak in some Victorian tones. You didn't think you'd slip this by me, did you?"

"Slip something by Ezra Fontaine? You do me an injustice, sir."

He smiled wryly at that.

"Have you shown it to the client yet?"

"No. I'll do it after today's meeting. I think she'll be in a proper frame of mind to appreciate it then."

"What if she doesn't like it?"

"I think she will. She is deeply invested in the story of the house, in the people who lived here, in the man who built it. She will understand how right it is." She grinned. "And if not, that's why you're here today—the master of convincing clients you know what's better for them than they do themselves."

"Perhaps. But Marius was even better at it than I was."

"Interesting. And yet he said he liked my Lego house without trying to change one thing about it. I heard he had plenty to say about plans you showed him over the years."

"Wren, please. You were ten. He was being nice to a little girl."

"Yes. And Cadieux was so warm and loving that he would spare the feelings of a child. He was simply impressed with my vision. Your jealousy is so transparent."

CHAPTER TWENTY-FOUR

"All right then, have it your way. But for what it's worth, I like your design. I think it appropriate. I think Cadieux would've liked it, too." Wren felt a thrill go through her, but tried not to show it, to make it clear that she was not dependent on Daddy's approval. Meanwhile, she knew her father well enough to expect more. "I will say that I sense a sadness there."

"That was deliberate. Despite the brightness, the angles add a touch of melancholy. That is why it matches Cadieux House. It took me a while to figure it out. I know that now. And I know why."

"Perhaps…" and that wry smile again, "perhaps I need to bow to your greater knowledge. But you do need to explain yourself in more detail."

"I will. People will be coming soon. It will be clear."

In the end, everyone accepted Wren's invitation, some happily, some reluctantly, but ultimately, those who didn't want to come did show up if for no other reason than they didn't want to be left out, fearing that someone else would be telling the story and they wouldn't be there to correct it.

And Wren had promised a story.

Fitzgerald and a few other detectives arrived first, looking around the room. They had some coffee but didn't eat anything. Bronwyn and Darren came next. She looked curious—maybe a little worried? But Darren looked around the room like the detectives did, and then he had a few words with Fitzgerald.

Rafe came, followed shortly by Gareth. They shook hands and spoke briefly, then got their lunch and sat together. Shoshana and Millie made an entrance. Wren watched Millie get both of them some lunch while Shoshana walked over to Rafe. They had a quick talk. Rafe frowned, and then Shoshana joined Millie.

Lavinia and Erik drove in together. She winked at Wren when she arrived, and Erik's usual good humor had been restored. He had made peace with what Wren had put him through, she was glad to see, and gave her a thumbs-up. Erik happily helped himself to the buffet while Lavinia spoke to her father. Whatever she told him, he took seriously. Lavinia was one of the few people he'd defer to, and Wren hoped—expected—she was reassuring Ezra Fontaine about his daughter.

Last came Woody Blaine, looking like he was going to explode. He didn't want to come at all and only grudgingly gave in when Wren had told him Shoshana would be there. Of course, Woody's presence had ensured that Shoshana would come, too.

Woody helped himself to some lunch and then sat by himself. Wren saw her father take a seat against the back wall, where he could get a look at both his daughter and their client, and Ezra and Lavinia sat with him. Wren had hung back, talking with Hadley, to discourage any of the guests from trying to get a private word with her before the presentation. They would all get the information at the same time.

Everyone was now waiting for her.

"I've got it," said Wren to Hadley.

"Of course you do." Yes. She had written out what she wanted to say and rehearsed it for hours. And as much as she didn't want to deal with people, she knew that it was really about the house, and houses were never a problem for her. Wren liked to think that Marius Cadieux would be amused at the presentation she was about the delivery. And maybe even proud. She stood and faced her audience, with her back to the windows, so everyone was well-lit.

"Thank you all for coming. One way or another, all of us here have a connection to this house, this magnificent, unique home, built specifically for Rebecca Blaine." She glanced at Shoshana, who pursed her lips. She was not happy about that. *But it's going to get worse for you. Much worse.*

"In the 1930s, recently married couple Dennis and Rebecca Blaine visited France and were introduced to Marius Cadieux, a young architect who was already making a name for himself. Perhaps I am saying something everyone here already knows, but it seems every man who met Rebecca fell in love with her."

She had hoped that would get at least a chuckle, but everyone was serious. At least Hadley winked at her. *Yes, it's a tough crowd, Little Bird.*

"I don't know what happened. I don't think anyone can ever know—the parties immediately involved are long gone. But I can tell you for certain that Rebecca Blaine had joined the OSS—a wartime U.S. intelligence agency."

CHAPTER TWENTY-FOUR

That got everyone's attention. Wren glanced at Shoshana, who was sitting straight and watching her intently, but Wren couldn't tell what she was thinking.

"I would give anything to know the details, but I can tell you this: Rebecca slipped into France to smuggle out Marius Cadieux. For anyone, especially a Jewish-American, it was incredibly brave. We do know it was a successful mission, and they made their way to London, and then New York. I think that bonded them in a way we can't even imagine. How would any of us thank someone for risking her own life to save ours? We know what Marius did. He built her this house. Don't we all wish we could've received a thank-you like this?"

This time, she got a smile from everyone—except Shoshana. She didn't come to listen to Wren tell everyone that this was really her mother's house, not hers.

"That should be the end of the story, but it wasn't," continued Wren.

"A pity," called out Bronwyn. "Because so far, it sounds like one of my novels."

"Yes, it does," said Wren. "And we'll come back to that." Bronwyn raised an eyebrow, and Wren took a moment to remember where she was.

"It was not the end, because this house is very complicated. It is the most complicated house I've ever worked on, and I will probably never get to work on something like this again." Her father *loved* that line. "Someone called this house a fun house and meant it as an insult, but they were more right than they knew." Rafe didn't react to that. He may have been proud of saying that—but no matter. "A funhouse reflects us again and again until we're dizzy. And that's what Marius Cadieux did here. I don't know if it was intentional or just a subconscious genius, but this house reflected the brilliant, interesting, and passionate people who lived here or even just visited. And they reflected back their deep feelings for each other and the house. The line blurred. And then it disappeared."

Ezra hid a satisfied grin behind his hand. Another convert to the Church of Cadieux.

"As strange as that was, everything might've been all right, but then one glittering night, in his strangely beautiful house, Dennis Blaine committed suicide."

Woody Blaine jumped up, as Wren expected, and at a glance, she saw Fitzgerald tense himself.

"That's a ridiculous lie. He was murdered. Dennis had no reason to kill himself." Wren just looked at him, not wanting to add more fuel to the fire. Woody clearly hoped for more support, but seeing there wasn't any, slowly sat back down.

"He killed himself," said Wren, "because he thought he had lost Rebecca, his one great love, to Cadieux, the man Rebecca had risked her life to save. What was tragic was that I don't think he had. I think Rebecca had every intention of staying with Dennis. I do think, I would like to think, that Rebecca Blaine and Marius Cadieux loved each other, but it was about this house. This house is how he gave his love. And living in this house is how she remained aware of it."

"So you're saying it wasn't physical?" asked Shoshana. *Physical, as with me?*

"What is more physical than a house?"

That infuriated Shoshana. "How dare you joke about that! Maybe my mother paid him, but it was me he loved. It was me he gave a son to!"

That hit everyone. Several people started to talk—but quickly stopped.

"You and your mother," said Wren, forcing herself to remain calm. "Both of you so beautiful, so…I guess I'll have to steal a word from real estate. So *desirable*. Everyone wanted the most beautiful mother-daughter pair in New York. Gareth Archer is here with us today. I understand that his grandfather Percival was madly in love with Rebecca. She must've been something! I've been accused of being an old-fashioned girl, so I'd like to think that Rebecca was loyal to her husband for the entirety of their marriage. But then again, I understand this house. I understand that Cadieux took the complicated Rebecca, the beautiful and brave Rebecca, and put her into this house. She knew it. He knew it. But not everyone did."

"You're wrong," said Shoshana, and Wren was glad of the interruption, because the comment—half-snark, half-sulk—would make the next part easier.

CHAPTER TWENTY-FOUR

"I'm *right*," said Wren. "You never understood this house. You saw yourself in competition with your mother for the love of Marius Cadieux. You've been lying to yourself your entire adult life."

"How dare you?" said Shoshana. It was literal—no one dared anything around her. Wren saw she was actually shaking. Millie was trying to calm her, but Shoshana didn't even seem to notice. "How *dare* you?" She repeated. Won't this be a great legacy, killing someone at a worksite, thought Wren.

"I have proof that Dennis killed himself. I think you were so enraged at your failure to seduce Cadieux that you told your father you had caught your mother and Cadieux together. You never changed, did you? Still the little girl who saw her mother curled up with Marius Cadieux in the back of any army transport plane, a horrific mix of jealousy and disgust."

The little color left in Shoshana's face drained out. She knew her story was out, and she was aware that Wren knew it and could publicize it. And was about to. *Oh, that hit home.* "How awful to have that image in your mind and then, as an impressionable teen, move into the house built by a man who loved your mother. Not you, your mother, and you had to live in it every day, enraged the man you loved didn't build you a house. Of course, you had other options." *Don't make me spell them out. I don't want to, but I will.*

"I don't have to listen to this," said Shoshana. "Millie—we're going."

"I'm afraid not," said Fitzgerald. "I need everyone here for a while longer. But we've made sure there's another room where you can wait in comfort."

Shoshana looked like she wanted to argue the point, but then muttered, "Fine," and she and a weary-looking Millie left, accompanied by one of Fitzgerald's men.

Wren took a breath. It was proceeding, and it could've been worse. If nothing else, this would show her father just how well she could hold her own with difficult people—difficult clients.

"Let's think on Dennis Blaine," said Wren. "I don't have a full understanding of the man, but I don't think he fully understood this house either. Marius Cadieux was not his rival, although maybe this house made him think so. It was...the *consummation* of the affair, not a *symbol* of one. I barely understand it myself. But I think Rebecca did, if no one else." A smiling Hadley gave her another thumbs up, and best of all, her father nodded. *I understand, too.*

"And so he killed himself, thanks in part to a daughter who didn't understand him either. So that's 1955. Did Rebecca feel the house was now—profaned—and she had to move? I don't know. But she did. And that takes us to the present."

"Umm," said Bronwyn, slowly raising her hand. "So Rafe is not Cadieux's son?" Wren looked at Rafe. He knew now he wasn't stupid. Maybe, at some level, he had always known. "We'll get to that later," said Wren. "But for now, let's go to the murders of Tristan Archer and Karen Weston." She watched Fitzgerald stiffen, no doubt balancing his wish to grab a suspect against his knowledge he had no proof at all.

"This house was empty for more than sixty years. The estate finally sells it. I have to think why. Shoshana Blaine is getting very old. And then comes Bronwyn Merrick, novelist. She had already learned about the Dennis Blaine killing. She had even referenced it in a novel." Bronwyn nodded. *Yes, guilty as charged.* "And she wanted to take the next step: a novelization of the story with a miniseries. Lots of money, I'm sure, but for the key person involved, there's much more than that. There's a chance to write her own story about her connection with Cadieux House. A chance to make sure everyone knows how it really happened."

"What can I say?" called out Bronwyn. "Everyone likes a good story. And one way or another, I was going to deliver one."

"I'm sure. You managed to get Shoshana to cooperate, didn't you? She wanted everyone to know that she was Marius Cadieux's lover and bore his child. All right, we all know that Cadieux was a world-class womanizer and that was going to come out, too. But Shoshana was special—she and she alone inspired one of the greatest homes of the 20th century. But you did have a couple of hurdles to clear. Woody Blaine. Why would he cooperate? In fact, he wanted everything quiet. Also, he and Shoshana disliked each other intensely. He was not going to go out of his way to give her something she wanted."

Bronwyn was very curious now. Even worried?

"And then Tristan Archer was killed—he knew everything, didn't he? The

CHAPTER TWENTY-FOUR

family lawyer, the son of Rebecca's ardent suitor. He doubtless had his own agenda, and it had to do with respect for the Blaines, the Rodriguezes, and the Archers. He had his own agenda. And then that deluded fan, Karen Weston. I thought it strange at the time—she said something like 'not here, not in this house.' She had oddly connected Bronwyn's controversial novel with the Dennis Blaine murder. How did she know all that, so quickly? This was old news, of course. However, Bronwyn, it was going to be difficult, maybe impossible, to keep everyone happy. You hadn't counted on all these deep emotions after all this time. After all, it's been seventy years. But for some people, it was like yesterday. When it comes to people like this, to homes like this...you can go to Europe and see people still worked up over events that happened seven hundred years ago. Meanwhile, you bought the house, hired our firm, signed contracts with publishers and TV producers, and now you see everything is falling apart..."

Darren, sitting next to her, became livid. Wren could see the tension in his shoulders, and his arms were crossed. His rage wasn't unexpected—he was being accused of serving as his employer's hired assassin. Who in that room had access to guns? Who knew how to commit a murder and leave no clues?

But Bronwyn herself didn't seem upset at all. She knew what was happening. She was fine with it, even amused. After all, she was a writer. But Wren didn't dare look at her father. What would he say: "Thank you so much, Wren, for accusing our client of cold-blooded murder."

"We keep coming back to the house. Who inspired it? Who was connected most closely with Marius Cadieux, who built it? Who would control its future and how it would be perceived?" That got a nod from Bronwyn. "But let's not forget the man who ended it all—Dennis Blaine. He's the forgotten man here, isn't he?"

Now, it was Woody's turn to tense up. Good—she had been right. "Few seem to remember him. What I know is mostly from the family financial manager, Woodrow Blaine. Woody—you went along with the show in the end because you were promised he'd be portrayed well. But that wasn't going to happen, was it? You could see what was going to happen. Meanwhile, you were going on about your overseas deals, about the embarrassment to the family, and that was just too much, wasn't it? You were just like Shoshana. You never understood this house, either. You never understood it was not as much a *gift* as a *tribute*. All you could see was Dennis, your kinsman—like you, a true Blaine—humiliated by being forced to live in a house designed by his wife's lover. And then finding—as I'm sure Shoshana told him—that he was her lover as well. This was in addition to being the father of his future grandchild. My God, what a mess."

He was really angry now, wasn't he? This wasn't like Darren, who had just felt insulted. This was going back to some very old, very dark places, to the Blaines being overshadowed by the lively, exotic Rodriguezes, to Woody today, having to face the humiliation of this all coming out, as he remained the public face of the family. Wren wished she could really know just how furious he was. Did she need to push him a little further…?

"And now we have the distinguished Bronwyn Merrick writing about the Blaines, and you just knew that Tristan Archer, keeper of secrets, was going to reveal it all. It was time to share the details for the next generations. For God's sake, even Bronwyn's readers were finding out—an idle mention slipping out at a book signing, and a crazed fan shows up here."

Time for the coup de grace. Wren took a breath.

"The whole world was about to find out what you knew all along. Cadieux built this house for Rebecca—born a Rodriguez. It was really hers. The complexity of this Sephardic Jewish beauty, this brilliant and entrancing woman, was woven into this house. Never mind the Blaines—Dennis in particular. Just another batch of dull protestant bankers." *My goodness—I think he's stopped breathing.*

Wren paused for the final line, one she had written and modified and rehearsed a dozen times, and looked closely at Woody. "I'm going to say what you know in your heart. The Blaines have never been worthy of this house."

That did it. Wren wouldn't have thought a sedentary man in his fifties could move so fast, but he was up and at her before she realized it. She jumped back instinctively, but then he came down as Darren took him out in a flying tackle. The state police followed a moment later, cuffing him

CHAPTER TWENTY-FOUR

and leading him away as he screamed incoherently about the Blaines, their power, their importance.

"Take him to a room and, for now, charge him with attempted assault. Read him his rights and see that he speaks with no one," said Fitzgerald. Then he turned to another detective. "This should get us a warrant. He lives in Manhattan. I bet the gun is in his apartment. Take care of that immediately."

Wren had wanted to stand and look smug and triumphant, but that wasn't going to happen. The last bit of energy had poured out of her, and she had to lean on Hadley to wobble her way to a chair in the corner. Hadley pressed a glass into her hand, something sweet and citrusy. She closed her eyes and settled deeply into the cushions for a while and tuned out all the sounds.

Her father was next. "Wren. Do we need a doctor? The police can take you to the hospital." She saw an unusual expression on her father's face, and it took her a minute to decipher it. It was concern.

"I'm fine. Just a little rattled." Then she giggled. "Look where I'm sitting. Cadieux designed it for this house—his famous Solace chair. Is there any hospital in the world that could give me greater comfort?"

Ezra nodded. "A deep appreciation for Marius Cadieux—so nothing wrong with your brain."

But Erik Leopold came over and started taking her pulse. "Congratulations," he said, "you're the first live person I've worked on since medical school." A few questions, and he pronounced her "all right" but advised her to sit for a while. Darren and Bronwyn joined her.

"That was a hell of a show," said Darren. "You're lucky I'm fast. You're lucky he didn't bring his gun with him."

"Yes, thank you," said Wren. "And I'm sorry if I seemed to imply that you and Bronwyn were killers."

Bronwyn laughed. "It's all right, sweetie. I just explained to Darren what was going on. Just a bit of theater. It was a little 'old hat' for a writer like me, but I have to say you pulled it off. Although I think I'm still missing a few points."

"I'm a historian," said Lavinia. "I get some of this—and I knew you were working with Erik, so I'm seeing where you're going. But finish the juice and give me your sources if you want an 'A' in this class."

Wren said she was okay, and Hadley had her catering assistant arrange the chairs in a circle. Rafe Rodriguez and Gareth Archer were talking to each other in a corner but occasionally looked up, as if unsure what to do next.

"Join us, please," said Wren. "I mean, if you want to learn more about what happened, you're welcome, but it's up to you."

They both murmured their thanks and came over, still looking a little overwhelmed. Wren thought about inviting Shoshana, but then realized she didn't want her there, didn't even want to face her ever again. She had lived her life, and there was not going to be any change now, not with her.

As for Fitzgerald and the police—if they wanted more information, they knew where to find her, and everyone would be more comfortable without them.

Hadley meanwhile produced more of her magic juice—everyone was in need of a good restorative.

"Can I ask what's in it?" asked Rafe.

"You work in a country club, right? Hire me to offer consulting to your culinary staff."

"How do you know we need a culinary consultant?"

"I never met a country club that didn't. Meanwhile, enjoy."

It lightened the mood, and then Wren felt everyone looking at her. Rafe and Gareth were curious. Her father, perhaps seeing Wren wasn't going to tank their firm, also looked expectant. Maybe proud, too? Lavinia and Erik were smiling—they were finding this entertaining. Wren took a seat, to discuss rather than lecture, and organized her thoughts.

"This is about people who understood this house and people who didn't. I wonder what Cadieux would make of that. He might be appalled. He'd probably be amused. But we have someone here who knows much more than I do. Ezra Fontaine studied under Cadieux and knew him well. He is considered an authority on his work as well as being a leading modernist architect in his own right. He is also the managing partner of our firm and my father. Ezra, what do you think Marius Cadieux would've made of our

CHAPTER TWENTY-FOUR

understanding of this house?"

Her father leaned back and looked at her. *Thank you so much for landing me in this. Nevertheless, I'm going to be just fine.*

"Cadieux would've been surprised," said Ezra in his perfectly measured baritone. "For all his meticulous planning, he believed the way people reacted to the houses he built was, and indeed, should be instinctual. He wanted everyone, especially the residents, to have a quick and emotional connection to the homes he built for them. I am sure from what I know—and from what my partner Wren has said—that Rebecca did. But no Cadieux residence was dependent on just one person. Bronwyn, you have the honor of being the second mistress of Cadieux House. So tell me, what does it say to you?"

She hadn't expected that, but like Ezra, she wasn't going to admit that.

"I am secure here. And yet, I am also free."

"You are lucky," said Wren. "Because that's why he built it. When I was ten, Cadieux told me each house needed to match the personality of the person he was building it for. It may have been a lot for a child to absorb, but it's been bouncing around my mind for twenty years. The lively, adventurous Rebecca needed to be free. But this OSS veteran also needed to be safe. So Cadieux gave her a house as free as an eagle's nest and secure as a gopher hole. I got that pretty quickly. But there is more here. I can't find the exact word. Perhaps wistfulness, a sense that as grand as the ceilings are, they are not as high as we would like them to be, and as open as the rooms are, we are still enclosed. Cadieux was the perfect architect, and from what I hear, Rebecca was the perfect woman." That got some smiles, which she was pleased to see. "But to a certain extent, this house was also about the imperfections. Indeed, the imperfections in their relationship. And that is what I feel." She paused. "More than that. I know it to be true."

She looked around. Everyone seemed to be giving thought to what she had said, especially Bronwyn.

"Are you actually saying Cadieux was imperfect?" Ezra asked. But he was smiling now as well.

"Yes, but deliberately so, if that doesn't sound odd. We long for things we have lost, or could never have, and this house reminds us of that. That's what

Cadieux House says to me." She paused to make sure she had everyone's attention. "So much for the house. Now for the reason why. Now for the people."

Chapter Twenty-Five

"Marius Cadieux loved Rebecca Blaine," said Wren. "It appears they first met in 1937 when Dennis and Rebecca visited France. Cadieux was just twenty-five, but already attracting attention, and Rebecca was thirty-two. She was alluring, as it is said, and bright and witty. He was handsome and brilliant. We could spend days discussing this young man who was probably psychologically incapable of making a commitment to just one woman. I'm sure Rebecca, who may have been taken with him, knew that. I think she was shrewd and didn't suffer from illusions. She was a married woman with a child."

Rafe laughed. "I don't know how you got all that, but I think you have a good sense of my grandmother, as I remember her."

"Thank you," said Wren. "I appreciate that. I can't say I really know what I'm talking about, you see. Marius Cadieux saw a woman and gave her a house. I am looking at the house and trying to give you a woman. In 1937, they had…what they had. And then separated. Cadieux might've promised her a house someday."

"Oh yes," said Ezra. "That would be just the kind of grand gesture he would make."

"And thank you, too. I'm clearly on the right track. Then comes the war. Rebecca spoke perfect French and managed to get herself into the OSS. That would be a story in itself. But the important part for us was how she got Cadieux out of France. She had language skills and already knew him. He could be invaluable for the war effort. And she did it. Rebecca succeeded."

"'We'll always have Paris,'" quoted Hadley. "'We didn't have—we'd lost it until you came to Casablanca. We got it back last night.'"

"And we're back again to Casablanca," said Lavinia. Everyone else looked confused.

"'Life imitates art far more than art imitates life,'" said Wren. "That's Oscar Wilde. But as romantic as we might want to think this was, we cannot be sure. We have a hint that they were curled up together on their flight to the U.S., but it may have been for warmth. From what I've read, I don't think the Douglas C-54 Skymaster plane was well-suited for lovemaking."

A chuckle now. Everyone was relaxing, at least for the time being.

"The war ended. Cadieux became a star of post-war architecture. He kept his promise and came back to New York to build a house for Rebecca. He also met Shoshana again. She had been a little girl, welcoming her mother home after she rescued Cadieux. But now she was a young woman. Maybe she felt in competition with her beautiful, extroverted mother." She had trouble getting that out.

Wren remembered when her own mother was dying. To the day she died, Wren thought her mother was the most beautiful woman in the world, so obviously more beautiful than she was. And yet, there was never competition. She fought back tears before continuing.

"At any rate, Shoshana fell in love with Cadieux. She was twenty and beautiful. He was forty-three, handsome, and charming. Shoshana probably became obsessed with him, and again, we come back to this house. He was building it as a tribute to Rebecca, the woman he loved, at some level, and who saved his life. But Shoshana convinced herself it was for her. And we are never more self-absorbed than when we are twenty. We can't be sure how far this went—"

"Oh, I think we can," said Rafe with an amused smile.

"We'll come to that in a moment," said Wren, more sharply than she intended. "I promise. Meanwhile, I just want to set the stage. Also around at this time was Percival Archer, the family lawyer and—surprise, surprise—he loved Rebecca too."

Now, Gareth spoke. "Some scene, right? Grandpa is running a distant third behind the husband and a handsome Frenchman who had given her a

CHAPTER TWENTY-FIVE

house. I mean, a *house*."

"Don't sell your grandfather short," said Wren. "He was an urbane, well-educated man, a very successful lawyer, and I'm going to give him a pass for falling for Rebecca when she was seven years older than he was." She took a breath. "Nevertheless, just because he was lovesick and so was Shoshana, there was no excuse for him to take advantage of a vulnerable twenty-year-old-girl and have a child with her."

That kept everyone quiet for a while. Rafe spoke first.

"So that was the test arranged for by Dr. Leopold," he said, glancing at Erik, who gave him a quick salute.

"Yes," said Wren. "We were able to make comparisons. You are an Archer, Rafe. You are not a Cadieux."

"I'm sorry—I'm the child of Percival Archer, the family lawyer, and Shoshana Blaine?"

"No doubt about it," said Erik.

Rafe looked stunned for a few moments. "I assume my mother knew that?"

"I don't think..." started Wren. "I mean, you can ask her. But I do not think there could be confusion in her own mind."

Rafe shook his head and started to laugh. "She made sure I was named 'Rodriguez' and not 'Blaine.' She always felt she was emotionally more a Rodriguez than a Blaine. And then she always told me I was a Rodriguez and a Cadieux, and nothing could be a better mix than that. You know, when it became clear, I thought she hated me because I was gay—an embarrassment to the family. But was it really about my not fitting neatly into her idea of what I should be as Marius Cadieux's son? Did I make it impossible for her to even pretend anymore?"

"Masculine vs. feminine energy. A theory in architecture," said Wren. "Your mother, Shoshana, clearly ascribed to that. The masculine energy of Cadieux combined with the feminine energy of the Rodriguezes, running so deeply in Rebecca and Shoshana. That's how she saw it, as far as I can tell."

"I guess being gay sort of threw a monkey wrench into that," said Rafe. "Her bitterness...as long as I was aware...was because I couldn't let her live her dream of being the mother of Cadieux's son, being the woman who gave us the perfect Cadieux *masculine* to the perfect Rodriguez *feminine*? Is that what was going on here?"

"Feminine and masculine..." broke in Ezra. "Even if you accept its way of looking at architecture, it has to do with the architects' skill and perception, not their gender. Yes, you can make jokes about Cadieux and his womanizing, but he understood women. This house is proof of that—one of many." He turned to Rafe. "I am sorry for the way your mother treated you. I am sorry for her inability to understand this house and the way Cadieux worked with Rebecca on it."

"Thank you," said Rafe. "I mean it. But it's going to take me a while to process it."

"There's more in this," said Wren. "This involves how others viewed this house, others who didn't understand it. Three people are dead because of that. Let's go back to Woodrow Blaine. He discouraged me from meeting with you, Rafe. He had the same misunderstanding you had and didn't want me to find out that Cadieux had seduced Dennis's wife *and* daughter. Shoshana was bad enough, but to have shamed Dennis like that—it was too much. That's how he saw it."

She turned now to Gareth. "Your father knew everything. Behind the scenes were the legal and financial implications of what everyone did, and Tristan was the gatekeeper. The sale of the house was going to be a good time to reveal secrets, so that future generations knew what happened here. With the upcoming book and miniseries, there would be no hiding it. But Woodrow couldn't accept that. He used the excuse of a big deal in France for everyone to keep quiet. But, ultimately, he was protective of Dennis, of the history of the Blaines, and didn't want that to get out at all. He wanted to quiet Tristan, permanently, and hoped that you, Gareth, wouldn't dig too deeply. After all, you had walked away from the firm and its clients. And when he saw Bronwyn had apparently leaked details to her fan base, as shown by Karen Weston's behavior, she had to go too."

"How did I manage to escape him?" asked Bronwyn with an uncertain smile. "My death would've solved a lot of problems." She slipped her hand into Darren's.

CHAPTER TWENTY-FIVE

"You were lucky. The obsession with your book character that led you to hire a bodyguard stopped him. You were too well protected. But if this had gone on further—he might've risked it anyway. I have a feeling that the police are figuring out right now the extent of Woody Blaine's obsession."

Gareth shook his head. "Poor Dad. I knew there was a reason I walked away from all of them." He waved his arm to encompass the house. "From this."

"This is going to sound like an odd question," said Rafe, a little uncertainly. "But I would think Woody would want to kill my mother."

"I gave that some thought, too," said Wren. "For all the two of them disliked each other, however, they were unwitting partners in the same delusion. Woody's main concern was protecting Dennis and the Blaine name generally. Shoshana was all about her connection to Cadieux and Rafe's parentage. That worked with Woody's point of view, although he knew enough to suspect Rebecca had been involved with Cadieux, too. He wondered if Tristan knew even more."

"And can you share your...contretemps with the Central Intelligence Agency?" asked Lavinia.

"Woody at work again, I'm sure. I'm sure they'll find a family or business connection somewhere. The Blaines had fingers in a lot of pies and the intelligence community had long recruited from the old families. All he had to do was drop some words about Rebecca and her OSS past, and the possibilities of both family and political embarrassment. They happily picked me up to warn me away from researching Rebecca because of some World War II derring-do."

Wren looked around. Everyone was lost in their own thoughts. Rafe and Gareth were no doubt reflecting on their own parents, the decisions they made. And speaking of parents, what was her father thinking of? Would he tell her if she asked?

Across the circle, Hadley gave her a little wave.

Investigator Fitzgerald came back. "Ms. Fontaine? A few minutes of your time?"

"Of course," she said and felt relief. She needed to get away from the family now, and even a police questioning was welcome. He took her into the site office—and took her chair.

"This is my office," she said without even thinking about it. Fitzgerald laughed.

"Do I have your permission to use it while we wind this up?" he asked.

"Yes, of course. I just want you to know that while I am working on this house, it is mine. Perhaps not in a strictly legal sense but in a practical and emotional one, and I congratulate myself that I understand it at last, and I think Marius Cadieux would be amused. I think you understand it too, at least in part."

"Oh, at least *in part*," he said. "A great compliment from a distinguished architect such as yourself."

"There is no need to joke about it," said Wren. "Your wisdom was seeing the connection to the house and using me—the term is a cat's paw—to find it out. My wisdom was seeing what you were doing. I suppose we are both the better for it."

"My apologies—you're right on everything. Anyway, you might like to know we got a warrant quickly and found Woodrow Blaine's gun in his bedroom. The ballistics tests are ongoing, but the ammunition type is a match, and they're confident it'll provide proof that he was the killer. That was unexpectedly clever of you, driving him to give himself away."

"Unexpected?" asked Wren, raising an eyebrow.

"I had thought you were all about the house, not people. But that was shrewd."

"It was shrewd about this house. If I had been better about people, I wouldn't have goaded him into attacking me, which I didn't expect or welcome."

"All's well that ends well, as they say, but we were all lucky. Anyway, I wanted to tell you that about the gun, because you were such a big help, but just keep it to yourself for now, as it's still undergoing tests." He stood and held out his hand. "Thank you for your help. And for letting me see this house. You can have your office back now."

"Shoshana?" asked Wren. It was all she could do to bring herself to ask.

CHAPTER TWENTY-FIVE

"She left a few minutes ago. Ms. Blaine is no longer a subject of any state police investigation and is not believed to have committed any crimes."

"She probably goaded Woodrow, twisted people's lives," said Wren. "She's the last person left who was truly a part of this house. I knew I wasn't going to change her. That would be as possible as changing this house itself. This house is what it is."

"So you still aren't sure if you like it?" asked Fitzgerald, smiling.

"It's impressive. And beautiful. But I'm still happiest in the 19th century. That says as much about me as it does about Marius Cadieux. And I'd like to think that he, of all people, would understand that."

"Would he have pity for Shoshana, for Rebecca's daughter?"

"Ohh...that's so far above what I could possibly figure out," said Wren. "I'm not a psychologist or moralist. All I can tell you is that Shoshana has a lot to answer for."

Fitzgerald laughed. "Take it from a cop, my architect friend: we all do." He gave her a fond slap on her shoulder and left, shaking his head.

Wren realized he was right, but didn't have long to contemplate the philosophical implications when two visitors slipped in after them, Hadley and her father.

"Oh, Wren, you were super. You were just *completely super*," said Hadley and gave her a hug.

Her father, meanwhile, just gave her his usual wry look. "Yes. Nicely done, indeed. This is going to make next Monday's staff meeting a little livelier than usual."

They all sat.

"I have to say, father, that modern architecture has really caught on with me. I am understanding it. I am even getting inspired by it. How can one not? I just wish I could understand the people better."

"I think you understand them better than you think," said Hadley. "You understand people—you just don't like them very much."

Wren laughed. "All right, fair enough. But I do like you two, and I will tell you that seeing the people and seeing the house made me realize that Cadieux inspires passion, and it's well-deserved. I can't say I will ever fully understand the love between Rebecca and Cadieux, but he built this house for her, and for decades, Shoshana has tried to tell herself it was built for her, that Cadieux loved her and Woody, seeing it as an affront to the Blaine family, and Dennis killing himself in humiliation over it, and Percival taking to bed a woman young enough to be his daughter in a desperate attempt to forget the woman he couldn't have because he couldn't give her a house like this. And I suppose we have Marius Cadieux to thank for it."

"What a nice, backhanded compliment," said Ezra.

"He'd have loved it. And I want you to know I may say the house inspired a lot of deep feelings, but I can separate art from the artists, and I'm not laying this at his door."

Ezra nodded. "Well said. For my part, as much as I admired Marius, he might've thought twice. There was too much intensity in building something like this for a woman he clearly had strong feelings for. And thinking about it now, I know he must have had strong feelings. He definitely thought more about her than any other woman. I know this because, for the most part, he was an open book, delighted to share his thoughts on friends, lovers, and clients, but he was mostly quiet on her. Those of us who knew him thought it was because she didn't mean that much to him, just the woman whose commission established his reputation. But it was because he felt so deeply that he kept his feelings for Rebecca quiet until the day he died."

Wren flashed back again to the ten-year-old girl building a Lego mansion. *Oh, but he shared them with me, dear father, he shared them with me.*

Epilogue

Wren decided, for reasons she couldn't immediately identify, to unveil the final design of Bronwyn's ADU in her firm's offices rather than in Cadieux House. She had always told herself that she liked running important events in the homes she was working on, because she felt comfortable there. But wasn't her firm, the firm where she was a partner, just as much her domain as any home?

Darren escorted Bronwyn up as usual. They were still playing it cool, although Wren figured it wouldn't be long before the gossip pages got ahold of it. Woody Blaine's arrest was all over the news, and reporters were digging into every corner of all the major players.

Bronwyn said she wanted to see the plans alone, as this would be a special mini-residence just for her. Darren seemed fine, putting his feet up on the desk in an empty office, sipping coffee, and reading the sports pages.

The conference room was all set up. Wren flicked on the laptop and watched Bronwyn's face as the ADU filled the screen. She could see from her client's face that she had it right. Bronwyn didn't speak for a while.

"That's it. It works for me, but just as important, it works in conjunction with the main house." Bronwyn kept looking. It was those Victorian touches, Wren knew. It gave it the necessary flavor alongside the relentless openness of the modernist lines.

"Did you ever read a book that you liked but couldn't immediately say why?" asked Bronwyn.

"All the time," said Wren.

"That's what I'm feeling now. I mean, I know I'm happy with it. You gave me what I asked for, but there's something else there."

"Sadness," said Wren. "Or maybe 'melancholy' is a better word. It took me a while, but I saw that's what Cadieux put into the house. I thought at first it was as simple as a statement from a man who loved a woman he couldn't have. But it's a little more than that—he loved her, yes, but knew he couldn't make her happy, not provide the life she wanted, or that he thought she wanted, anyway. And even if he was overlooking that, would she have been happy going through life just as Mrs. Marius Cadieux?" Wren shrugged. "I can't say. But there was sadness there, in Cadieux House. And I wanted your writer's house to match it."

"And it does. Nicely done, Wren. Now, you can feel free to tell me I'm an architectural illiterate—"

"I can't. You're a paying customer," said Wren.

"Ah, but we're both artists, you with buildings and me with words, so we can be honest with each other. There is more than one style. I'd guess you call it, in my tiny house, right?"

"Yes. You're completely right. And that's something else I got from Cadieux. Do you know what someone told me about Rebecca? That she was an actress who was always playing a role. And that's another side of Cadieux House, the confusion many feel inside it may actually have been an attempt to give Rebecca's different personalities their own—habitats, I guess you'd say."

"Oh! Do you mean multiple personality disorder, like Sybil, that Sally Fields movie back in the 1970s?"

"No, nothing so blatant. More like personas she liked to live through. Think about her, in some ways, a traditional wife and hostess, but also a wartime secret agent, a woman who attended a synagogue but married outside her faith, a loyal wife but in a relationship with Cadieux that defied categorization. But was she much of a wife? Much of a mother? I don't really know. Her only child seemed to dislike her, and everyone says Dennis loved her far more than she loved him. I'm wondering if she ever gave herself fully, if she was ever honest, even with herself."

"You wonder if she was even happy?" asked Bronwyn.

EPILOGUE

"I do," said Wren. "Perhaps there is another layer to the house I didn't even see. That is, even if so many of us feel a dissociative sense at first entering the house, perhaps it worked for Rebecca, who may have spent her whole life disassociated from herself. Cadieux knew this."

Bronwyn seemed very serious. "This is going to sound strange, but I was glad you said you wanted to show me the final of the ADU in your office rather than at Cadieux House, and not just because it saved me the commute. Do I sound crazy if I say I need a break from a world-renowned home I just paid thirty million dollars for? A home that suited the 'mad Rebecca' but perhaps not a reasonably sane book author?"

"Not at all," said Wren. "It has been a lot, for all of us. Maybe I stressed the importance of Rebecca and Cadieux too much." She forced a smile. Wren knew she'd have to explain it again. "Consider that I'm an architect, not a psychologist. When it comes to the people, I may not even know what I'm talking about. I'm so far out on a limb I can't even see the tree trunk anymore."

"All right then. But I guess, after everything, I can't stop thinking about the past."

"Hadley keeps telling me I get lost in the past when I work on old homes, so I know what you're feeling. But Rebecca and Cadieux are long gone." Wren knew how to handle this—right out of the Ezra Fontaine playbook for soothing clients. "At the end of the day, it's a house, it's your house, yours and Darren's. I need periodic reminding that people make it a home. And I know Cadieux would agree with that. I would like to think you and Darren will make it a home. A happy home, as Cadieux intended."

"Thank you—that puts it all in perspective."

"Well, I'm hoping to have years to consider it, with Darren," Bronwyn said, clearly relaxing. "And I'm looking forward to seeing my tiny house built—I have a book and a TV script to revise," she said, and now Wren saw the grimace on her face.

"Going through with it, then?"

"Oh yes. Shoshana still wants it. We have the proof now of what was really going on, and now Rafe Rodriguez and Gareth Blaine are in the mix. They have a stake in seeing what we show, and the lawyers are working it out. I can tell you one thing, Shoshana is saying we can't prove she didn't have an affair with Cadieux. In her sad little mind, she did, never mind the child wasn't his. It's almost immaterial to her—she's lost in her own little world, I'm afraid."

"Do you like Sherlock Holmes?" asked Wren.

"Oh! Yes, of course. I read those books again and again in my childhood."

"From *A Case of Identity*. Holmes quotes an Indian writer, I think it was. 'There is danger for him who taketh the tiger cub, and danger also for whoso snatches a delusion from a woman.'"

Bronwyn nodded. "And while we're talking about Sherlock Holmes, maybe we can think of Cadieux and Rebecca as having a similar relationship to Holmes and Irene Adler: 'To Sherlock Holmes, she is always the woman.'"

Wren took Bronwyn to her office for a few papers they needed to review and sign—and Wren was delighted with her client's surprise at the photo of Cadieux House on her office wall.

"It's beautiful! It really captures it."

"I hired a photographer to memorialize it for me. If you want, I can send you a copy."

"That would be kind." She looked around the office at the pictures of Regency and Victorian mansions and Gothic castles.

"This is the only post-war house you have on your wall," said Bronwyn.

"I see it as a diploma, of sorts, to announce my recognition of the beauty and even importance of modern architecture, even if my heart is in another era. My father was delighted when I hung it up."

"Promise me you'll put a photo of my tiny house when it's done. I just know it's going to be spectacular—you've given me something I didn't even know how to ask for, and you should have your triumph next to Cadieux's."

And Wren suddenly went back to being a little girl building her own take on a Victorian mansion while the elderly Cadieux leaned over her and gave her advice: "I had to figure out the owners and give them the homes I knew they wanted," he had said, "even if they didn't know themselves."

Acknowledgements

Many thanks to Verena Rose and the whole crew at LBB, who helped me bring Wren to life. My family was wonderful as always: my wife Elizabeth was again my first reader, and my daughters, Katie and Sophie, were my Millennial consultants, helping make sure Wren and Hadley were consistent for their generation. And great thanks to my agent, Cynthia Zigmund, for her years of wise counsel. The New York State Police assisted me with certain police details, but any errors are entirely my own. Finally, thanks to more writers than I have space to list: No one exceeds mystery writers in kindness and generosity.

About the Author

Over the years, R.J. Koreto has been a magazine writer, website manager, textbook editor, novelist and merchant seaman. He was born and raised in New York City, graduated from Vassar College, and has wanted to be a writer since reading *The Naked and the Dead*. In addition to his novels, he has published short stories in *Ellery Queen's Mystery Magazine, Alfred Hitchcock's Mystery Magazine*, the *2020 Bouchercon Anthology* and *Paranoia Blues: Crime Fiction Inspired by the Songs of Paul Simon*. His current series features Wren Fontaine, an architect who finds mysteries in the historic homes she renovates. He and his wife have two grown daughters, and they divide their time between Rockland County, N.Y., and Martha's Vineyard, Mass.

SOCIAL MEDIA HANDLES:
   https://www.facebook.com/RJKoreto/
   https://www.instagram.com/rjkoreto/
   https://twitter.com/rjkoreto

AUTHOR WEBSITE: www.rjkoreto.com

Also by R.J. Koreto

Historic Homes Mysteries
  The Greenleaf Murders
  The Turnbull Murders

Milton Keynes UK
Ingram Content Group UK Ltd.
UKHW030628071024
449371UK00001B/249